A CLEAR NORTH LIGHT

BOOK ONE OF THE LITHUANIAN TRILOGY

Laurel B Schunk

LAUREL B. SCHUNK

ST KITTS PRESS ◆ WICHITA, KANSAS

PUBLISHED BY ST KITTS PRESS
A division of S-K Publications
PO Box 8173 • Wichita, KS 67208
316-685-3201 • Toll-free 888-705-4887 • FAX 316-685-6650
stkitts@skpub.com • www.StKittsPress.com

The name St Kitts and its logo are registered trademarks.

Edited by Elizabeth Whiteker
Cover design by Diana Tillison
Cover illustration by Sally Toh

First Edition 2001

Library of Congress Cataloging-in-Publication Data

Schunk, Laurel.
  A clear north light / Laurel B. Schunk.-- 1st ed.
    p. cm. -- (The Lithuanian trilogy ; bk. 1)
  ISBN 0-9661879-6-2 (alk. paper)
  1. World War, 1939-1945--Lithuania--Fiction. 2. Holocaust, Jewish
(1939-1945)--Lithuania--Fiction. 3. Lithuania--Fiction. 4. Young
men--Fiction. I. Title.
  PS3569.C55533 C57 2001
  813'.54--dc21
                                    00-012788

ADVANCE PRAISE FOR
A CLEAR NORTH LIGHT

Laurel Schunk's new novel, *A Clear North Light*, is set in Lithuania – a fragment of Europe unfamiliar to many readers – during the early months of World War II. An engaging young man's struggle to live a decent life in a decent little country pinched between Nazi Germany and the Soviet Union dramatically illuminates the effect of deadly global politics on the private lives of all-too-human individuals caught up in events not of their making.

Gretchen Sprague, author of *Maquette for Murder*

Set in Lithuania in the World War II era, *A Clear North Light* pulls one into an historical drama with excitement and moral persuasiveness as Petras fights and searches for faith, meaning, and love when Principalities and Powers – first Nazi, then Communist Russian invasions – divide his beloved homeland and shred the spirits of his people.

James D. Yoder, author of *Lucy of the Trail of Tears*

OTHER BOOKS BY ST KITTS PRESS

PO Box 8173 ▸ Wichita KS 67208
888-705-4887 (toll-free) ▸ 316-685-3201
FAX 316-685-6650
stkitts@skpub.com ▸ www.StKittsPress.com

The Voice He Loved by Laurel Schunk

"...a masterful tale that reaches into the inner workings of a bruised and battered psyche, while keeping the plot moving at a breathless pace." —*The Charlotte Austin Review* (www.charlotteaustinreviewltd.com, reviewed by Nancy Mehl)

Black and Secret Midnight by Laurel Schunk

"Beth Anne's appealing child's-eye view of the world and the subtle Christian message should make this appealing to fans of Christian and mainstream mysteries." —*Library Journal*

"Beth Anne is at times touchingly naive..." —*Publishers Weekly*

"...a memorable picture of racism that is variously stark and nuanced." —*Small Press Book Review*

"...a good look at racial relations in the south...with a mysterious twist." —*The Pilot* (Southern Pines, NC)

"The story is so gripping that I worried [Beth Anne] would be killed before the end." —*Murder: Past Tense* (The Hist. Mys. Apprec. Soc.)

"...Schunk's adult novels are serious, skillfully crafted works."
—*nwsbrfs* (Wichita Press Women, Inc.)

"...a light in the darkness and a novel to sink your teeth and your heart into."
—*The Charlotte Austin Review*
(www.charlotteaustinreviewltd.com,
reviewed by Nancy Mehl)

Hyænas by Sandy Dengler

"Highly recommended."
—*Library Journal*

"Dengler has crafted a masterpiece. *Hyaenas* proves that there are still new slants to the mystery genre."
—*The Charlotte Austin Review*
(www.charlotteaustinreviewltd.com,
reviewed by Nancy Mehl)

"*Hyænas* is both a terrific murder mystery and a work of unique, flawless written exploration of prehistoric antiquity."
—*Internet Bookwatch* (The Midwest Book Review)

Death in Exile by Laurel Schunk

"What could have been a straightforward Regency romance is elevated by apt social commentary in this offering from Schunk..."
—*Library Journal*

"Schunk is a good writer who has a good grasp of story and character."
—*The Pilot* (Southern Pines, NC)

"This beautifully written Regency novel...will throw you into another time, and you won't want to leave."
—*The Charlotte Austin Review*
(www.charlotteaustinreviewltd.com,
reviewed by Nancy Mehl)

"Laurel Schunk is a masterful storyteller."
—*Murder: Past Tense* (The Hist. Mys. Apprec. Soc.)

Under the Wolf's Head by Kate Cameron

"The gardening tips seeded throughout the narrative are a clever ploy, echoing the inclusion of cooking tips in the ever-popular culinary mysteries..."   —*Publishers Weekly*

"Plenty of gardening filler and allusions to inept local law enforcement lighten the atmosphere, as do the often humorous sisterly 'fights' and the speedy prose."   —*Library Journal*

"You'll laugh at the sisters' relationship and grow to love the two women just as Callista's plants grow through her loving care."
—*GRIT: American Life & Traditions*

"Schunk in the past has tackled child abuse and racism; her first gardening mystery provides a message about ageism and the value placed on elderly lives..."   —*Norwich Bulletin* (Norwich, CT)

"Highly recommended."   —*The Charlotte Austin Review*
(www.charlotteaustinreviewltd.com,
reviewed by Nancy Mehl)

"*Under the Wolf's Head* is a wonderful new release by Kate Cameron."   —*About.com* (reviewed by Renie Dugwyler)

"...a quick and pleasant read..."
—*nwsbrfs* (Wichita Press Women, Inc.)

Shaded Light by N.J. Lindquist

"...a cozy that will delight fans who appreciate solid, modern detection."   —*Publishers Weekly*

"Detailed characterization, surprising relationships, and nefarious plot twists."   —*Library Journal*

"A very good novel by an accomplished writer."
—*Rapport Magazine*

"This most enjoyable novel is written in the style of Agatha

Christie...Follow the clues to a bang-up ending."
                                        —*The Pilot* (Southern Pines, NC)

"...an admirable first outing for a pair of detectives readers will
look forward to hearing from again."   —*The Mystery Reader*
                              (reviewed by Jennifer Monahan Winberry)

"With any luck, we'll see more of Manziuk and Ryan in years
to come."   —*The Charlotte Austin Review*
                                     (www.charlotteaustinreviewltd.com,
                                                      reviewed by PJ Nunn)

"This excellently plotted novel is the first in a projected series of
Manziuk and Ryan mysteries."   —*I Love a Mystery*

"Paul and [Jacquie] make a fabulous team as their divergent per-
sonalities harmoniously clash to the benefit of the reader."
              —*Internet Bookwatch* (The Midwest Book Review)

"A cozy reminiscent of the best Agatha Christie had to offer."
              —*Midwest Book Review* (reviewed by Leann Arndt)

The Heart of Matthew Jade by Ralph Allen

"...a compassionate view into religious, familial and romantic
love..."   —*Publishers Weekly*

"…an eye-opener. *The Heart of Matthew Jade* is a compelling
novel that will stay with you long after you put it down."
                                      —*The Charlotte Austin Review*
                                     (www.charlotteaustinreviewltd.com,
                                                  reviewed by Nancy Mehl)

"...this novel's strength is in the behind the scenes glimpses of
faith behind bars."   —*The Bookdragon Review*
                                          (www.bookdragonreview.com
                                            reviewed by Melanie C. Duncan)

NOTE

For the purposes of this story, some liberty has been taken with the chronology of the Holocaust in Lithuania. For example, the massacre of 300 children in the Šiauliai ghetto occurred in 1944, not 1940.

LANGUAGE NOTES

Orthography in Lithuanian is different from English, including diacritical marks lacking in English. The most unusual for the English reader is the "little bird," a small V sometimes placed over the letters C, S, and Z. The mark adds an H sound to the letters: č becomes ch, š becomes sh, and ž becomes zh.

In this book the main character's name is Petras; the E in the first syllable is pronounced like a short A in English: PAT-ris.

Unlike English, in Lithuanian the last names of different members of a family have different endings to denote gender and marital status. Petras's last name is Simonaitis, his mother's is Simonaitienė, to show she is a married woman, and his unmarried sister's is Simonaitytė.

Religion that is pure and undefiled
before God and the Father is this:
to visit orphans and widows in their affliction,
and to keep oneself unstained from the world.

James 1:27 (RSV)

Petras – 1939
Autumn

Chapter 1

Petras* Simonaitis walked to work in the dark that October morning. Along the street he could see only the rooftops of houses and buildings weakly backlit by the moon.

It was his twentieth birthday, but he doubted anyone would remember. The pittance he earned today would go to his mother for meat, milk, and flour. Nothing left for frivolous things like birthdays.

He didn't expect anything else. His family had been rock poor for a long time. He didn't mind that his mother couldn't give him presents or make him a cake. That wasn't very important, really. He did mind that he couldn't do anything for her.

He blew on his chilled hands. He loved the red, gold,

Petras [PAT-ris]: Peter

and bronze of autumn but not the increasing dark, nor the damp cold. Soon the trees would be stark sticks against a lowering winter sky, and the days short, only seven hours long at the Winter Solstice. They weren't much longer in October. He ached at times for sunlight, which at best he saw only on his half-day Thursday or on Sunday. If it was raining, or if it was foggy, a leaden sky weighed down his spirits.

"Petras," a voice called from behind.

He knew the voice, and he didn't want to hear what the voice would say to him.

"Petras Simonaitis," Father Juodas* repeated.

Silencing a heavy sigh, Petras turned to look at the priest. "Yes, Father?" he asked, his voice cold. Petras was not Catholic, but as a child he had attended the Catholic school, under Juodas.

"Good morning." The priest emerged from the shadow of the church. Dressed in black as he was, he was invisible out of the light.

"*Labas.*" •

"You don't wait for me to catch up with you, my friend? Surely you know I am getting old and slow." The priest smiled, a street light glinting off his large front teeth. His black cassock and hat were black holes in the dark, with only his teeth and narrow yellow eyes showing. The priest's name – Juodas, meaning black – suited him.

"Oh, you seem to get around quite well, Father."

"I need your help. I wonder if you could drop by the rectory this evening."

Petras stared at the priest. "This evening?"

Juodas [you-O-dus]
labas [LOB-us]: hello

Father Juodas nodded. "Yes, some naughty boys – you know how boys are – " he said with a smug, sleek smile that Petras hated " – some boys threw stones and broke my windows. I need them replaced before the winter sets in."

At last the sigh Petras had suppressed hissed out through tight lips. "Yes. Of course. I will stop by this evening. You know that Antanas keeps me after hours these days, so it will be late." Very late. With the extra duty, it would be nearly midnight before he could return home.

Father Juodas waved a scrawny hand. "I understand. It won't bother me to wait for you."

But it would bother Petras to come late to help him. "Which windows?"

"The two in my study, overlooking the back orchard. Small windows they are."

Petras shook his head. "Not so small – at least a meter wide. You will take a chill when they let in the north wind. I'll come."

"Good. And I have another issue to talk to you about. Something to your benefit."

"Really? What is it?" Petras asked warily.

"A proposal. I'll talk to you tonight. Don't be late."

No thanks from the priest, just an order. But Petras expected nothing else. His back stiff, he strode on to work. He remembered the Christmas ten years ago, just after his father died, when his mother had nothing to feed him and his sister – the first time the priest deceived him. Would this be another betrayal at the hands of the tall, dark, cadaverous man?

Petras entered the old, brick, two-story building that housed the glass works, into a hot, black room with flares of molten fire in the ovens. It reminded him of a cave, dark and protected, the heat welcome on such a raw morning.

He had worked for Antanas Paškas,* glassmaker, as his apprentice for two years and was soon due to be made a master glassmaker himself. Antanas had once promised to help him set up his own glass works, but Petras didn't dare bring it up now, for Antanas was avoiding all talk of that. The town didn't have enough money or business for two master glassmakers.

"Petras," Antanas said warmly. He was a friendly, robust man whose round face was always red, gleaming crimson in the oven's glare; sweat poured down his cheeks and stained his navy shirt. His voice, high and squeaky, didn't match his looks; it had taken Petras a long time to get used to it. "I'm glad you're here. We have much to do today." The short, rotund man rubbed his hands together. "That big window for the Baron's salon comes first – he'll pay well."

"But –"

"But what?" Antanas asked, impatience in his voice.

"But Widow Kazlauskienė needs her window repaired."

"But she won't pay on time. It will be a few *litai* * now and an old, tough rooster later."

"She'll freeze. Antanas, you know of her weak lungs – how can you put her off again?"

Antanas put on a stern look that was not common to his broad, jolly face. "No arguing about this, Petras. You are a good boy, but you have no business sense. Now you must work – and on the Baron's stained glass."

Petras clamped his mouth shut, turned away from Antanas, and put on his leather apron and gloves. He would work for the Baron, but he would do his best to put a curse

---

Paškas: [PASH-kus]
litai [LEE-tai]: unit of paper money, pl.

on the glass so it would bring the arrogant man no pleasure. What if his mother knew his thoughts? He wasn't supposed to be thinking of spells and curses.

But if you scratched any Lithuanian, Christian or not, you'd find a bit of the old pagan underneath.

Nearly asleep on his feet, Petras dragged himself out of the glass works and to the priest's house. The cold took his breath away. The ancient hands on the clock in the town centre pointed to 11, so late after a day at work. The heat from the ovens sapped a man's strength, if long hours and a small supper hadn't already killed it off. The shops hunched over him as he walked; they felt menacing in the dark, but in daylight they sported pastel paint on stucco and their windows sparkled in the sun.

The handles of his heavy packet, the two glass panes set in a wooden carrier and padded with batting and canvas, cut into his hand. He shifted it to his other hand, then raised the knocker on the heavy wooden door to the priest's large, gray stone house. Unable to avoid making comparisons, he noted the heft of the door, its tight fit, the imposing façade of the two-story mansion that housed the priest. For one man, luxurious indeed compared to the small cottage Petras's family shared. He shrugged – no reason to harbor bitterness about it, for it would change nothing; yet he admitted to the bitterness within him.

A cold wind swirled around his ears. He shivered. Why was that old priest taking so long? The man knew he was coming.

At last the door opened, and Caterina, the priest's housemaid, peered distrustfully at Petras. "What do you want?"

"Father Juodas asked me to come, to repair the broken

windows."

She shrugged and opened the door barely wide enough for Petras to squeeze by her. He tried not to touch her, but she drew too close to him. He had heard tales about her, but he didn't want to think about them.

Her gray skin, sour demeanor, and rotten teeth repulsed him. Yet behind her distasteful appearance he thought at times he saw another Caterina, once young and lovely.

"Come see me later, Petras," she wheedled.

"Not I, Caterina," he said stiffly. "I'm too busy."

She shook her head. "Now, now. Don't be rude. I know how to teach you some things."

Unable to speak, he turned away and strode down the long hall of the house. Lined with dark woods and sparse sconces with dying candles in them, the hall was darker than the grave.

"You know the room, don't you?" she called after him. He didn't respond to her – why bother?

He knocked loudly on the door. Again he was made to wait. How dare this wicked old man expect a late-night call but then keep him standing about? Shoving open the door to the study, he walked in without waiting for a word from Father Juodas. Immediately he noticed something was missing: a breeze from the broken windows he'd been summoned to replace.

He heard the old priest's voice and realized someone else was in the room with Juodas. It was the Baron, Pavel Gerulaitis.

The Baron spoke. "You will let me know soon about the annulment. I don't have a lot of time to wait for this, Juodas." He looked up as Petras entered and blanched. "What are you doing, Simonaitis, eavesdropping?"

"Ah, Pavel," Juodas said, "you have nothing to fear from

Petras."

Pavel lowered his voice, yet Petras still heard his words clearly, as if the man were on stage and whispering in a way to be sure his audience heard him. "I don't want him hearing my business; he knows too many people and can spread gossip about it."

"No one pays him any mind – he doesn't earn enough in a month to redeem a cat from the pawnbroker."

Petras felt blood rush to his head in anger, but he struggled to control it. It wouldn't do to lose his temper here. Instead he took a moment to survey the gloomy, square room.

In front of a large marble fireplace the two men were sitting at a small round table spread with tea things. Petras eyed the crystal tea glasses set in filigreed silver holders. At home his family drank hot tea from pottery mugs, chipped ones at that. The remains of the tea, half a loaf of white bread, cherry jam, some ham slices and four slices of fresh white cheese could have made a whole meal for his family, but here they were merely leftovers.

The Baron – tall, hefty, with black hair, a scowl on his dark face and fleshy, sensual lips – turned to look at Petras and smiled like a fox who had discovered a nest of baby chicks.

"Why are you spying on us anyway?" the priest asked.

Petras scowled, his anger hot enough to burn his brain. "You didn't ask me to come here tonight? You didn't hear me pounding at the door? You didn't see me enter?"

The Baron stood and grabbed Petras's arm. "Watch how you speak to your elder and superior, boy!"

Petras pulled away from the Baron, shrugging his shoulders to straighten his coat. "Yes, sir," he said coldly, glaring at the large man.

"You don't sound as if you mean it," the Baron said.

It galled him, but he said what the man expected. "Oh, I mean it – sir."

The gaunt old priest shooed the Baron off. "Go on home now, Pavel. Petras must replace the glass. It is late for the boy to be out."

The Baron smiled, but it was an ugly smile. "I'm leaving, Juodas, but I'll be back." To Petras he said, "I will be checking on you to make sure you do the work right."

Petras bridled and began to speak, but saw a quick negative gesture from Juodas, which he obeyed automatically.

Once the Baron left, Petras made a cursory check for the broken windows, but he couldn't see them. At last he realized that they were behind a heavy tapestry. For some irrational reason that made him even angrier: the widow Kazlauskienė would not have a heavy tapestry like this one, in reds and deep blues and gold, to cover her broken window. He resolved to fix her window on his next half-day. Why should these odious people be warm and dry when that kind old woman suffered? And who was more generous with her widow's mite than she was?

Juodas gestured to the end of the room. "They're covered for now, but you know a mere piece of cloth won't stop any winter blasts for long," he said.

Petras didn't try to answer him. Instead, he set to work replacing the broken glass.

Juodas talked as Petras worked, not about anything interesting to Petras. Then, once Petras had finished his work, Juodas cleared his throat and said, "I have a proposition for you." He rubbed the black stubble on his chin.

"What is it, Juodas?"

Juodas flicked his eyes around the room. "It is a small thing, but I need some help. A little matter of administrative work for the parish."

Petras stared at him. "What?"

"It's not much, but you're the best candidate for secretary for me."

"I can't work for the parish. The church would never accept me."

"I can get you a good stipend for it."

Petras shook his head, but Juodas held up his hand. "Listen. I'd register you on the parish rolls, quietly, not to make a fuss. There'd be no question."

"I can't!"

"I need you. No one else is as meticulous, and I know you're honest." Seeing Petras's face, he changed tactics. "You have to do it. You have no choice."

"You can't force me to do this!"

Again Juodas rubbed his chin. "I don't want to threaten you, Petras."

"With what? I don't belong to you!"

Juodas started to stammer, then stopped and began to speak very slowly. "I'll speak to Antanas about your position. You want to be a master glassmaker. I can keep that from happening."

Petras stared at him. "But why? There are many other people in your parish better suited to working for you."

"No. I want you." Juodas then switched topics. "I think I should tell you, Petras – since we are such old friends – Pavel is interested in Rima."

Petras tensed; he stared at the priest. Did he know Petras himself was interested in Rima? And why did Juodas care? Rima was Catholic and out of his reach, in Juodas's eyes. He turned to look at him. "And?"

Juodas smiled at him, a greasy smile, Petras thought. "Isn't it true that you are romantically involved with Rima?"

"'Romantically involved'? What do you mean by that?" He carefully controlled his panic to keep it out of his voice. Her father and brothers would follow Petras in the dark some night and beat him without mercy if they knew he was interested in Rima. He'd never done more than speak to her because he figured he had no chance with her.

Juodas laughed. "Do you not hunger for that slim, yet luscious female form, are you not encouraged by the cow's eyes she makes at you?"

"Isn't Pavel married? What are you implying?"

"Marriage vows have meant nothing to him. You are enough of a man to know that. And she is very lovely."

Petras had to count to ten, slowly. If he didn't control his anger, he would perhaps go for the priest's throat. If he did, however, where would his mother and sister be? "I don't like the way you discuss her, *Father*," he said slowly. "Is there a bit of lust in you, perhaps?"

At that Juodas's face purpled, and he struggled to speak. At last he sputtered, "Why, you devil's spawn! How dare you speak to me this way? I am your spiritual father. You will have much to answer for in confession."

Petras smiled. "But you forget. I am not one of your little flock. I am *bambizas*." * He hurled back at the priest the word that had hurt so when Petras was a child, a pupil in Juodas's classroom. "Remember? My family are not members of your church. Praise the good Lord – I want no part of you."

Juodas recoiled as if he'd been struck. "After all I've done for you. I have treated you as if you were my own son."

---

bambizas [bam-BEE-zus]: of the Reformed church; a derisory term meaning not of quality

"I'm glad I wasn't!"

"When I corrected you, years ago in school, it was for your own good," he said through gritted teeth, "to make you a man. I thought you appreciated all I've tried to do for you!"

"Like with the lottery?"

"Lottery?"

"Yes, the one where I won twenty kilos of beef; you betrayed me."

"What?"

"You talked me into trading it for more tickets, you said so that I could win the prize of two hundred *litai*, do you recall? Instead I ended up with a pencil and a pad of cheap paper."

Once again Juodas's face turned purple, and a shaft of pain crossed it, mingled with something else Petras didn't recognize.

Petras pressed on, knowing that he could perhaps win this battle with the priest but never the whole war. Not as long as the Church was a power as great as the government, aligned as it was with rich landowners like the Baron.

With a shock he realized the truth. "There was no two hundred *litai* prize, was there? It was promised by the Baron's father, but it didn't exist, did it? That beef would have fed my family for a whole winter." He ran shaking fingers through his hair. But – why would a rich man bilk poor people that way?

Juodas's cheekbones pressing white against his pale skin, his yellow eyes narrowing. "You don't know anything about it. There was no beef either, you stupid boy. Just go back to your work, but remember my words – Pavel is after Rima." With that he turned on his heel and left the room.

Petras's heart sank. What had he done? Had he turned

this man into his enemy? Or rather, had he let Juodas know he considered him an enemy?

No beef, Juodas had said! There'd been no prizes at all, except for the cheap pencils and paper and a few rulers, for school children? His heart had broken when Juodas deceived him long ago, and now he realized Juodas had deceived everyone. But why? Why had there been no prizes?

He thought back to his school days. He'd been a bright pupil, which was both good and bad in Juodas's eyes. Depending on his mood, he used Petras either as a shining example of a hardworking, bright boy, or as a butt of his anger when he tried to shame the others, the Catholic boys, to outdo this *bambizas*, this *other*.

One day Petras would have his seat in the scholars' row, the next in the dunce's seat, depending on how bad a day Juodas was having. He grimaced as he remembered his first day of school. He had looked forward to going; his parents had already taught him to read and do simple math, they had talked to him about European politics and history, and he knew he could learn new things.

The classroom was warm with a good gas fire because the priest hated to be cold. There were many books lined up behind Juodas's desk, and Petras's hands itched to hold them and read them.

Within two weeks Juodas knew Petras was bright. Rain hissed at the windows and the wind whistled in the chimney when Juodas marched him up to the top form where he had Petras recite the names of all the Russian, German, and Polish rulers, from 1750 on. Juodas showed him off to shame the others, but the end result was that the bigger boys waylaid Petras after school and beat him up. He'd refused to cry, until he got home and his mother saw his cuts and the blood running down his face and chin. He'd blubbered in her arms for a full ten minutes and swore he'd not step foot inside that school again. But he did. And when he came back, day after day, the older boys still bullied him, but with time they grew to respect the tough, wiry boy who would not cry.

Except once, when Papa died, and Juodas refused to let him be buried in the cemetery. Because Jona Simonaitis was not Catholic, his body had to be taken to Latvia by train, to be buried in a Protestant cemetery there. The rejection of being "other" still stung when he thought of that time.

Coming back to the present, he thought of Rima. Pavel Gerulaitis was noted for his depravity and cruelty. But what could Petras do to save her? She was off-limits to him, forever.

CHAPTER 2

Early in the morning, when it was still dark, Rima Baltrunaitė climbed the steps to the mammoth oak doors of the church. With carvings on each side, bas-relief likenesses of saints Peter and Paul, the doors seemed to forbid her to cross the portal, but she was always driven to enter, to confess her sins. At times, the two saints appeared in her dreams and turned into gargoyles, or into devils that chased her into the sea, where she became imbedded in amber. From inside the amber she'd scream and cry for help, and although men looked at her and knew she screamed, they did not try to help her.

Five men passed by the church singly, on their way to work. Was Petras one of them? She thought so, the one at the front of the line. He walked straight and purposefully, but the others looked old, hunched over against the wind.

Rima shivered, drew her coat around her, rounding her shoulders to hide her feminine figure. Several of the men in town acted as if they lusted after her, so she tried to shrink inside her clothes, which she wore too large in order to hide her appearance. She had not asked to be beautiful or attractive to the wrong kind of men. She wanted to wear beautiful clothes in festive, light shades, white and pink and pale blue, but instead she disguised herself in the rusty black of old women.

She found none of the men around her appealing, except for Petras, who was too often engrossed in his work or family worries and rarely spoke to her. They'd been friends when younger, but now he seemed to have forgotten her.

And the Baron? He frightened her. She prayed every day she could find work somewhere else, rather than for him at his estate. It was a lovely building, a manor built in the 1700's by the Russian Catherine for one of her many lovers, but Rima hated the thought of going back there.

A stiff breeze stirred the dry, papery leaves littering the marble stairs. Rima pulled her scarf closer about her face, for she feared a relapse of the influenza she'd had for the past month. One good thing about illness: it kept her feeble, thin, tired – and at home, out of the town centre on market days and out of the Baron's Castle.

She pulled the heavy doors open just wide enough to squeeze through. The smell of incense and dust, and of chrysanthemums, bit at her nose.

Three women sat separately around the church, all saying their rosaries. She heard the mumble of holy, devout voices, the kind of voices she hungered for.

Rima dipped cold fingers into colder holy water and crossed herself. She passed under the tympanum to a row halfway down the aisle, genuflected, and eased herself silently onto the kneeling bench. "Hail, Mary, full of grace, the Lord is with you," she whispered, at ease now that she was safe inside.

Still needing to confess, however, confess her desire for Petras, she did not let herself relax too much. That would be wrong. She still needed to suffer yet a little while. And perhaps she would, what with war threatening. But what suffering it would be, with too much death and destruction.

As she rose, a prayer sprang up in her heart: "Oh, God, give us peace!"

Firelight in the ale house common room cast glints of light onto the ruddy faces of the men. The Baron, Pavel Gerulaitis – a Lithuanian with a Russian name but German sympathies – surveyed the room, and the other men in it. The fire in the large stone fireplace winked in the copper kettles on the walls and in the glasses lined behind the bar. Pavel sat back in the shadows, to be unobtrusive and able to listen and observe the men across the room, hoping they would forget his presence. Only two of them mattered: Petras, compact and wiry, intense and driving, fair, with Slavic cheekbones; Kazys,* tall, slim, ascetic. Both were idealists.

And then there was the Jew, Joelis,* with whom Petras was entirely too friendly.

And the two Communists, from Russia, pragmatists like himself. But he'd already sized them up: they lacked his black strength, a gift from the *velnias*.*

Kazys [kuh-ZEES]
Joelis [YO-el-is]: Joel
velnias [VEL-nyas]: pagan Lithuanian demons or the devil

The last man was from the United States and of absolutely no interest to Pavel; the man said he was a journalist, but Pavel doubted it. Few Americans ever visited Lithuania and none cared about its welfare; it was too small and too far off the beaten path for Americans.

"I tell you, Kazys, this is the time to push for change. Come with us to the union rally tomorrow night." Joelis gestured toward the American, Robert Branson. "Robert tells me this can help us."

Petras reached across the heavy wooden table for the earthenware jug of ale. Splashing some of the dark ale out on Kazys Palauskas's pile of books in his haste, he poured more for himself and the American and gestured to ask Kazys whether he wanted more.

Kazys, a philosophy professor in Vilnius,* shook his head and used his sleeve to wipe the frothy ale off his books. "Careful, Petras," he growled. "These are new books for the classes I'll be teaching – I'd rather not ruin them before I get to read them."

"Ah, dump them," Joelis said.

Petras hurried to cover for his friend. "It's just that Joelis thinks this meeting coming up is more important."

Kazys stiffened. "I doubt that, Joelis. And Petras, *mano drauge,** you need to know it's only education that will last."

In spite of the fact that the comment was directed to Petras, Joelis responded. Irrepressible, he grinned crookedly. "Maybe, but not likely," he said. "At least come see what's going on."

Kazys shook his head, offense on his face. "I'm too busy. You know that, Petras."

Vilnius [VILL-nyas]: capital of Lithuania
mano drauge [MAH-no DROW-gheh]: my friend

To the Baron the interchange looked like a tennis match, with Petras as the net. Joelis and Kazys were playing the game, and Petras couldn't take in what was going on.

Yet the Baron knew that in reality he and the Communists were the real players in the game.

Pavel leaned back to hide the smile on his face. Perhaps Kazys and Petras, close friends as they were, would argue and fall out; at that point he could move in and control this group of hotheads for his own purposes.

Still the men argued back and forth. The Baron shook his head, the smile still on his face. If only they knew what was to come. The two coarse, crude Communists and the sleek, well-fed American had no idea, although they thought they had.

"Look, Petras," Kazys said crossly to his friend as they strode through the town centre late that night. A heavy mist haloed the streetlights, and a hint of frost etched the men's breath in the night air. "I'm not coming to this rally Joelis spoke of. You go if you wish. I must prepare for class."

"Why? What is to prepare? You know more philosophy than all the Jesuits at that university. How can you waste your time this way? The fate of Lithuania – !"

"'Fate of Lithuania,'" Kazys repeated, scorn on his long, narrow face. "You won't change the course of history, *mano drauge.*"

Petras stopped in the middle of the street. "This from you, my idealistic friend? You can't be serious!"

Kazys faced him. "I am serious. There is still a worldwide depression. Until it ends, we are in danger of someone – Russia or Germany, who knows which one – gulping us down. Again."

Petras grabbed his friend's arm and shook it. "That's precisely what Joelis was talking about. This is the time to make a difference. If we form unions ourselves, the Soviets will leave us be."

"Never."

"Why do you do this, act so pigheaded? It can make a difference. People want economic justice, but not communism. We can forestall the Soviets. And the Nazis. They look at Baltic ports too hungrily."

Kazys shook his head, the light, thin hair blowing like dandelion fluff. "You will not succeed."

"We have to. Didn't you understand a thing Joelis was saying? This is the time – 'strike when the iron is hot,' you understand."

"So earnest, so serious," Kazys said lightly.

Stung, Petras pulled his hand back. "Earnest? Such a dire failing to have. But, yes, I'm earnest." He glared at Kazys, whose eyes sparked in the streetlights. Turning on his heel, Petras strode off in the other direction.

"Oh, please don't be angry," Kazys called after him.

Petras did not reply. He was so angry-hot, who knew what he would say? He dreaded going home now, for to be sure his mother would be awake and waiting to hear about his day, and she would see how angry he was.

He decided to take his time getting home by circling through the old crooked streets in hopes of walking off the rage. He often wondered whether his anger would burn holes – like acid, or fire eating old crimson tapestries – in his brain and heart. Yet he didn't want to give it up; at times he found it purifying, for it kept his eyes focused on important things.

When he reached home about thirty minutes later, one

small lamp burned behind the white lace that curtained the front window. He fervently hoped his mother wouldn't be up, waiting for him. He was afraid he'd see in her eyes the knowledge that he would never be a fully mature, real man. Think of the pittance he earned, in spite of how hard he worked.

The moment he stepped into the room, Petras heard a chilling sound, a woman sobbing. He closed the door silently, then paused. Was it his mother or his sister? He left his boots and coat in the hall and entered the parlor.

His mother, Donata, stood and came to him slowly, moving through the narrow hall like an old woman. Her gray cotton dress was wrinkled, her hair hidden under a dark blue babushka. She lifted her apron to rub at her eyes and dash away any telltale tears. "Petras, come in. How was your day?" He could make out Ona sitting on the sofa in a darkened corner of the parlor, out of the light. She was covered with a thin white blanket, her feet drawn up under her.

"What's wrong with her, Mamytė?" ˙

"I'm so sorry, Petras. This will make your hard day harder," she said, her sorrow dragging down her voice. "You get too upset, your stomach so sensitive."

"Mamytė, forget my stupid stomach! What is going on? Tell me!"

"The Baron, he…"

"What did that beast do?"

His sister Ona threw off the blanket and stood up. She stepped into the pool of light. He was struck again by his sister's beauty – her thick blond hair and brilliantly blue eyes, her peach and ivory coloring, her healthy body. To-

Mamytė [mah-MEE-tah]: Mommy

night she wore a dark red sweater Mamytė had knitted for her, over white slacks. She looked like a fashion model.

Hers was a strong, outdoors beauty, unlike Rima's more ethereal type. "Stop growling at Mamytė," she said. "You sound like a bear."

"What happened? If I have to drag it out of you, I will be a bear."

She looked at him, then slid her eyes away. "The Baron has told me I have to live at the Castle now. I can no longer come home at night."

"What else?"

A deep intake of breath shook Ona's body. "He says he plans to 'groom' me to be his wife. To be his *Vilkmerga*,* he said – he's so melodramatic."

"What?" he shouted. "The man is married! His wife is pregnant, due to deliver soon. How in Heaven's name – ?"

She covered both ears with her hands. "I don't know, I don't know! Don't yell at me, it won't make me say something I don't know. I just think…"

"What?"

"That it would be a wise move for me."

Petras stared at her. When he spoke, his tone was still strident. "This makes no sense." He paused and ran a hand over his face. He was so tired, he could fall asleep on his feet. "You want to go?"

She nodded slightly.

He forced himself to soften his voice. "Why?"

She shook her head. "I can't explain, really."

He looked at their mother and asked, as gently as he could, "What do you think is going on, Mamytė?"

Donata covered her mouth with her hand and turned

Vilkmerga [vilk-MEHR-geh]: the wolf's woman, or bride

away.

Petras stared at them both, then plopped down in a wooden chair next to a small round table and disarranged the lace tablecloth as he sat. "He'll never marry you, you know that. You're not noble, you're not wealthy. You're not telling me everything."

"He'll get me lessons with Stranski," Ona said, her voice flat. "You know how I have wanted to continue with my violin."

"That can't be reason enough."

"We're poor, have you noticed, Petras? And he will help us."

He stared at her. He'd never known her to be so calculating. "But why? At what price?" Petras asked.

"Please don't worry about it, Petras. You are just a boy," Donata said. "You do not need to carry more burdens."

He stood up rapidly, knocking the chair down behind him. "I am no longer a boy, Mother," he said through clenched teeth. "Tell me now – has he touched you, Ona?"

She laughed mirthlessly. "Don't ask such a question," she said, ice in her words. "Stay out of this, Petras. There's nothing we can do. It is a bad situation that a hothead like you will only make worse."

"No!"

"Yes. Stay out of it."

He picked up the chair and prepared to throw it into the front window.

"Petras! No!" his mother said quietly. "Put it down. We can't pay for a new window, even if you do work for Antanas. We are going to stop and think and pray about this."

"Pray?" Ona repeated her mother's word, icy sarcasm in her voice. "You may pray for a solution, Mamytė, but I will live with the problem." With those words, she folded the blanket, very precisely, and put it back in the cedar blanket box, very precisely, then left the room, her back straight, stiff.

Her shoulders bowed, Donata looked as if she'd aged two decades that night. She turned a shocked face to her son. "I don't know, Petras. Perhaps my faith is not strong enough for this."

He put his arm around his mother's shoulder. A lump in his throat threatened to choke him, but he forced his words out. "Don't say that, Mamytė. Your faith has to carry us all."

She looked up at his face. "You don't believe anymore?"

He dropped his arms and glanced away. "I…I don't know. Why must we all suffer this way, either under the Germans, or the Russians, or with our own people lording it over us through the Church or their land or money? I cannot understand a good God allowing this, Mamytė." Exhausted, tired enough to sleep on his feet, he rubbed his face with both hands. "I can't protect you and Ona."

She didn't reply, merely examined his face. At last she said, "Come, I have saved you some supper. You need to eat."

"I can't. I'm too weary to eat. I stopped to have some ale with Kazys, and that wolf Pavel was there. He's waiting to take us over. I think he plans to devour us, one way or another. He would love to see the Nazis goosestep into Lithuania, to see them fight off the Russians, who want us again, to use Lithuanian bodies as fodder in the battles. He's an evil man, Mamytė, and I'm helpless, like a boy, a child. I cannot fight him, and no one else sees what he is up to. Now he'll take my sister, split up our family, and I'm helpless."

He removed his boots and coat and placed them in the

hall. "Don't stay up to clean my boots, Mamytė. I will go to work with them dirty and clean them next half-day."

"I don't mind cleaning them, it gives me something to…"

"Don't!" he shouted. "Don't touch them! I'll clean them myself! Go to bed, now!"

She recoiled as if struck. "*Taip,* *taip, taip,* Petras, don't worry, I won't touch them."

Sorry he'd yelled, he couldn't bring himself to apologize. He was heartsick, knowing just how helpless he was.

Illogically, Petras thought of Joelis. Why did he think of him? Because he seemed helpless too, trapped by the people and events around him, not from any personal lack?

They had become friends instantaneously, once they'd looked each other in the eye, recognizing each other immediately, knowing what they were: smart, different, able to see the truth under the façade of daily life, the façade of Lithuanians living as if all were well.

Joelis had black eyes that sparkled, straight black hair, and a finely honed face shaped like a triangle that broke easily into sardonic smiles. Petras had liked him from the first moment they had taken in each other's presence.

He'd never told anyone of his friendship with Joelis, the times he visited his home in the Jewish quarter and learned the truth. While Lithuanians in general were tolerant of other faiths, there were still some who were anti-Semitic. In most of Europe, Jews had been forced to be moneylenders in the Middle Ages, since Christians couldn't touch "filthy lucre," but the money the Jews handled made them suspect and easily scapegoated for any economic or health problem that developed. If there was a recession, it

---

taip [type]: yes

was the Jews' fault. If there was a crop failure, blame it on the Jews. If cholera swept northern Europe, the filthy Jews had spread it on purpose, even though their people died of it too. If a child disappeared, it was because the Jews were kidnapping Christian children to use in unspeakable Satanic rituals.

On their part, Jews learned to mistrust and fear all Christians and told horrendous tales of *their* personal lives too.

Most Lithuanians allowed others their different faiths, but still distrust separated Jews and Christians. Perhaps the *Others* were guilty of some atrocities, some reasoned.

Petras knew better, as did Joelis. They heard the tales from both sides and exchanged looks, looks that said these might be good people, but they believed in lies.

Petras's head began to pound, for he'd lost his temper too many times today. *Sleep*, he told himself, *just sleep*. Not looking back at his mother, he staggered off to bed, to his small room up in the attic, under the eaves. Exhausted, he fell asleep immediately.

It seemed only moments later that he began to dream. He was driving an old panel truck, German make, in a snowstorm. He didn't know how to drive, but in his dream he did his best. He drove and drove, knowing he needed to get home before the snow got any worse. Soon he would not be able to see the road, nor the edge of the ravine yawning off to his left.

At last, on the road ahead he glimpsed a large house, like a country estate, with many yellow windows lit up; it seemed to be waiting for him to arrive, to come in out of the storm. He navigated the narrow drive and stopped beside the house. He recognized the house, yet he couldn't name who lived there.

He got out of the truck and went inside the house, where he found the Baron and Juodas awaiting him. They smiled at him and offered him a hearty repast: thick, hot soup and fresh bread with butter and jam, and steaming hot coffee full of cream and sugar. Their laughter echoed in the cavernous room, for before he could take a bite, the Baron spoke up. "You'd better get back on the road to deliver that body. You mustn't waste time this way."

So he went out into the snow and started up the truck; he was amazed that it started in the bitter cold. He drove down the drive, and the tail end of the truck began sliding off the road, down the steep ravine that was now on his right. He looked out the back window to see his cargo – a coffin – sliding out of the back of the truck. The coffin lid flew open. In stark terror he saw for the first time who was in it: Ona, her face contorted from the screams of her death. His heart split open in deep rents of pain out of the love he felt for her. He could see his heart beating and spurting blood, and he knew his heart was large, full of love for family and friends, and for his country, and even big enough to nurse hatred for the priest and the Baron.

Panic overcame him and he tried to scream, but at that point, the snow engulfed the truck and began to fill the cab. He was suffocating, drowning in tons of snow and his own blood, and there was nothing he could do about it.

Petras awoke from the dream, knew he'd tried to scream and couldn't. Tears burned his chilled face, for the north wind whipped around the house and sneaked in under the eaves, and he gasped for air. He was helpless to stem the tide about to deluge his country and his family. No one else saw, except those who wanted the flood, the ones who directed the flood, whose aim was to destroy the common people of Lithuania.

CHAPTER 3

On his next half-day, Petras decided to go hear Kazys lecture. Thursday afternoons Kazys taught Lithuanian history to high school students who were quick learners and needed more challenging school work. Petras had liked learning when he'd had the luxury. Besides, it was a good excuse not to go home. Petras still could not face his mother after shouting at her on Monday night.

Petras had been a good student but lost his powers of concentration the last two years of school when he'd had to go to work to support his mother and Ona. His mother would not let him quit before his last year, but he worked after school and weekends for Antanas, learning the trade. With no energy left for studies, he wondered whether he had missed something he needed to know now.

He took a seat in the back of the old, dusty room that

smelled of chalk and wet wool. Kazys nodded when he saw Petras enter but stayed in front, before the chalkboard and a pull-down map of Lithuania and surrounding countries.

When Kazys spoke, he used his long, thin hands expressively. He looked very professorial in a gray tweed jacket and wool slacks. His fine light brown hair fell over his eyes, and he pushed it back from time to time as he strode across the front of the room.

Now he was lecturing about the Lithuanian language, one of the oldest in Europe, an Indo-European language kin to the Prussian the Germans had annihilated centuries before. The Russians had tried to eradicate Lithuanian during the seventy-five years they had dominated the country in the nineteenth century and early twentieth, but the people were too stubborn to give it up.

He spoke of the fact that Lithuania had been a major European power seven hundred years before, and the last European country to become Christian. Crusades were fought in Lithuania over its refusal to join Christendom, yet at last it became a Christian country peacefully through the marriage of a Lithuanian grand duke and a Polish princess.

Yet in spite of its professed Christianity, Lithuania still bowed to its old pagan gods, the *velnias* – the demons – and the spirits in trees and forests, in the sea, and in its finest fruit, amber.

Roadside crosses featured the suffering Christ, meek and mild, but Lithuanians believed that Perkunas, the old god of thunder, conferred power – earthly power, the power of nature.

Petras knew these facts, but the overriding idea he gleaned from Kazys's teaching that day was the extreme stubbornness of the Lithuanians. Kazys spoke of it with pride, and Petras's heart lifted. He was stubborn, so he was a true Lith. But was he strong enough to resist the massive armies moving toward Lithuania at this moment?

How, he didn't know, but he would fight the German and Russian tides, and refuse to drown while doing so. He envisioned years of swimming against bloody tides, but also an eventual safe beaching, on the white sands of the Baltic. The Germans had infiltrated Klaipėda with their phony sports teams and now called it Memel, claiming it was German and always had been, just so they could have Nida and the only ice-free Baltic port. But some day it would be returned to Lithuania, in perpetuity.

Enough! He ordered himself to stop daydreaming. If he was going to spend time sitting in class, he needed to listen and learn something. Kazys was speaking now of Lithuania's religious ties to Catholic Poland and ethnic and language ties to Protestant Latvia.

Petras didn't know whether he was disappointed or relieved that he already knew this tangled history. His thoughts trailed off to the Baron and the huge stained glass window he was to begin installing the next day. Once again he'd handle the rich shades of the heavy leaded glass, once again he'd be allowed to arrange the pieces as if he were a painter with glass for his paints and his fingers as his brushes. Antanas was not one to praise much, but he made sure Petras knew how much his talent was prized.

Antanas had told him that even the Baron acknowledged that Petras was an artist with stained glass; even he respected the young man with the eyes of an artist.

When the students in the room stood to leave class, Petras shook himself. Time to concentrate.

"Well," Kazys said, "you didn't pay much attention after the first few minutes. I was going to ask how well you thought I taught, but you really can't answer, can you?"

"I'm sorry. I thought you did well, very well, in fact, but I also realized I'd learned most of what you taught. I was grateful for that small plum at least."

Kazys nodded, then began to gather up his books and papers. "You know all about my subject today, but there is more you can learn. I know you work long hours at the glass works, but I beg you not to neglect your mind."

Petras shrugged and stared down at his toes. "It's kind of you to encourage me. You're right – I could learn much from you."

"Ah, such courtesy between old friends. You're still hurt that I argued with you the other night."

"Never! I don't get hurt," Petras replied, knowing in his heart this was a lie. He hated lies and tried never to tell them, yet sometimes he had to preserve the social graces.

Kazys's mouth twisted wryly. "Whatever you say, *mano drauge*. Will I see you later?"

Petras glanced away. "Perhaps. Yes, I will certainly try to return."

He and Kazys walked out of the classroom. Kazys said, "I hope…"

"What?

He shook his head. "Nothing. Well, can you go for beer Saturday night?"

"I'll try to come. It depends on how things go at home." He sighed.

Kazys examined his face closely. "What's wrong?"

Petras shrugged. "I'm not sure, precisely. I think Ona is having problems with the Baron." He didn't add that Ona had packed her few possessions and moved to the Castle in a deep, dragging depression.

"His reputation…"

Petras glared at him. "I know. You think I am an ignorant child?"

"Of course not, Petras, for heaven's sake. You are so touchy." He looked down the length of the town centre ahead of them. "I always had hopes I could marry Ona. She is a beauty. But I won't earn enough to take a wife for some time."

"And it will be too late for her by then."

Kazys reached out to touch Petras's shoulder. "I'm so sorry. She was a lovely girl."

Was? "Right." Petras turned and walked off, with no leave taking. What was there to say? How could Kazys sound so distant about Ona, whom he supposedly loved? Petras didn't understand him anymore, that was the truth.

About two blocks down the promenade of the centre, Petras glimpsed Rima Baltrunaitė stepping into a dairy shop. He hadn't spoken to her in some time; he should speak to her now, to see how she was doing. What did Juodas's warning about Pavel's lust for Rima mean, now that he had taken Ona into his lair? Why would the priest expect Petras, a Baptist, to marry a Catholic girl?

And what of Pavel's wife? Did he plan to build a harem?

A woman nodded to him. The widow Kazlauskienė, a short, round woman, with brown hair and brown eyes – she reminded him of a wren – stood in front of the dairy store jiggling the handle of a baby buggy. Her grandchild, a blond two-year-old girl, wailed from inside the carriage.

"Good day, Mrs. Kazlauskienė," Petras said. "How is Marija's girl today?" Marija was the widow's daughter-in-law, married to Jona, a Baptist minister who had recently been called to a small church in Klaipėda. They were poor people too, like Petras's own family.

"Still suffering from her stomach. She cannot tolerate

cow's milk. We will try goat's milk today; that may help."

"Ah, yes. I hope it will. Mother had the same problem with me."

"I recall," she said with a smile, "but look at what a sturdy young man you have become!"

"Thank you," he said shyly, feeling awkward.

"Rima is inside," she whispered conspiratorially. "Will you join her?"

He blushed. "Oh, is she? I didn't know."

"Don't waste too much time claiming her, Petras. She would be a good wife for you," she said.

"But she's Catholic. Why do people expect us to marry?"

She shrugged. "Don't let the Baron get his hands on her, as he has…" She stopped, confusion reddening her face.

His face burned too. "Yes, Mrs. Kazlauskienė, I know."

He nodded to her, then left her to go sit on a bench across from the store. Fuming, he tried to understand why these people were behaving so much out of character, but he couldn't. He decided to wait for Rima here, and see what her face told him when she looked at him.

When she came out of the store, she saw him across the promenade. She smiled and crossed to him. The sun shone on her bright hair, and the cool, crisp air had put healthy color in her face.

He was sorry, however, to see her in dark, worn clothing, wishing instead to see her in a new rose dress he'd seen in a shop window a few days ago, but he knew her family couldn't afford new clothes.

He stood and took her bag from her. "May I carry this for you?"

She smiled and blushed. "Yes, of course." They fell to walking side by side, and she went on. "I've been thinking about you. How is your work going?"

"I start installing the large stained glass window at the Baron's tomorrow."

"Oh," she said, looking away, then back at him. "That's an honor, to be entrusted with such a task, isn't it?"

"Antanas says it is." They walked silently down the promenade. At last Petras spoke. "How is your family doing? And you? I heard you've been quite ill."

"Yes, I was, but I'm better now. My family does well enough, but I must soon go work for the Baron."

He stopped and gazed into her eyes. "Must you?"

She shook her head in denial of his concern. "Papa can't hold a job. The gas in the Great War damaged his lungs so badly, you know."

"Yes. I'm sorry." He didn't ask about her father's drinking because he knew how that was going.

He cursed himself for carrying on this prosaic conversation with the most beautiful young woman in the world. What exciting topic could he come up with to speak to her about?

They resumed walking, in silence. Was it an easy silence or a strained one for her? He peeked at her face and saw there a slight smile, and roses on her fine cheekbones. Perhaps she was content just to be with him.

At last he thought of something to say. "On Sunday, do you think you can go to the country with me? I want to fix the Widow Kazlauskienė's window."

"Antanas won't let you do it on his time, will he?"

"No, he says she can't pay anything but a tough old rooster, but even a tough rooster can be boiled down for broth. It wouldn't be a fancy outing for you, but I would like your company, if you care to come."

She took his free hand and squeezed it. "I would love

to go with you, Petras," she whispered. "It sounds like a lovely idea. And I can see Marija's little girl. She is so adorable."

"You like children?"

"Love them! And the little one is so precious, but my father won't let me associate with Baptists, you know. Oh! Sorry, Petras."

"Baptists are dangerous types," he said with a laugh.

She smiled shyly. "Yes," she whispered.

Keeping her hand in his, Petras led the way to her small frame house on the edge of town. They spoke easily of everyday matters, and the tightness around Petras's heart lifted so he could breathe. She was happy in his company, and that was all that mattered. He left her standing at her door, a shy smile on her lovely face. Rima cared for him – sweet, beautiful Rima.

His heart high, he watched as she entered her house with a wave to him and turned toward home. He was hardly fifty yards from the house when someone hailed him. "Petras," the man yelled. "Wait up."

He turned to face Alfonsas, Rima's older brother. "What is it?" he asked, still a bit euphoric.

Alfonsas had long, straight, reddish hair and high color in his pudgy cheeks. He looked, even now at 25, like a child. "Our father asked me to speak to you." Alfonsas turned both palms up to soften what he'd come to say. "I apologize, but it is my father's wish."

A chill ran up Petras's spine. "Yes? What is it – spit it out."

Alfonsas rubbed one toe in the dirt. "It's about Rima. We have – my father, that is, has nothing against you. He knows your family and how hardworking you are."

"And?" Anger rose in him once again. Were the people

in this town destined to anger him every time he encountered one of them? Other than the Kazlauskas family or Rima herself, or Joelis – the outcasts, he guessed.

"He says she has a great opportunity before her, to live at the Castle and learn gracious living. She will be able to move among the best."

Petras spat on the ground. "You are joking! The Baron will defile her!"

"Please, Petras," Alfonsas begged. "Don't say it. That will not happen to my sister. The Baron has promised."

"You do know he's taken over *my* sister and her life, don't you? How do you think Rima will fare any better?"

"Oh, Petras, you don't get it. Your family has always been on the outside, not even being in the Church. Always poor, always defiant. My father has gone along with the Baron and the priest, in whatever they ask, so we're safe in the authorities' arms, you know? Rima must not miss out on her one great chance."

"You're a fool, Alfonsas. It won't happen that way!"

"It will!" he shouted. "Please stay away from her, and don't interfere." With those words, he turned on his heel and left Petras glaring after him.

Their father, Eugenijus Baltrunas, his beer gut hanging over his belt, stood at the rickety gate in front of their house. He looked sober for once, and stern. He raised his fist in anger. "Stay away!" he yelled.

Petras heard him but didn't plan to heed him. He would wait to hear from Rima herself how she felt about her father's edict.

Chapter 4

The Baron, Pavel Gerulaitis, stood in his study, hands clenched behind his back, and stared out the large window facing the forest to the north. Birch and pine marched up the distant hills, their vigor making him smile. To him they symbolized what he knew Hitler could do to make this lazy, good-for-nothing country straighten up and work!

So many moony artist-types in Lithuania, idealists like that fool Petras. Life would change under the hands of the Nazis, with him at the forefront of the movement, as Hitler's co-leader.

His man rapped on the door to the study.

"Enter!" Pavel barked.

A trim, erect man with neatly combed, thinning brown hair, Walther Funk entered the room. He wore a tight-fitting gray wool suit, collar buttoned up to his neck. He was from Memel, a city on the Baltic often claimed by Germany; Pavel tried to hire only Germans because he valued efficiency. Funk didn't click his heels, however; the Baron didn't want all the trappings of the Reich, at least not yet. "Sir, Miss Simonaitytė is here. You'd asked her to come to you, she says."

Petras's sister at last. "Ah, yes. Send her in." He seated himself behind his desk and busied himself with some papers.

Ona Simonaitytė entered, head held high. He ran his eyes slowly over her strong, firm body, voluptuous, shapely. She wore a badly cut suit, in brown tweed, that he would replace very soon. By the hair of Perkunas's head, it was an ugly thing.

Her skin was like a sun-ripened peach. Her deep blue eyes, like lapis, returned his gaze boldly. He wondered who would break eye contact first. The golden blond hair that he wanted to grab and pull, hard, gleamed in the light from the chandeliers of the study.

He smiled, but she didn't smile back. "So, Ona. Are you thankful to have this opportunity to live at the Castle and to better yourself?"

"Thankful?" she repeated coolly. "Thankful?" She paused, then said, a slight sneer on those full lips, "Oh, yes, Baron, I'm very thankful."

He didn't correct her. The foolish young woman would learn her place soon enough.

She still held his eyes. "May I have a cigarette?"

"Cigarette," he repeated, smile on his lips. "A nice girl like you?"

"Oh, you'll make sure I'm no longer a nice girl, won't you, Pavel?"

He pulled himself upright and glared at her. "You are

not to call me that in front of any of the help, do you understand? You are to call me Baron at all times" – he paused – "except when we are, shall we say, intimate. I want this all to look perfectly correct."

"I understand – Pavel."

He glared at her. Her mocking tone and the look in her eyes told him that she planned to buck his authority at every turn; he relished the thought of teaching her to regret such behavior.

Danielius Martinaitis stopped his car in front of the widow Simonaitienė's house. He said a brief prayer, got out, hunched into his old leather jacket against the cold north wind, and opened the back door to remove a parcel on the floor behind his seat. He had heard from Herr Zeller, his pastor, that Donata needed some kind words now that the Baron had "hired" Ona away, perhaps for life. Danielius and his wife were only lay people, but they were noted in the small church for their gentle concern for others.

A language teacher at the new free church high school, recent competition to the state-supported Catholic school, he knew he was unprepossessing and that people overlooked him, but he took that as a gift from the Lord: he could do His work surreptitiously and no one interfered. Hair and eyes the color of creek water, a medium physique, a pleasant but not handsome face – he smiled: it made a good cover.

Danielius was a man who believed in prayer. He loved to pray, he lived to pray, yet he knew not all his prayers were answered as he sent them up. He couldn't guess why, but he kept praying anyway.

His thoughts returned to Ona and her mother, and

the others he prayed for daily. What was hardest for the people of their congregation? The living in fear of the Nazis' overrunning the land or just the day-to-day grind of working and trying to keep house and family together? He thought of the position Conrad Zeller found himself in now, pastor of the small church here, only ten families, yet a German citizen – to whom did the man owe his loyalties? Zeller was paid very little by the congregation, that he knew, yet he lived well enough, even with four growing sons to feed, the oldest nineteen and a hulking great man now. Did he have private wealth or another source of income? Danielius didn't know and wasn't sure he wanted to.

One family who had recently left the church complained about Zeller's sermons, calling them exhortations to work hard and obey the authorities rather than food for weary souls seeking God. Danielius thought that criticism was a little harsh although it did have some truth in it. He wasn't one to enter into gossip, however, so he did his best to do what he felt called to do, not what others might expect of him.

Tucking the awkwardly wrapped parcel more firmly under his arm, he tapped lightly on the door. He'd heard Mrs. Simonaitienė wasn't taking her daughter's loss well – and how could she? Everyone in town knew what this move to the Castle meant: the girl's ruin, and near enslavement under the Baron's heel. As he stood waiting for Donata, he resolved to go talk to the priest; surely Juodas had some influence over the Baron.

Donata Simonaitienė looked pale and sickly in the half-light of her small house. Her round, plain face was twisted with worry. "Come in," she said. "May I offer you some tea?"

He smiled at the woman. "If you are having some, yes,

thank you."

"It's brewing now," she said. He knew that was probably not true, but he wanted to leave her dignity intact. He doubted she had moved from her chair by the window all day, praying for Ona's return while knowing it would never happen. At best, when or if she returned, she would be much changed from the fresh, beautiful young woman she had been when she left.

Donata bustled back into the parlor with a tea tray. On the tray she had placed two flowered china cups, one cracked, her teapot under a crocheted cozy, and chocolate biscuits on a matching plate. Danielius wondered if the cups were the last pieces of her wedding china. His heart wrenched for her and her effort to be hospitable.

"So how is your wife?" she asked.

"Marita? Oh, she is fine," he said, adding his thanks when she served him tea with two lumps of sugar. "Donata, I hesitate to intrude on your sorrow, but I'm here about Ona."

She straightened, eyes downcast, and covered quivering lips with her left hand.

"This must be so painful for you."

She nodded and dashed tears from her eyes.

"I've brought a token of our affection for you and Petras – a small cake, some tea, and a book – just a copy of Marita's favorite book of poetry. It will not repair your loss, or even touch it, but we want you to know we're thinking of you."

Tears shimmered in her eyes. She couldn't bring herself to speak.

"You and your family have been special to us; you were the first to welcome us when we moved here." His words, he realized, were worthless, so he gave up trying to say the right thing. "I am so sorry, Donata. What can I do for you?

Is there any news from Ona?"

"Nothing, not even a note to say she's well. Which is reasonable – how can she be well, trapped up there at that monster's mercy – lack of mercy?" She raised tortured eyes to him. "It's tragic what this is doing to her, to me, but I worry now what it's doing to Petras. He has become so hard, so angry. I fear…"

Danielius stared at her. Surely, no matter how badly this affected Petras, Ona's situation was much worse. He didn't voice this, however; his job was to sit and listen, not to judge.

She glanced at him. "You think I am wrong to be so concerned about Petras?"

"No, I – "

"It's that he's so sensitive, you see. He is young and strong, yet he feels helpless. He fights so hard to change things he cannot change."

"God can change things. Does he pray?"

She shook her head, her eyes glittering unnaturally.

"And you – do you pray?"

"But of course! Without ceasing, as Saint Paul told us to, yet I see no change for us. God works slowly at times."

"Yes," Danielius said. "We want him to move like lightning."

"You see what I mean," she whispered, "you know how it is." She sighed, then gestured. "Drink your tea before it turns cold. Surely it has already. Let me refill your cup."

"No, Donata, this is fine." He drank his tea in three sips, not one gulp to indicate he wanted to leave. He cared about this family, yet felt helpless to aid them. Perhaps Conrad Zeller could advise him.

Soon he took his leave. "I'll pray for you, as will Marita. This is very hard." He put his hand on the tiny woman's shoulder. "Blessings, dear Donata. We won't forget you."

Now the threatening tears came. "You are both good friends, and I thank the good God for you. We'll be all right. Don't worry too much about us."

Petras started to whistle on his way to work, but he stopped himself. His heart had no reason to fly high today; nothing had changed in the days that had gone before. Ona was gone from their family for good; perhaps Rima would also vanish into the Castle maw.

No – she wouldn't. He wouldn't let that happen. Perhaps soon he would think of a way to save her. Perhaps he could do something that made a difference.

The early morning, still dark, was cold but clear. The chill in the air made his nose run and reminded him of childhood days when he and his friends went sledding. The brightest days were always the coldest, but being able to see the sun in winter always cheered him. Perhaps later today he could see the sun.

This was the day he was to go to the Baron's to install some of the new stained glass. It would take several days, perhaps a week or more, to complete the task. Perhaps while he was in the Castle he could learn something to help him solve the double problems of Ona and Rima, and the overriding one of the Baron's mistreatment of so many people in town.

Ona's and Rima's plights made the Baron's wickedness personal for Petras. But what to do?

He saw a familiar figure ahead – Joelis, his Jewish friend, dressed in a black suit and long overcoat that were a bit too large for his small frame.

"Petras!" Joelis called. "How are you? I haven't seen you

since that night at the pub."

"What are you doing these days?" Petras asked Joelis. "Are you working now?"

He grimaced, his finely chiseled face contorted under the spiky black hair. "After a fashion. My parents expect me, still, to finish up one more year of Sabbath school, then go to Vilnius for rabbinical school. You know my grandfather and father want me to be a rabbi. In spite of the political situation."

"Being a rabbi sounds right for you, always a good student."

"But pointless at this time in history, I think. Didn't you hear?"

"What?"

"Of the crazy Jewish boy who shot a minor Nazi official in Paris. Germany is sure to extract vengeance here too, as they have in Krakow. Hitler will decide to punish even unimportant Jews like us in Shavli,˙ you know."

"No, why do you say that? The Germans stay mostly in Klaipėda, not here."

"But what of men like Pavel? Do you think the Baron is the only cruel Nazi? He ruins all the lovely young Aryan women here – "

Petras grunted as if punched in the solar plexus.

Joelis put a long, slim hand on his friend's arm. "I'm sorry. I heard about Ona, Petras, and know it must be terrible for you. But he hates us Jews, you know, and wants to torture us, I think."

"But why? Surely he doesn't know of your existence."

Joelis's face froze. "He knows. He knows."

Shavli: Jewish name for Šiauliai; major Jewish center, also major ones in Vilnius (Vilno) and Kaunas (Kovno)

"I – I detest such vermin as he is, but maybe you are too pessimistic."

"I warn you, my friend." He turned to walk on.

Petras at that moment remembered something Kazys had told him the night before. "Wait! Did you hear about the German Gymnasium coming to town?"

Joelis turned a bleak face to Petras. "No. Tell me," he said, lead in his voice.

"Kazys has heard that German athletes are coming to Lithuanian cities to hold sporting events, supposedly to teach some skills to boys and young men. But it sounds suspicious to me."

A lashing of anger crossed Joelis's face. "This may be the way they get us. Petras, do you believe in prayer?"

Petras felt the blood rush to his face. "I – I'm not sure. My mother does."

"Please ask her to pray for us, the Jews of Lithuania." He turned on his heel and strode off.

Petras watched him go. He didn't know what to do for Joelis, or for himself, for that matter. Everything looked easy, innocuous, on the surface, but he felt a maelstrom building that would engulf them all.

Did he believe in prayer? He wasn't sure, but he nevertheless lifted a short one up to God: *If you are there and if you care, protect Joelis and all of us too.*

He went on to the glass works to pick up the central pieces of glass for the Baron's massive rose window. Once he'd wrapped them securely, he set off, Antanas's words to be cautious ringing in his ears. What else would he be, with fifty pounds of costly glass?

He decided to take a shortcut between the Zellers' house and the old cemetery. The glass was heavy, and he could save some steps. Near the Zellers' outbuildings he saw a familiar figure, a young man who now looked toward him and waved.

"Petras!" It was Hans Zeller, the Baptist pastor's son, who was about Petras's age. Hans had never hung out with Petras and his friends, but had always been cordial. "Where are you going?" Hans asked, a friendly smile on his broad face. Hans had always seemed a fresh-faced puppy-dog sort of person, although hanging around on the edge of groups, never part of them, not quite fitting in. He seemed friendly but flew into rages with slight provocation, so the other guys didn't trust him.

Today he wore the hated Nazi brown-shirt uniform and a leather pistol holster at his side. "You're a Nazi," Petras said.

"Oh, yes. That's why I wanted to speak to you. You need to come join us, Petras. Hitler's Army is the wave of the future. You would like the order, the uniforms and flags, the marching. It's thrilling."

Petras laughed out loud. "Me, like marching and uniforms? Oh, Hans, you don't know me, do you?" He sobered as he thought how stifled his artistic needs would be if he had to join the military, how damaged his pride would be if he were forced to support a foreign country's domination of his beloved Lithuania. "Never in a thousand years," he said through gritted teeth.

Hans's face suffused with blood, as if he'd been slapped. "You must not speak that way, Petras. I'm warning you." He fumbled with the flap over the pistol in the holster, withdrew the gun, and pointed it at Petras. "If I were to shoot at you," he said, his voice trembling in fury, "you could not possibly escape. You could try to run, but you could not hide, because the power of this pistol would overwhelm your puny strength. The same is true of Lithuania and Germany – Lithuania can run but it will never succeed in hiding from us and our onslaught."

Petras, ice now rising in his veins, replied, "You're correct about that, Hans." He stopped and looked into the man's pale blue eyes. "But you, the pastor's son – how could you? How could you?" He turned his back on Hans Zeller and walked away, sure that the barrel of the gun was aimed between his shoulder blades. Would Hans shoot him now, in cold blood? No, nothing that easy. The Nazis would rather suck his blood out, slowly and painfully.

"You never told me where you're going, Petras." Hans's voice held a hint of threat, so Petras knew he should answer.

Without stopping, he called over his shoulder, "To install a stained glass window for the Baron." He added, knowing full well that he shouldn't, "Is that all right with you, *Herr* Zeller?"

"I warn you, Petras, for your own good. Be careful."

Petras didn't reply but trudged on to the Castle, his heart heavy. Hans, he hated to say, was right: they were like rabbits in a stoned-in garden, with no boltholes.

The Castle rose before him, three stories of stone, with long, narrow windows and a large, round turret that rose above the roofline. Not really a castle, rather a baronial manor, it was relatively plain but impressive enough. Until Pavel took over after his father's death, it was called the Manor, but that hadn't been enough for the new baron.

At the Castle, the butler, Walther Funk, opened the door to Petras. "Come in," he said softly and gestured for Petras to enter. Even this mild-mannered servant of the Baron's irritated him; Funk seemed like a kicked dog, slavering at the Baron's heels.

Petras shook his head in disgust, once more hoisted

the packet of glass, and entered. Every thought of the Baron angered him.

"Follow me," Funk said, his manner calm and courteous. "The Baron is out, but he has left orders for you. I'm sure you will have no problems."

Petras didn't know whether he was relieved not to face the man or angry that Pavel hadn't paid him the courtesy of being available. Either way was an irritation.

Ona! he thought. "My sister, Ona," he said to Funk. "Can I see her?"

Funk looked rueful. "No, Petras, I'm sorry. She is also gone. I believe they are boar hunting."

"Boar hunting? Ona?"

Funk shrugged slightly. "She looked lovely in her green velvet riding habit. You would have been proud to see her." He led Petras into the large salon where he was to install the stained glass. "You know what to do, I understand," he said kindly. "Is there anything you need?"

Petras looked around the large, square room. It was overwhelmingly opulent, with its gilt and cream-colored paint, with touches of peacock blues and greens and royal reds. He felt sure others thought it beautiful, but it repelled him with its overdone opulence. The sight of the room infuriated him, but there was no call to vent it on this mild-mannered butler. He felt sure Funk had nothing to do with the Baron's vileness. "I was told there would be a scaffold here. Do you know where it is?"

"Vanya was supposed to build it. I thought he would be here by now. I suppose you are a bit early? No matter. I'm sure he'll put it up for you in no time." He gestured to a gilded chair, upholstered in gold damask. "You may sit there until he comes if you wish."

Petras sat in the chair. It seemed he'd been on his feet

for hours. Yet even so, he could not settle, could not relax. He looked around the great hall and wondered whose blood bought that Turkish rug, whose flesh withered for the grand piano, whose gold teeth were yanked for the heavy tapestry above the blazing fireplace.

Other than the spitting, hissing sounds of the wood burning in the fireplace, there was no sound in the room. If it hadn't been for the fire, he might have wondered if he had gone deaf.

The warmth of the room made him drowsy. He fought against the rising sleepiness, but he decided to rest his eyes for a moment. Vanya would come with the wood scaffolding, and he'd get to work. Nothing he could do now anyway.

Chapter 5

As Petras dozed, images of small, crying orphans and old, hunched-over widows shivered before his mind's eye as they strained to hold up the walls of the Castle, for in his dream they'd been used as foundation blocks for the building. He ached for them, wanted to cry with them, but he couldn't reach them.

He must have slept a minute or two. He heard the clomp of heavy boots and jerked awake to see Vanya, Pavel's young brother, entering the room, carrying eight-foot lengths of lumber on broad shoulders.

About Petras's own age, Vanya was tall and thin, but his hands and feet promised a bull-like strength when he matured fully. His black hair spiked around a heavy head, brilliant blue eyes darted here and there, looking fearfully around the room for who knew what – Petras assumed it was Pavel the poor man feared. His mouth hung slack around large, mottled, protruding teeth. There was a strange odor about him, of cooking grease and a strong perfume, not precisely bad but not good either.

At last his eyes landed on Petras, and he tugged at the sleeves of his ill-fitting shirt. "Oh, Petras," he said, "sorry. I was supposed to have this up before you came, Pavel said. I'm late."

"It's all right," Petras said. "We'll get it up in no time."

Relief washed over Vanya's pinched face. "Thanks. You're a good guy. I don't know why Pavel hates you."

Petras felt the blood rush to his head, shocked at Vanya's honesty.

Vanya must have noticed for he said, "Sorry, guess I shouldn't have said that."

Yet it was to be expected: if he hated Pavel, why wouldn't the man hate him back? "Don't worry. It's no surprise." He gestured to the window. "I guess we should get the table up." Petras would build the window on a waist-high table and have a crew of men set it in place once it was completed.

They worked companionably for some time and got the fifteen-by-fifteen structure in place. It wasn't quite the craftsman-like job Petras would have built on his own, but it would do. Vanya talked to Petras the whole time and told him about his latest girlfriend, a dairyman's daughter. "But don't tell Pavel," Vanya implored. "He'll beat me if he knows."

"He'll beat you? Why?"

"He says Niela is beneath my station, but I know I have no station. My brain isn't good; I can only do some physical labor. But I do work hard." He gazed fondly at the braced table. "It's not bad, is it?"

Petras glanced over the wooden structure; the wood wasn't aligned perfectly and some of the nails holding it together had been hammered in crooked, but it was sturdy enough. "It looks as if it will do the job, Vanya." He clapped the young man on the shoulder. "I think you do fine work."

Vanya beamed at him. "Thanks, Petras. You're a good man, I know."

Petras blushed. A good man? A man who yelled at his poor mother and couldn't save his own sister from the Wolf of Šiauliai?* He didn't think so, yet he felt strangely blessed by Vanya's words, as if an idiot had special spiritual powers to bless him. "I'd better get to work."

Vanya nodded, a wide smile on his large, loose mouth. "Can I watch?"

Petras hid a sigh. He really didn't want to be watched. He feared an observer would hinder the artistry and skill of inlaying the glass pieces. Yet he hated to disappoint the man-child.

Man-child. That was an insulting label others could apply to him also. "For a bit. I may want you to leave later if I get behind schedule."

Vanya grinned. "Oh, thank you, Petras, thank you. I'll sit over here and be very quiet."

"Hmph, we'll see." With those words Petras set to laying out the glass, piece by piece, that would eventually make up the huge window.

A thought came to him; perhaps Vanya could tell him frankly what the situation was with Pavel's present wife. How could he marry Ona if he was already married?

"Vanya, I need to ask you. How is Pavel's wife doing? What is her name – Ana?"

Šiauliai [show-LAY]

"Oh, not well at all. You know Pavel hates her now. She is dark like us, and he wants only blond children."

"The Aryan type? But he's dark, as you say! How will he sire blond children?"

"Our mother was blond; he counts on her blood showing through."

"She was German, right?"

"Half-German, half-Russian. That's why we have these silly Russian names."

"But isn't Ana's baby due soon?"

Vanya's eyes slid away, to hide something, Petras thought.

"What is it?"

"She is not doing well. Don't tell anyone – he'll kill me – he beats her, you know, terribly."

"How bad?" Petras asked, his heart sinking. Did it really matter how badly? A large man beating a small woman?

"Bad, Petras. Sometimes she lies for hours in her own blood, unconscious. He's my brother, but he's wicked. I guess I am too, that's why my brain is not so good." He rubbed a drop of spittle off the corner of his loose lips. "Don't tell, please, Petras, don't tell," he begged.

Petras nodded. He'd vowed he'd call a curse down on the window and the Castle and its owner as he worked, and now he knew he'd been right to want to. He set to work, his heart heavy.

But it was hard to concentrate on curses as he handled the beautiful glass in myriad hues. Each piece was two layers, like a flat bottle. The layers caught the light and refracted it, giving depth and life to the design.

The central glass in the window was a representation of the Castle itself. The first row around that was a six-sided design of clamshells, which were consecrated to the

Lord's brother James. That struck a false note to Petras; the Wolf had no touch of true faith, of that he was sure. The next ring of designs in the window was of dark fir trees, the next ring a wolf's head repeated twenty-four times.

He figured he could easily finish that part of the window today. Vanya talked to him from time to time but didn't disturb his concentration. After an hour or so he heard voices, muffled by the heavy doors of the salon but resonating in the hall.

"Oh!" Vanya said, "Pavel's back! He'll kill me..." A look of stark terror blanched his face.

Petras stared at him. "How badly does he mistreat you?"

Vanya laughed a high, whinnying laugh. "He...! Never mind, forget I said anything." He raced across the room, ducked behind brocaded drapes, and disappeared from sight. A gust of air pulled the drapes into the long French windows, then ruffled them back into the room. Did Vanya have several boltholes throughout the Castle?

Within seconds of Vanya's disappearance, Pavel strode into the salon, through a door directly opposite the window Vanya had just left, carrying with him the scent of autumn leaves, cordite, and horses. "You're at work at last. Is it going well?"

"But of course, what else would you think?" Petras growled.

"Don't bother playing the temperamental artist, Petras. It won't work." With those words the Baron turned on his heel and left the room, returning in just moments. "Oh, by the way, you may speak to your sister before you leave. Tell Walther when you want her. I will tell her to hold herself ready for you."

"Excuse me, Baron, but is such formality necessary? Why can't she come in here and visit while I work?"

The Baron stared at him. "You don't know your place, do you?"

"My place? As her brother?"

"That hardly matters here. Get on with your work." Before stomping out of the room, again using the door opposite to Vanya's window, he turned and looked at Petras, a smirk on his face saying, *I've got you now.*

Petras had a strange vision of the Gerulaitis brothers as small, carved figures in a Black Forest cuckoo clock, attached to opposite ends of a plank that kept them bobbing in and out of the room in an elaborate, ridiculous, mechanized dance, where only one could be inside the room at a time. He paused to see whether Vanya would now bob back in, but he didn't.

Belatedly, rage with Pavel and his arrogance rose in his head, and he looked around for something to throw at the closed door. He glanced at the wolf's heads in stained glass – sienna, dark green, and black – and considered throwing them, but couldn't bring himself to do it. How could he destroy any of this work, even if it had been commissioned by someone as detestable as the Baron?

Petras always worked carefully, with no wasted motions. He rarely broke anything, and left no waste materials behind him. He worked quietly.

The large ballroom was too quiet, however, with Vanya gone, without even the Baron there to make irritating conversation, so silent he felt as if it had been wrapped in cotton wool around its perimeter by large, supernatural hands. The quiet was not comforting, but eerie.

At five in the afternoon Petras finished for the day. Although he'd done only a small part of the entire window, he knew he had accomplished a great deal. He gazed over the center of the large window braced on the wooden table before him and smiled. Even if it was for the Baron, it was a good work.

He gathered the padding and heavy canvas he had used to carry the pieces in this morning. He would need the packaging the next day.

Now to ask Walther Funk to seek out Ona for him. He took a big breath. He was almost afraid. Would she want to see him?

He exhaled loudly and hoisted up the rolled packing material. He felt weighed down, like an old man.

Upon opening the door, he found Walther waiting for him. "The Baron said I could see Ona."

"Yes, I was just coming to see how close you were to finishing. She is waiting for you in her salon."

Petras grunted. *Her salon – how she has risen above us,* he thought bitterly. After placing his packet by the door in the front hall, he followed the Baron's man up the wide and curving stairs to the second floor. It was narrower and darker than the main hall below, with lighted alcoves every few feet. His sister's salon was the second door on the left, and he shivered when Walther Funk knocked at the door.

"Your brother is here, miss."

Petras ran his sweating hands over his hair, to smooth it, to dry them off. How could he be so nervous about his own sister?

"Hello, Petras," she said. She stood lounging by a marble fireplace and held a cigarette in a long holder, her hair bleached blonder than the last time he saw her. She wore a long, black jersey dress, the sleeves long, covering her arms. She looked like a movie star, the room like a movie set, its chairs and divans upholstered in gold velvet, the marble fireplace and marble pillars set around the room, and old Turkish carpets on hardwood floors.

A magnificent violin had been left carelessly on a sofa, and sheet music lay open nearby on a stand. She was getting to play some; that was good, at least. All the surfaces looked foreign to Petras, with only one homely touch, a fat white kitten with blue eyes playing with the hem of Ona's dress. Yet no, even the kitten was foreign, a Persian.

She looked so different from the Ona he knew. "Ona, can it be you?"

"But of course." She took a drag off the cigarette, then used it to point to a chair by the fireplace. "Please sit."

He sat where she directed, then stared at her a long time without speaking. She returned his look, a wry smile on her lips. At last she said, "Well?"

"I don't know. You seem so different, yet you're the old Ona too. I want to tell you we love you and miss you."

"We? You must say 'we'?"

"I miss you, very much. We – I – this is hard for me, Ona. I've been worried about you. How are you doing? You look like a million *litai*, but how are you really?"

A dozen emotions flitted across her face, like a summer rain across the marshes. "But I am fine," she said, "can you not see? Mamytė worries about every cent, and I have nearly unlimited money to spend. I have lovely clothes, fascinating parties, exciting outings, important people to…" At that point, her voice broke and her face crumpled. "I have nothing to complain about."

Petras got up and crossed over to where she stood and put his arms around her. Her expensive perfume enveloped him as she collapsed in his arms and sobbed. "I miss you so!" she said. "I want to come home!"

Suddenly the door jerked open, and Pavel entered the

room. Ona leaped back away from Petras and stared wide-eyed at Pavel. "My, my, what a touching scene. The home-sick, ungrateful girl sobbing on her worthless brother's shoulder." He strode across the room and kicked the kit-ten out of the way. The kitten yelped, dashed away, and then curled into a ball in a corner.

"Pavel, don't!" she cried.

The Baron ignored her, roughly grabbing her elbow and gesturing with his head for Petras to get out. "Keep to your work from now on, and forget about upsetting my fiancée. Do you understand?"

"You're a maggot, you know," Petras said quietly.

Pavel gritted his teeth and squeezed Ona's elbow tighter, and she grimaced in pain.

"Don't hurt her!"

"Don't interfere, or I'll hurt her more."

Petras glared at the man who stared back at him, gave up the fight for the moment, bowed his head, then turned and fled the room. Snagging the wrappings for the glass, he dashed out the front door without waiting for Funk to show him out. Rage, disgust, and fear warred within him. He didn't understand men like Pavel. It was easy to say that he was evil, or merely that he was used to doing things his way.

Yet Ona had money and expensive clothing; certainly she would never worry about starving. She seemed torn, wanting to be there, yet afraid too.

Petras didn't understand Pavel, or why Ona had come to the Castle willingly. He would never understand Pavel's cruelty. If he could, he would know how to counter him.

CHAPTER 6

Outside the weather had changed. The bright, clear air of the morning had fled, and a storm was blowing in from the north. The wind threatened the white steeple and red roofs of St. Peter and Paul, yet Petras knew the proud, up-thrusting cathedral would survive but the little houses like his own, huddled along the ground, would be devastated. Powerful winds worked that way.

His jacket was too thin for such a day, so he lifted the canvas wrap up to shield his face from the tiny shards of sand nicking his skin. He put it down from time to time to get the long view of where he was going, not just a view of his feet, and he came straight up against a kiosk with a new flyer tacked to it:

Come One and All: German Gymnasium at the School Grounds on Saturday, November 19. Learn How to

Play Soccer with Germany's Top Athletes.

A shiver ran up his spine. This was what Kazys had warned him about. This was the day the Nazis would use to overpower reason and punish Lithuania.

His throat closed. He knew what roiled under all the recent rage he'd experienced toward Pavel – its true name was fear, bone-deep, emasculating fear. He was afraid of what would happen to him if he had to face Pavel or other Nazis in a real battle. What would he do? Would he humiliate himself? Probably, he thought wryly. He was always making grand gestures that signified nothing.

Oh, if only the good God above cared enough for him to keep him from that, help him save face, help him save his family and friends from the fate to come. If only he believed, as his mother did, in the power of a simple prayer.

He stood at the edge of the town centre and watched people scurry in and out of the shops, buying milk and bread before the storm hit. Behind him he heard the rumble of large equipment, felt it move the earth under his feet. He knew without looking what it foretold, and his knees turned to mush, his stomach heaved, his bowels loosened.

People at the shops turned to look, some smiling, some alarmed, some blasé. They had no idea what the trucks meant.

Some day, if not today, that sound, that movement under his feet would mean German tanks in Lithuania.

Today it was large trucks painted white with red letters on them. *Their owners want to make sure they are visible, eh?* The sound of running feet presaged the rush of children and young people following the truck. They wanted to see what was going on, be there for the big party to come.

He looked across the town centre and saw Joelis watching him. He raised his hand in greeting. The trucks rumbled between them and obstructed the sight of his friend.

It was too late to effect any change in Lithuania, too late, perhaps forever.

"Petras," his mother called up the attic stairs, awakening him from a deep sleep, "come quick. It's the Baron at the door for you."

"Tell him I'm not here. I'm not at his call today."

"Oh, Petras," she whispered, "come. I cannot tell him a lie."

Petras groaned and rolled over. He couldn't let Mamytė cover for him. He sluiced his face and hair with cold water and rinsed his teeth. Did Pavel come calling when he knew Petras would be at his worst, bad breath and all? What a rotter the man was. But in the past two weeks, since the German athletes came and took over town with their charm and warm invitations and lowering presence, Petras had given up fighting the man.

Pavel was in the parlor. "What is it?" Petras asked when he entered and saw the Baron fingering Mamytė's books. "You do not have a library at the Castle?"

The Baron turned from the books, wiped his hands together as if to knock off any dust – as if Mamytė allowed dust to gather! – and grinned at him, showing large white teeth. "Now, now, none of your sarcasm, Petras. You know I have the best library in town, better even than Juodas. I am here to invite you to the Gymnasium next Saturday. You are nearly done with my window." At this the Baron leaned back and spread his hands across his large chest, in pride of ownership. "I'll give you the day off so you can attend. It's been brought to my attention that because of the work you're doing for me, you are the only young man in the region who has missed all the previous Gymnasia. I hate for you to be neglected."

The thought of Joelis flashed across his mind. He doubted Joelis had been included, so he surely was not the only neglected young man in the area.

On a whim Petras thought he would join the Baron's game of exaggerated courtesy. "How kind of you to think of me, sir, but I prefer to finish my work. So if you're through?" Petras gestured to the door, as if to usher the tall, heavy man out of their house.

The Baron stiffened, his affable expression gone. "You don't understand," he said, very low, his voice rumbling, a dog's preliminary growl at an interloper. "I am ordering you to attend. Do not mistake my forbearance with you. You are to turn up Saturday at 7 AM; do not fail to be there." He flicked his fingers at the books behind him. "Pathetic bunch of books. Why none by the great German thinkers, Petras? I know you are poor, but surely you can find some spare change for the important books of Europe." He marched out of the room and slammed the door behind him.

Petras smiled. He had cut the overbearing man to the quick, enough to make him abandon his pretense of pleasantness.

A week until the Gymnasium. He shuddered. He hated the sight of Germans these days, since *Kristallnacht* and the destruction of synagogues, homes, and businesses in the great Jewish centers throughout Germany, Poland, in Lithuania at Vilnius too. He thought of the bonfires of the Talmud, the Ark in each synagogue, the piles of learning sent up in flames. The Germans were barbarians.

Even the rich ones like the Baron – perhaps especially the rich ones like him.

CHAPTER 7

Petras awoke the next Saturday in the dark, well before the clock went off. He dreaded spending the morning with a bunch of German sports fanatics.

To think that just weeks ago, some poor crazed Jewish boy from Poland had shot a German embassy worker in Paris, because no one would let his parents leave Poland safely. And two days later the onslaught took place – Jewish synagogues and businesses broken into, destroyed, by Brownshirts out of uniform, so the Nazis could say it was a spontaneous outpouring of common folks' wrath at the Jews!

The brown-garbed, brown-faced Russians – in brown like the Nazis, more like them, he feared, than different – had whispered to him at the pub the night before that just such an attack had been planned for over six years; the

Nazis had waited for some provocation, and that pathetic Herschel Greenspan had fallen right into their hands.

Now, today, with Nazi athletes in Šiauliai, he knew he had to face some of the German beasts. He dressed slowly, for he was in no hurry to get there. His stomach was queasy from staying up late the night before, talking with the Communists and drinking too much ale with Kazys, in town briefly from his teaching in Vilnius.

He didn't think he could eat much, but he had better put something in his stomach. "Mamytė," he called, "no breakfast for me, just a cup of tea and some bread and butter."

"Yes, Petras," she called back from the kitchen. "I am fixing it for you."

He hated it when she acted so subservient with him, yet he didn't know how to talk to her about it. How to say it? *Stop waiting on me hand and foot, Mamytė. I should be waiting on you.*

He could just say it, but the thought frightened him, for she was likely to make a scene, and he couldn't bear that right now. She would cry and carry on – no, truthfully she rarely did that. He felt ashamed for believing she was melodramatic. And ashamed to want distance from her. He knew he wanted distance – yet from his mother, the lady who fed him and worked to make a home for him and lost sleep over him? Why was he ungrateful to her?

"Here, sit, Petras. You need to eat." She set before him three slices of fat bacon, a pile of scrambled eggs, and two large slices of bread, too thick to get into his mouth!

"Mamytė! I told you I cannot eat much this morning!" Blessedly he was able to soften his tone so that it wasn't as harsh as it could have been. She wasn't the one who angered him, not really. She was merely the butt of his wrath at times. "Please, forgive me if I don't eat all this food. It looks wonderful." He took a small bite of bread. "Have you eaten yet?"

"No, I'll eat once you are gone."

He stood rapidly, the chair squealing back along the wood floor. "Sit and I will get you a plate."

"Oh, no, Petras! I will do it later!" She looked flushed, embarrassed.

"Sit, Mamytė. Humor me in this." He busied himself waiting on her, and his old love for his mother flickered to life in his cold heart.

Once he'd served her, they sat silent, a bit strained with each other, but Petras hoped that would change with time. He needed to treat her better.

At last he stood. "There, I ate more than I meant to. You have stuffed me. Some day I will be as fat as the mayor, with a fine gold watch and chain straining across my belly, just because you overfeed me!"

He carried the dishes to the wash basin for her and grabbed his coat. "I'm off to see what those d – " he caught himself " – what those stupid Germans are up to with their 'Gymnasium.' Do you think they are looking over our young men to see who is good enough to be in their service?"

"Oh, don't say that, Petras. I would die if you were drafted."

He laughed at her, ruefully, then put on his coat. "I'm gone."

He stepped out the front door and froze in his tracks. Before him on the steps lay a still white scrap of fur. "Oh, no," he groaned. He knelt down to look at it, fearful he knew already. "No, no!" He lifted his head and shouted to the sky. "I cannot believe he would do such a thing!"

"What is it?" Donata said as she rushed to join him.

"Go back in, Mamytė. I will need to…"

With the toe of his boot, he turned the scrap of fur over. Ona's white kitten had been gutted, its fur matted with blackened blood along the cut up its belly.

Petras turned away. His gullet rising, he headed for a shrub by the steps and lost his breakfast. "Oh, dear God, how does this man live with himself? Has he no conscience?" He knew that was a stupid question the minute he uttered it.

"But what – what man? Who did this? Whose kitten is it?" Donata knelt down and scooped the stiffened body up in her trembling hands. "It must have been a beautiful little thing." She looked at Petras, pain in her eyes. "Some boys this cruel? How?"

"Not boys, a man – if he is such. The Baron did this –"

"No! It isn't possible!"

"He did it. This kitten was Ona's, I'm sure. It's a Persian, and I saw it playing at her feet, just days ago."

Donata shivered. "But what if – Ona?"

"Mamytė, if you believe in prayer, this is the time to pray your heart out," he said through gritted teeth. "I must go, but I'll bury this poor creature first. Go inside, please."

After digging a grave near the trash burner for the kitten and throwing a handful of lime from the garden shed over the small body and replacing the dirt, Petras went to the well to rinse out his mouth, bile-sour. Shoving his hands into his pockets, he forced himself to set one foot in front of the other as he set off to the secondary school, the morning still dark, the sun not up yet, now in late November.

This senseless death had pierced through his protective armor of anger: Pavel frightened him nearly to the point of stopping his breath, of being past the sensation of pain because his fear had numbed him.

He could not stop the man and his overriding ambition and cruelty.

Once at the athletic field outside the school, Petras took a deep breath to steel himself for the ordeal ahead. *Just get in and out as quick as you can. Let Pavel see you, then go.*

Inside the field he was surprised to see so many young men there. Surely they represented more than just Šiauliai; he would know more of them otherwise. There were three distinct groups: young Lithuanian Christians in rough work clothes, Lithuanian Jews in well-cut but worn woolen coats and pants – he gestured slightly to Joelis, who nodded surreptitiously back – and a cadre of men dressed in well-pressed brown shirts and pants, with perfectly combed, slicked back hair and looks on their faces that to Petras said: *See how superior we, Hitler's soldiers, are? You all look like bums next to us!*

Still another group of obviously German young men came running out of the dressing rooms at the south end of the field. All of Aryan type, as were the brown-shirted soldiers, they wore sports uniforms of one sort or another, not identical but spiffy compared to the garb of the Lithuanians. Petras shook his head and ran his hand over his chin in bewilderment. Perhaps there would be no athletic contest, just a style show, at which the Germans and German-sympathizing Lithuanians obviously excelled! At that he perked up a bit, his head clearing with a wisp of humor floating through his brain.

An old friend from childhood, Saulis* Kazlauskas, left the group of Lithuanian Christians and came to join Petras.

Saulis [SOW-lis]

Rima's brother Alfonsas was in that group, looking as frightened as Petras felt. Behind the Lithuanians stood the American journalist who'd been hanging around town for the
last month or so – what was his name? Branson – Robert
Branson, he thought. The man had a strange expression
on his face, rather sad. He dropped his eyes when Petras
caught his glance. Was he ashamed, perhaps?

"What's up, do you think?" Saulis asked, scraping long,
straight brown hair off his forehead. Saulis had a long, bony
face and small eyes, and a thin but strong physique. He'd
been an aggressive soccer player in school, invariably surprising opponents who never expected so much fight from
such a skinny kid.

Petras shrugged. "I don't know. Haven't you attended
one of these before?"

"Yes, but the two I went to weren't like this. They were
just the athletes teaching us poor, benighted Lithuanians
how to play soccer."

Petras grinned at him. "Yes, because we don't know
how already."

Saulis punched his arm. "Like we didn't win soccer
matches in school."

Saulis pointed to two men standing off to the left of
the German Brownshirts, the Baron and Father Juodas.

Petras froze. "Why is Juodas here?"

"Even more," Saulis added, "why is he watching you so
closely? And the Baron – he also has an eye on you. Why
are they so interested in you?"

"I don't know!"

"You've always wanted to be invisible to others, to their
sort in particular. What's up?"

Petras felt his belly muscles begin to tremble. "I don't
know. I had promised myself I wouldn't come, then the

Baron made a point of coming to our house to invite me, no questions asked. It spooked my mother."

"You were our star soccer player. Maybe they want to recruit you?"

"Oh, dear God, don't say such a thing. I could not stomach any span of time with such toads!"

"Look!" Saulis said. "There's Hans Zeller, in a Nazi uniform! What's he up to?"

"Oh, yes, I ran into him a while back and found out he was a Nazi."

"He's wearing a gun!"

"Yes, and he threatened me with it."

"Why?"

Petras shrugged. "I guess I wasn't properly respectful of his garb or his fearless leader." He leaned over to spit on the grass.

"You think he's dangerous?"

"He's in a Nazi uniform, isn't he?"

Hans began working his way around the other Brownshirts and headed for Petras and Saulis. "Uh," Saulis said, "I think I'm being called elsewhere."

"Coward."

Saulis grinned at him over one shoulder. "Bye, buddy."

"Simonaitis," Hans said, "I see you've finally arrived. I need you to join me over here at the starting line."

"Me? Why me?"

Hans turned a pinched face toward him. "Don't push me, Petras," he said in a low voice. "You'll be sorry if you do."

"Right. Lead on," Petras said with a cocky grin he pasted on but couldn't feel. He glanced over at the priest and the Baron. Both were watching him, the Baron with cold hatred, Juodas with nervous eyes. The priest began to wring his hands and whisper something in an agitated fashion to the Baron. What was so interesting to them about a glassmaker's apprentice, especially one as difficult as he was? He couldn't even guess what was going on in their petty, wicked minds.

When they reached the starting line, the athletes moved closer to Hans and Petras, at the head of the field. Hans nodded curtly to the other Brownshirts, and the desultory scene before him broke open into sound and motion. One of them, whom Petras couldn't see, spat out some order in incomprehensible German, and the soldiers began trotting to circle the huddle of Jews at one side of the field. Once the Jews were surrounded, the soldiers drew their pistols and began pushing the Jews to line up on the field, then to lie, face down on the ground, next to each other. When some were slow to obey, four or five soldiers began pistol-whipping their heads. One of the first to fall, his face bloodied, was Joelis.

"No!" Petras screamed and tried to race to his friend's side. "Stop it!"

Four of the German athletes jumped him and pinned him. "You're going nowhere, you Lithuanian savage!" one snarled in his ear.

"You call me a savage, and you allow your beasts to attack defenseless men?"

One of the athletes, one a little shorter than the others, silenced him with a left jab to the ear. The ear began to ring, and he could feel blood spurting hot from it. It went numb, and he couldn't hear out of that ear at all.

He watched in pain and horror as the soldiers kicked the Jewish men lying on the ground. Some he recognized as businessmen, others as professionals or students. Their wounded dignity made Petras's heart constrict in pain. Oh, to be a man, a respected doctor or lawyer or teacher and be treated like a despised cur! His eyes burned as he watched still another soldier hit Joelis in the head with the butt of his pistol.

Surely, dear God, this horror will end!

CHAPTER 8

The horror didn't end, it only worsened. The Nazi troopers lined up the Lithuanians and held their guns on them. Petras knew it was do what they said or die.

Perhaps today he'd die. He could not torture Joelis, or his people. He would not.

Hans came up and stuck his gun against Petras's head. "Now, sir, you will lead the march."

Petras gave an involuntary shake of his head.

Hans shoved the pistol harder into his skull. "You will," he growled.

One of the athletes stepped forward, and with a smug grin on his face began to speak. "Now we will begin the games. You Lithuanians will begin running across the bodies of the dirty Jews on the ground. They're not real people, so you don't need to consider their feelings. You, Simonaitis,

you poor wretch. Don't you know these filthy Jews have
robbed you of money, of food, of a decent life? We are here
to help you. Look at them, fat and well-dressed, and then
look at your scrawny, pathetic countrymen!"

"No!" Petras said.

Hans hit him in the solar plexus. "Shut up!"

Pain seared Petras's belly, and he longed to lie on the
ground and not move. But, doubled over, clutching his
stomach, he forced himself to speak. "Funny how you try
to help a poor man like me."

Hans laughed. "You'll see how, soon enough. Now – I
want you to race each other by running across the backs of
the men on the ground. Saulis, you start the race. Our star,
Petras, is a bit discommoded."

Saulis looked at Petras, terror in his eyes. "What can I
do, Petras?"

A Brownshirt approached him, hit him in the gut with
the butt of his gun. Saulis grunted and struck at him. The
soldier hit him in the mouth, and Saulis spat blood. The
Brownshirt shouted at him, "Start running. That's simple
enough for even an idiot like you, isn't it?"

"No!" Petras shouted. With great effort, he forced himself to take a deep breath and straighten up. "I'll lead it.
Give me a minute to catch my breath."

He heard Hans laughing softly behind him. "Now we
see how idealistic our dear Petras is, don't we, Baron?"

"Yes," the Baron said, "at last."

Petras saw a sheen of red before his eyes. He wished he
could grab a gun and kill them both.

Joelis turned his head and looked Petras in the eye.
Petras figured the look meant, *I told you so.*

"Now," Hans said, "you need to run as fast as you can,

stomping on the backs and heads of these scum as hard as you can. I want you to be sure, Petras, to kick that Jewboy there, the one called Joelis, in the face, as hard as you can. Do you understand?"

Terror and shame shook Petras's whole body. "Yes," he whispered, "I understand."

"Go!" Hans shouted, and fired his pistol straight up in the air.

Petras leapt forward involuntarily, from fear at the sound of the gun, and began to run. No one else moved.

He ran across the prostrate Jews' legs, doing his best to miss them, but sometimes kicking them. He began to cry, saying, "Sorry, sorry, I'm so sorry." He reached Joelis, who was watching him with no emotion on his face. At that point, Petras dropped to the ground, over his friend, and shielded him with his body.

"Petras!" Joelis cried. "What are you doing? They'll kill you!"

"And I'll thank God for it. Be quiet, and hide your face in your arms. It's not much protection, but some."

Joelis did as he was told. Petras could feel his friend's body wracked with sobs. His own tears had dried up when he dropped down over Joelis's body.

"Simonaitis!" the Baron barked. "Get off that vermin! Who knows what filth will be on you now? Get up!"

Petras hid his face in his own arms and began to laugh. What a stupid thing to threaten him with. Did the Baron have no brains at all? Here he was about to be killed and buried under the ground, where the maggots could eat him, and he was to be concerned about dirt from his friend Joelis?

Out of the corner of his eye, he saw Saulis running toward them. He looked strong, cool and calm.

"Dear God," he cried, "protect us!" At that point, he heard a huge boom, as of cannon firing, then heard no more.

Petras had no idea where he was, what time of day it was. Pain washed over him in waves of red and purple, of sickly yellow-greens, and he could not surface from the powerful undertow of his injuries. Nor did he want to – why would he want to come back to life? It hurt too much.

"Mamytė, he's stirring." It was Ona speaking, as if from a tunnel.

"Petras, my boy! You're alive." Mamytė began to cry.

"Oh, don't cry," he groaned. "I can't bear it." A strange odor he knew, of grease and a strong perfume, wafted past him. Vanya?

Ona laughed her familiar tinkling laugh. "He's going to be okay! He sounds like the old bear he's always been."

How could she laugh, at a time like this? Petras wanted to spit or throw something at her. He moved his head and was jolted by the searing pain in his left ear. The pain made him cringe, draw into himself, so he vowed not to move again any time soon. He looked around the room he was in. It was small, warm and dry, done in blue and white. A fire burned in a grate to his left, lighting up birch wood table and chairs, a rag rug on the floor, old Russian paintings on the wall. Even in his confusion, he could see it was an expensive room pretending to be humble, a cultured room pretending to look rustic.

"What happened?" He forced the words out over inflamed vocal cords, the effort hurting more than he would have thought possible. "Where am I?" he croaked.

"Here, with me."

He scowled in trying to remember the voice – ah, Vanya!
"With Vanya? Why?"

"He has a nice cottage on the Castle estate," Mamytė
explained.

"Yes, it was built for the first Baron's mother, you know,"
Vanya said.

Petras started to shake his head no, but thought better
of it. "Why?"

"Because she needed a place to stay."

"No, Vanya," Ona said, a lilt of happiness in her voice,
"he didn't mean that. He meant why is he here." To her
brother she said, "You were brought here because this will
be the safest place for you. It's clean and tight, and the
Baron –"

"– never comes here," Vanya said. "So he won't find
you."

"He's looking for me?" Petras asked, his voice failing,
his energy nearly gone from the effort of conversation.

"Well, of course!" Vanya said. "You really made him
mad this time."

An involuntary grin spread across Petras's face.

"Oh, my," Mamytė said, "if you could see how beat up
your face is, but praise be to God, it's good to see you smile!"

Petras scowled. "I can't remember. I know the Nazis
were trying to make us stomp and kick the crap out of the
Jews they'd humiliated – oh! How is Joelis?"

"Gone."

Petras tried to sit up, but the pain and his weakness
knocked him flat. "What?" A sob racked him. "Dead?" After
all he'd done?

"No, not dead," Ona said softly, one hand on his shoulder.

His eyes flew open; her voice had finally awakened his

memory. "Ona! How are you? And your kitten – !"

"Please don't try to move, Petras," she said. "You'll rip out your stitches. I'm fine, Joelis has been taken to a safe place, and it would be best if you don't know where."

He glared at her. "You must tell me!"

Mamytė began crying again. "Oh, you need to get better first!"

He glared at Mamytė but didn't reply. "Okay," he said to Ona, as patiently as he could, easier now that exhaustion had felled him, "tell me what happened. I fell down to cover Joelis, I heard a cannon, but what next?"

"A cannon? No cannon," Vanya said. "But Saulis grabbed Hans's gun, and –"

"No!" Ona shouted. "Not quite, Vanya!" she said, adding softly, "The gun went off."

Petras saw red. "You're not telling me the whole truth. Tell me this much at least." He raised his hand to Ona. "I'm not a boy anymore."

"Oh, Petras, can't we wait to tell you? This is not the right time," she said.

"Tell me," he begged.

"One of the Brownshirts shot Saulis," she whispered. "He was trying to protect you."

"He's dead?" Petras could hear his mother sobbing.

"Yes," Ona said. "One bullet also hit you, and that's why you have stitches. The doctor came and removed it from your shoulder, and sewed you up. But he couldn't heal your cuts and bruises."

"The other Jews there – where are they?"

Silence, no response.

"The Jews, the older men there – what happened to them?"

"Please, Petras," Mamytė begged, "just get well first."

"Where are they?" he growled.

"They're gone, Petras," Ona whispered. Her face crumpled. "The Germans shot them as they lay on the ground."

"Throughout the country," Mamytė said, tears in her eyes, "our Jews are being massacred by those monsters. Through the ages Lithuania has been the one country most open to them, but now..."

"And Joelis?"

"He got away," Ona said. "I already told you that."

Through gritted teeth, Petras spoke. "What day is this?"

"It's late Sunday; you slept over twenty-four hours."

"Get me out of this bed. I need to kill them." The pain immobilized him, and he swore.

"Petras!" Mamytė gasped.

"Mamytė," he said, "swearing is nothing compared to what these inhuman beasts are doing. Forgive me, but..." His voice trailed off.

"He can ask forgiveness later, Mamytė," Ona said. "If he kills any of them, he'll have more on his conscience anyway." Her dry tone underlined the sarcasm of her words, and Petras nodded, grimacing in pain, for the movement threatened to take the top off his head.

"We'll worry about that later," he said.

"Let me help you," Vanya said, "when you're ready to get even."

Mamytė gasped. "No!"

"We'll see, Vanya – I have to get out of bed first. Mamytė," he said gently, "please pray for rapid healing. I believe any good God will hear you." He recalled that his last thought before he was struck down was a prayer. It obviously hadn't been heard.

CHAPTER 9

Petras lay sick for several days. Mamytė said his youth hastened his healing. He wasn't so sure: his body felt like an old man's. One thing that didn't heal was his left eardrum, which throbbed with pain. The doctor, Saulis's grandfather, Sigitis Kazlauskas, said he knew little about such injuries, but felt the hearing loss was permanent. "If we had a lot of money, I could send you to Vilnius for care, but we don't."

This news set Mamytė to sobbing, and Petras didn't try to stop her. What would this mean for him in future? To lose one's hearing – what if he lost it all and could never hear Rachmaninoff or Bach again?

But he was alive and his muscles were knitting. Soon he'd be as close to normal as he'd ever be.

Late on Thursday evening, Vanya brought Rima to see

him. Her face was blotched from crying.

"Rima! You shouldn't be here!"

Bringing the fragrance of new rain and pine trees into the small, beautiful room with her, she knelt beside his bed and grasped his hand; she buried her face in the white and blue bedding. His heart twisted to see her dressed so poorly, in a too-large gray dress too thin for the weather.

She took his hands, and her long, thin fingers chilled him. "I begged them to let me come. I had to see for myself that you are alive. I thought…"

"Now, now. I'm too tough to kill off," he blustered. "No more tears, for me at least." Raindrops had turned her strawberry blond hair into red silk sparkling with diamonds. He ran his hand over her hair and scattered the diamond drops. Impatient at being an invalid, he struggled to sit up. Once he was upright, he leaned over to pull her up to sit beside him and kissed her hair. His voice husky, he whispered in her hair, "I'm glad to see you."

She turned to him and gently laid her lips on his, but then pulled back, her eyes gazing into his. "And I you. I love you." She blushed and pulled back. "Oh, now you'll think I'm too forward! I'm sorry!"

Out of the corner of his eye, Petras saw Vanya edge out of the room, leaving them alone. He wrapped his arms around her and kissed her back. "No, never. I love you, Rima, I love you."

He held her close, drew back and, holding her face in his hands, he smiled. "Will you marry me, Rima?"

"Oh, yes!"

"But we have to wait. You know I have no money, not much chance of making any. Antanas may have replaced me already, you know."

"He hasn't."

"Do you interrupt every man who proposes to you like this?" he teased.

She blushed charmingly and shook her head no.

"In the spring?" he asked.

"So long?" she wailed. "I can't wait!" She edged still closer to him.

He laughed at her. "I'm glad to know you're eager! But no, we have to wait; I need to save some money." He stood up then, and wavered a bit. "I'm dizzy – it's been so long since I've been up. But what of your father? He won't be pleased. He had your brother warn me off, you know."

Her face fell. "What will we do?"

"I'll have to think about it. Perhaps we'll have to marry secretly."

"Yes!"

"Your father – will he ever accept this?"

"Yes, he wants me to be happy, in the end. And Alfonsas is always on my side."

"But we still must wait."

Rima stood up and walked into his arms, molding her body into his. "Don't make me wait too long. I fear –"

His face in her hair, his mind on the warmth spreading through his body, he spoke at last. "What?"

"The Baron. Don't let him take me away."

Petras pulled back, held her out at arm's length. How had he forgotten? He began to pace, his muscles screaming from the beating he'd taken and the days of lying in bed. "We'll have to make plans soon." He stepped back to watch her face. "Will you mind a secret wedding? Have you always wished for a formal wedding?"

She walked back into his arms. "No," she whispered, "I have only wished for you."

By the weekend, one week after Petras's beating, he was up and moving, although he was still in considerable pain. The surge of energy from his anger when he first came to had vanished, and depression dogged him.

What could he do? What difference could he make? And what of Ona or Rima? Was there any hope for any of them?

He needed to return to work. Although Vanya and Ona had been feeding him and Mamytė all week, this situation could not go on much longer.

What of his work on the Baron's window? This, at least, he could ask of Vanya.

When Vanya came back late afternoon to serve him a meal, he wore oversized, greasy mechanic's clothes. Petras noticed Vanya's large, clumsy hands, which plucked at his clothes as if they were binding him.

Petras sat at the birch table and motioned to Vanya to join him as he ate and beleaguered the poor boy with questions.

"Does the Baron know where I am? Does he expect me to finish the rose window? Will he kill me on sight, or have me thrown into jail?"

Vanya shrugged eloquently. "I don't know, really. But he does want you to finish the window. Antanas offered to work on it, but Pavel shouted him out of the Castle. Pavel hates you, but only you can touch his cursed stained glass."

Petras didn't reply, but merely set to eating. He was hungry, famished, in fact, for the first time in a week. After finishing off his second bowl of soup and third slice of bread, he stopped a moment. "So what do you think? Can I just turn up Monday, ready to work?"

The overgrown boy nodded his head eagerly. "Yes."

"But what if he turns on me?"

Vanya grinned. "I'll show you some escape routes."

"That's right. You must have a few."

"Just ten or so. It often happens I need to get away before he can grab me."

"Tell me, Vanya. What in his life turned the Baron so brutal?"

Vanya pursed his lips and thought a moment. "It was my father – you know we had different fathers, right?"

Petras shook his head. "No, I know nothing."

"Our mother was odd enough in her ways, always putting on airs and acting as Russian as she could. And cold! Not a warm, loving mother at all."

Petras was amazed that Vanya could express himself so well.

"So what did your father do?"

"He was either gone on trips or home beating Pavel, who always questioned his authority. And my father was not one you questioned."

"Did he beat you too?"

"Oh, he'd backhand me from time to time, but I was good at disappearing. Pavel couldn't let him be, had to be defying him all the time." He pulled on his lower lip and scowled. "It was really bad at times. When I saw him beat Ana, I felt I was seeing him beaten by Father over again."

Petras felt sick to his stomach. "I'm sorry. And Ona? She's unsafe with him surely?"

Vanya shrugged. "She's stronger than Ana. Maybe she'll do okay."

"I can't figure out why she wants to be here with him!" Petras said.

Vanya looked at him, eyes wide. "Does she have a choice?"

Petras ran his hands over his face. "I don't know. I some-

times wonder – is she just looking for money and secu-
rity?"

"I think she wants your family to be safe from him,
and this is the way to get that."

"He's told her this will buy our safety?"

"In so many words."

Petras couldn't speak. He took a long time thinking
this over. It made him tired. How to fight against the man?

"And you?" Petras asked. "How do you handle him?"

"If I stay out of his sight long enough, he usually for-
gets what I did that made him mad."

Petras rubbed the back of his head. "I doubt he'll forget what I did."

"But you are just a stupid Lithuanian –"

Petras reared back and glared at him.

Vanya held up a hand to stop him. "His words, not
mine. He thinks you're stupid – he knows I am – so we're
not worth much effort, after his first big outburst of anger."

Petras smiled. The Baron's idiot brother was not such
an idiot after all.

They finished eating in companionable silence. At last
Petras rose and took his dishes to the small kitchen. He
looked at the clock. Five PM – dark out now. "I need to go
out. I have to check on Mamytė." He turned quickly. "The
funeral. When was Saulis's funeral?"

Vanya squirmed and looked at the floor. "This isn't
something Ona wants me to talk to you about. And I have
to please Ona. She is wonderful, you know," he said with
shining eyes.

"I won't tell her. The funeral?"

"It was Thursday. I'm sorry."

Petras nodded. "It's okay." He grabbed a coat off the

rack by the back door. "I'll be back before too late, I hope."

"Do you want me to go with you?"

"No need." He left quickly and lengthened his stride to cover ground as fast as he could. His muscles ached from his injuries and misuse, but soon they loosened up, and he felt good to be outside under the open sky, thankful for fresh air.

It was biting cold, but invigorating, especially after his illness, cooped up as he'd been. The night was black, clouds covering a pale moon. He decided to cut through the forest on the far side of the estate, emerging at the town cemetery. Once he reached the cemetery, the moon slid shyly from behind her cloud cover and lit his path.

He thought he should avoid the Zellers' land. He really didn't feel up to a confrontation with Hans, so he steered over to the north side of the cemetery. Just before he reached the far north fence, he heard a scrabbling in the bushes and the thud of feet – two or three men running away, he thought – leaving a white lump behind them. He listened as the sound of running feet disappeared in the distance. He knew, however, that with no hearing in his left ear, he was handicapped in judging just how close sounds were.

His heart dropped to his feet and he felt faint. He didn't want to face anyone. Coward, he thought – and the pain came back: he had called Saulis a coward. He'd been joking, but he'd branded his friend, who died in his place. Hot tears stung his eyes, but he blinked them back. He was afraid, afraid, down in his guts afraid to death of the Baron and his men.

Knowing he must find out what was such a secret over there, he took a deep breath and made himself walk as silently as he could to see what was going on.

He stopped and swallowed the bile in his throat. He

had to know.

Approaching the white shape on the ground, he feared he already knew what it was, but not who. He walked up to the body wrapped in a white sheet and looked around to make sure no one was there. He leaned over and carefully unwound the small body, small enough to be a child's.

Ana! It was Ana, the Baron's wife, and she was dead. She looked like a wraith, so thin, like a skeleton already in spite of recent death. An open grave yawned next to her, still not deep enough, shovels flung aside in the gravediggers' haste to get away when he arrived.

He felt around her body for wounds, finding none but finding something else: a naked infant, still sticky from birth, its skin chilling but a breath of life still in it. The baby opened its mouth and let out a wail.

Still alive! Oh, dear God in Heaven, help this little child!

Petras shook his head. Why was he praying for Pavel's child? Shouldn't he hate it as much as he did its father?

But he couldn't. The baby must be freezing! He picked it up and wrapped it in his coat, against his chest. Perhaps his body warmth would help it survive. He had to hurry, get it home to Mamytė.

She would know what to do – but then what? Mamytė was too old to take on the care of a child. Perhaps she knew of a wet nurse. Whatever they did would be wrong. Someone would find out the baby had disappeared from the gravesite; someone would tell the Baron that the Simonaitis family had added a mysterious baby to their household. Oh, God, what to do?

It didn't really matter, he guessed. He couldn't let a child die from exposure. Forgetting to take care, he began to run – no time to waste. His head pounded as he ran, but he didn't slow his pace. The child needed warmth and food.

Ana was dead. He wished now he could examine her in daylight; had she died in childbirth, or was she killed? Now Pavel was free to marry Ona. Would he? Should he? Surely not, not for Ona's best.

Mamytė gasped when he burst in the back door and filled the cozy yellow kitchen. "Petras, you frightened me – but you look so well! You look as if you never suffered."

He shook his head at her. "Mamytė, that's in the past. We have a new problem." He opened his coat to take the naked child out and to hand it – her – to his mother. It was a little girl, with curly black hair and Gypsy skin, surely not a baby an Aryan nationalist would value. But she looked like Vanya and Pavel too.

"Where –?"

"In the cemetery. Three men, I think, were digging a grave. Ana Gerulaitienė is dead, and this baby lay naked beside her. How it's alive, I do not know. Can you care for her, Mamytė?"

"She belongs to Pavel, not us. What will he do?" she asked, taking the child in her arms anyway and wrapping it in her apron. "I'll look in the chest for Ona's old things; I saved them all."

"Let me do that. Do you want to wash her up, fix her a bottle, something?"

"Yes, of course," she said, too flustered to think clearly, but she filled a basin with warm water from the back of the stove and began to wash the baby. The baby wasn't crying, hadn't since Petras picked her up and wrapped her in his coat. Was she dead, was all this effort too late?

He found an old well-washed pink baby dress of Ona's and some clean, bleached cloths in his mother's chest in her room. He dug deeper to find several blankets. That baby needed all the warmth she could get now. He remembered the wooden cradle up in the attic, and once he'd placed the clean clothes on the kitchen table, he went upstairs to bring it down. It was dusty, but he cleaned it up and looked around for the pads that would go in the bottom of the cradle. They could set up a perfectly fine nursery for that baby, for at least as long as she was in the house.

Carrying the cradle on his back so he'd fit through the narrow attic door, he climbed down the steps, wincing at the pain throughout his body, and rejoined Mamytė in the kitchen. She was wrapping the baby in a worn towel, her face twisted in grief.

"What?"

"Too late, oh, I'm sorry, Petras, we're too late. She is gone."

"No!" He swung the cradle down from his back and dropped it on the floor, then took the baby from her. Her face was still as porcelain, long black eyelashes on her sallow cheeks. Like a china doll, yet horribly different. A long-held breath shuddered out of him.

"Perhaps," Mamytė whispered, "it's for the best."

CHAPTER 10

Petras waited for two hours before he could force himself to take the dead baby back to her mother's grave. He knew it was the only way to protect his family from the Baron, yet his heart balked at it. A secret burial, with no one to mourn either Ana or her baby – so tragic.

Mamytė had wrapped the infant in an old white towel, ragged but clean. Petras shook his head. "Is there nothing better we can wrap her in?"

"I'll see. Maybe a linen tablecloth from my wedding."

"No, Mamytė, don't give that up. This is all right." Petras wanted to curse but didn't dare. It would upset Mamytė too much. Besides, if he gave in to his anger, he'd never be able to carry out the burial in the cold ground. This baby deserved better than they had. She deserved better than she'd got, in all respects. Putting on his heaviest

coat and wrapping the body inside it, he trudged out in
the new snow that was falling. The town felt so still, so
quiet in the snow, except for the soft crunch under his feet,
the whish of flakes past his right ear. At least he hadn't lost
all his hearing; maybe this handicap wouldn't be too hard
to live with.

As he approached the cemetery, his gut twisted. He
was afraid of who might be there. All he could do was hope
the place was empty, of living folks.

He stopped just outside the gate to listen. He heard
branches scraping against each other, and the soft plop of
snow sliding off a branch. With damaged hearing, he was
amazed at the minute sounds he could hear.

Glancing right and left, he tried to judge how far he'd
have to traverse open ground to Ana's grave. Perhaps forty
feet, he thought. Guarding against placing his feet too
loudly, he crossed the graveyard and held the poor dead
baby close to him. His head injuries, the beating he took
to his head and body, began to pain him, and immense
fatigue washed over him. How he wished he could go home
to sleep it off.

But he had this one job to do, before he could rest.
Pushing himself as hard as he could – within seconds, which
seemed like hours – he reached the place where the men
had earlier been digging. Closed! The body was gone and
the grave filled. He groaned. What to do with the baby's
body?

As he stood there thinking about his options, he heard
a rustling behind him. As he turned, a sharp blow to his
head felled him.

Petras awoke to a vaguely familiar odor, then heard a voice, way off above him. He ached so and his brain felt so confused. Where could he be, and why did he hurt so much? And why again?

"Wake up, Petras," the voice said, and Petras recognized it as Vanya's and the odor too as Vanya's. "If I don't get this broth down you, Ona's going to kill me."

"Does she mistreat you?" he asked, the conversation vaguely familiar to him.

Vanya laughed. "Oh, no, just Pavel hurts me. But if she's disappointed in me, it'll hurt more than he ever can." He placed pillows behind Petras in his attempts to prop him upright and began spooning hot broth into him, spilling some down his shirtfront.

"That's hot!" Petras barked.

"Sorry. I'll do better."

Petras tried to smile although the effort hurt; there was something so child-like about Vanya. It was too hard to smile, though, so he tried to open his eyes to look once again at the small, beautiful room in Vanya's cottage, but even that he couldn't manage. Oh, so tired, so sore! How he wished for death! Forcing the words out, he spoke. "What happened?"

"Your mother found you lying on a grave in the cemetery. She had to leave you to come to find Ona and me. You probably would have taken your death of cold if we hadn't found you." He sounded very proud of his own part in it.

"Thank you," he whispered.

"Then that Danielius Martinaitis from your mother's church came to pray over you. He's quite a nice man, but not very impressive."

Petras froze. "No! I'd rather not have anyone praying –
no, forget I said that." He couldn't hurt his mother by refusing prayers. Then Petras jerked fully awake. "The baby.
Did someone bury the baby?"

Vanya sighed and his hand shook, spilling soup on
Petras again. "Sorry. We couldn't find it."

"Do you know who –?"

"Hush! Let's not speak of this now."

"Is there no talk of Ana's disappearance? Does anyone
of the village know she's dead?"

"I doubt it. It will be a well-kept secret. But don't worry.
Ona is taking care of it all."

"I'm sure I was knocked out so I couldn't talk about
finding Ana and the baby."

"Maybe," Vanya said as he stuck another spoonful of
broth in Petras's mouth. "She's very efficient, you know,"
he said with a shy smile. "And beautiful, so beautiful."

He meant Ona. "Yes, she is." Petras wondered if Vanya
was in love with her.

The soup was flavorful, salty, and warming, welcome
because he was so cold. "What day is it?"

"Early Sunday morning. You lay there perhaps only an
hour or two. Stop talking, though, would you? You're making me spill worse."

"I'm full," Petras said.

"So go to sleep. No need to keep talking. Ona said to
feed you, then let you sleep, so that's what I'm doing. I'm
not leaving, though, so don't worry."

Petras closed his eyes, too weary to argue. He hurt worse
than he had a week before, and it was more than he could
bear. He tried to find a more comfortable position, but
any attempts to move made him cry out in pain. At last he
gave up and sleep overcame him.

Ona entered the small sitting room and pushed her long, glossy hair out of her face. Wearing a simple but well-cut forest green dress with cream-colored lace around the neck and cuffs, she looked like something out of a fashion magazine.

Vanya was trying to clean up around the sofa where Petras lay sleeping. "Has he come to?" she asked, worry etched around her eyes.

"Yes, and I fed him some. Spilled more than I got down him."

"Oh, be careful," she snapped. "It's hard enough to take care of an invalid, keep them clean in bed and all." She'd had her trials when she and Petras were children and their father lay dying. Older than Petras by two years and the young female in the family, she had been responsible for most of the nursing. It hadn't been easy.

Vanya cringed. "Sorry. I'm trying…"

"Yes, yes, forgive me. I shouldn't have scolded you. I'm too tightly strung. Please forgive me," she repeated.

"I will," he said softly, looking deep into her eyes.

The front door to the small house banged open, hitting the wall behind it. Ona jumped up and rushed out of the small room where Petras lay. She reached the front room in time to see Pavel enter, hate in his eyes. "Pavel!"

His face dark with anger, his tailored jacket unbuttoned displaying a wrinkled white shirt underneath, Pavel didn't look quite the militaristic Nazi he usually did. Now he gritted his teeth. "I understand you like spending time with my idiot brother. I didn't bring you to the Castle to groom you for him but for me."

"It's nothing!"

He grabbed her long, smooth blond hair and yanked it, pulling her toward him. "I will not be made a fool of."

"Let go! You're hurting me! You're yanking my head bald!"

"I mean to. Now get out of here. I'll deal with Vanya."

Through her pain, Ona realized Pavel did not know Petras was here. "Please, Pavel, I go on my knees to you. Believe me – there is nothing between Vanya and me. I was here to help him clean up a soup spill in the kitchen. He's trying to feed himself."

"Stupid! You are not his maid! Get someone from the house to help him. You are merely my consort, got that?"

"Yes, Pavel," she said through her tears, for the pain was considerable. "I understand."

He let up on the pressure, then pulled her to him. "I own you," he whispered through clenched teeth, and he began kissing her hard, his teeth against her lips, splitting them open and bringing blood. His expression softened, and he began licking blood from her mouth.

She shuddered but did not resist. He turned her stomach, but she couldn't let him know that now.

"Come," he said in a wheedling tone. "Let's go to the Castle. We'll make up for this little set-to there. You will be thankful for my concern for you then, my love."

Her stomach heaved, but she dared not show her feelings. Was this how it felt to be a lamb led to slaughter? So helpless – for some reason, that reminded her of Petras and his incessant fighting against the system. Was this what it was like for him all the time?

Yet he didn't give in, ever, and she was giving in now – but to save him, to save someone at least, from this ghastly life they all lived.

How long had it been? Five days, six? Ona felt that surely no human could suffer through the pain she'd been in and live. The room stunk of old candles, human sweat, and blood, all remnants of acts too gross to remember. She was surprised she was still alive, for Pavel had been practicing his version of paganism, he said, and she was the sacrifice. But he'd stopped short of killing her.

She stood and tried to find some clothing in the dark, but her head spun.

"Come back to bed," he growled.

"No more," she whispered, "not again. You're killing me."

He laughed, and her stomach rose in her gullet. She couldn't see where to vomit, so she just let the bile come, all over the carpet. Who cared?

"I'm not through."

"You're through. You've used me up, there's nothing left." She wondered how she could kill him, make sure he never touched her or anyone else again.

Silence. "All right. You see how reasonable I am. I will let you rest. And I will call someone to come clean up this pigsty. You are a filthy creature. You know the Bible verse, 'as women's filthy rags'?"

"You surprise me, Pavel, that you know any Bible at all," she said through gritted teeth.

"But of course. I was forced to go to church when a child."

"Too bad you didn't gain something from it."

"Be very careful," he snarled. "I can hurt you, you know."

She bit her lip. Much as she wanted to answer back, she did not dare. He would injure her but not kill her; if

she could count on death, she wouldn't mind – it was the
living that hurt.

The second Sunday in Advent, Ona knew she was carrying
Pavel's child. *God*, she raged, *I want to die! How could you
let this happen?*

It didn't take Pavel long to figure it out. "Since when
do you think you have the right to refuse me?" he'd asked
the night before, in the icy voice she'd come to fear.

"Pavel, please! Let me be. I cannot live through the
pain. Do you want to make me lose this child? You've already killed off your first child."

"What? Who told you?"

"I was here when you hired those men to bury Ana
and her baby!"

"You haven't told anyone, have you?" he asked, rare
panic in his voice.

"Of course not!"

He merely grunted, did not answer.

"Oh, Pavel, what kind of monster are you?"

She ground her teeth in frustration. How difficult to
deal with a man with no human feelings, with no capacity
for empathy for others, just the desire to control and to
hurt.

At last he spoke. "It's interesting to watch all those
emotions race across your face. It is really quite stunning,
you know." He ran the back of his hand down her cheek,
and it took all her power to keep from flinching. "So lovely,"
he said softly. "You know, if this child is fair, I will marry
you, make you my own."

He turned and made his way from the room. At the
door he tossed the next words over his shoulder, iciness

once more defining them. "But you really need to learn to control your expressions. Be a good poker face so you can move among the genteel classes."

He left her, and she turned and spat into the fire. "Genteel classes," she muttered. "You wouldn't recognize anything genteel if it struck you in the face."

She picked up the new black velvet robe he'd bought her and wrapped it around herself, curling up on the small sofa before the fire. The room had been cleaned; the stains of her degradation were gone. She stared into the fire and wondered how she could get the upper hand over him, take control of his cruelty.

The more she thought, the more she realized there was no way for her to escape him. Tears flowed down her face, for, truthfully, only one way to get at him was open to her. Could she kill herself? Did she have the strength of mind to do it?

Next week some fat German generals were coming to visit him, to discuss the next move the Nazis planned in their takeover of Lithuania, with the help of the ruling class, men like Smetona and Pavel. While the generals were here? In a bloody, ostentatious way? That would be poetic justice.

And it would be during Advent. While the world celebrated its welcome for the Christ Child, while she should be thinking in terms of precious babies like the infant Jesus, meek and mild.

Pavel's mention of a fair child brought up an image of a real baby – fuzzy hair, fat cheeks, curving rose-petal fingers. She could not bring this child into the world. If she saw its face, if she were to love it, could she stand letting him hurt it? No. Only one course would do, that was certain.

CHAPTER 11

Halfway through December already, Petras thought, trudging through the dark to work. He'd been sick so long, but at last he was beginning to feel normal. He thought of the possibility of running into another Nazi, another one of Pavel's toughs, and his stomach clenched. *I can't stand to be hurt again. Is this how they make cowards?*

He'd returned to work, with promises to his mother and to Antanas that he'd not get involved in politics. He wouldn't butt heads with Pavel, he wouldn't try to stand up for anything anymore.

Pavel waited for him in the hall every day, usually stood leaning against a tall gun cabinet there, and smirked at him when he arrived at the Castle to complete the stained glass. Soon he'd be done. He gritted his teeth: let Pavel do what he wished, let him defile the whole town with his lusts and cruelties – Petras would not try to stop him.

Pavel refused to let him see Ona these days. "She's in a delicate condition, you see. I cannot let her be upset. You only set her off, pining for some romantic notion she has of the noble peasant life," he said with a sneer.

"I really need to see her, Pavel. I must. This isn't at all necessary, to keep us apart. See how docile I am now, like a lap dog? I just want to speak to her for a minute or two." He heard the cringing in his voice but didn't mind at all.

"No. She is off-limits to you, forever."

The way he barked sounded like a military order. In his tight-fitting, tailored suit of tan wool, studded with metal buttons, he reminded Petras of something Kazys had said the last time they'd gone drinking together: "A poet I know said to me over ale last week that the Germans are turning Europe into a culture of camps. Everything is now a camp, from the Gymnasia they held all over Lithuania, to the concentration camps and detention camps, to the schools where they raise their children. All the finer things of life will disappear under such an *Achtung* approach to life."

"I did try to beg you to listen to me. I did warn you."

Kazys grimaced. "I hate know-it-all's." He shifted in his chair. "You don't really think we could have saved the world, do you?"

"Ah, your sarcasm held up like a shield. It keeps you safe, *mano drauge*."

Kazys shrugged and smiled. "Perhaps not. Let's speak of other things."

Petras's anger flashed through him like a spring flood. "Will it go away then?"

"No, it will not go away. But I can hope. Now, can I tell you of the latest stars I've been able to find with that telescope I built in the summer? It's very powerful!"

Petras had nodded, but he had listened with only half a mind as Kazys raved on about his stupid telescope. Had Kazys been so busy looking at stars far away that he was blind to life right here?

Now, facing the Baron, Petras glared at him. "Whatever you say, Baron."

"You'll be done by Friday, correct?"

"Yes, sir."

"Good," he said, rubbing his hands in a greedy fashion. "I want to show it off to the German dignitaries coming this weekend. Well, you're excused. Go on about your business."

"Certainly. Whatever you say." Unable to see Ona, he gave up; he needed to leave immediately and go see Rima. She could revive his spirits. The day they could marry kept being put off, but he still hoped it would be in the next year.

The fat German generals arrived on Saturday, and Ona learned they were not all fat, but certainly well-fed, their skin glossy, creamy. She'd had to play the gracious hostess last evening at the dinner Pavel held for them. She'd not been able to eat more than a few bites, but she had fortified herself well with plenty of brandy. Then, this afternoon, while the sun still lit up the sky, and the glass, Pavel had held the unveiling of the rose window.

What an affair it had been. Antanas Smetona stood at Pavel's side and conferred his status on the Wolf of Šiauliai. He'd made sure all the German generals, dressed in their uniforms and hung with medals honoring their service to the Fatherland, paid their respects to Pavel Gerulaitis. Even

lowly sorts like Hans Zeller – he had always made Ona's
flesh crawl, even when young, especially when he started
pursuing her just two years ago. Now he watched her with
glittering eyes and, to Ona, a stupid smile on his face.

She had played her violin for them, accompanied by a
concert pianist from Berlin. They'd played Bach and
Mozart, and Ona had wished her mother were there to see
these gilded foreigners pay tribute to her two children and
their differing artistry.

Throughout the passing day, the colors in the glass had
grown and receded, the reds and oranges and yellows glowing with the sun, the blues and purples emerging with the
sunset. Ona found the window breathtaking as it brought
tears to her eyes, tears for her brother's skill.

Pavel had been gracious about Petras. "I'm sorry to say
the man who built this rose window cannot be here tonight to receive your acclaim," he said, after the sincere
applause for the glory of the glass had died down. "He is
quite a talented artist but one that is unduly shy. He made
his apologies, and I promised to relay them to you."

Ona knew Pavel hadn't invited Petras. He admitted
earlier to her that he didn't want some scruffy peasant in-
terrupting an evening of culture and refinement.

"How nicely you speak of my brother, Pavel," she'd
said, ice in her tone.

He had started to slap her, but she spoke. "You don't
want your property marred, with the generals here now,
do you, Pavel?"

Now the unveiling was over, and the *soirée* that followed it. Soon she would put her plan into effect. There
would be no better time.

She stood beside the tall floor-to-ceiling windows in
her room and fingered the dark red damask drapes as she

looked out at the cold, dreary landscape before her. The drapes were new, as were the rugs and all her bedding. After Pavel's orgy of some weeks back, everything had needed to be replaced. Her stomach heaved when she thought of it.

The room was warm enough, but she was freezing. The shivering began in her stomach and spread over her whole body so that her knees and hands shook. What if it didn't work? She couldn't face failing, yet could she stomach succeeding?

Clenching her hands until the nails bit into her palms, she took a deep breath and stood straight. She had no choice.

Unbidden, grief overwhelmed her, and she sobbed and sobbed. Oh, how she wished she could talk to Petras! He could hold her for a moment and comfort her. He would understand.

"Just help me to bear the pain, Father God. I know you care about me, even though I am abandoned here in this devil's den. And, dear Father, help Mamytė and Petras understand why I'm doing this."

She turned from the window, for it was time. She'd hidden a length of rope under her bed; as suspicious as he was, Pavel never searched there.

First, before tying it to the foot of the bed, she went to the door and opened it. She jumped; there was Walther Funk coming toward her room.

"Madam," he said, "there's a gentleman here to see you, Danielius Martinaitis. What shall I tell him? Will you see him?"

"Danielius!" She hesitated, scowling.

"I can send him away if you wish. It's very late."

"No, just wait a moment – I'm thinking." Would she

lose her nerve if she halted now in her plan? Perhaps. Did she want to lose her nerve? Yes, surely. "I'll see him. Give me a moment."

Inside her room, she felt panic rising. What to do, what to do?

First, she needed to wash her face; it felt sticky from her tears. Once she'd done that, she looked in the mirror to brush her hair and straighten the skirt on her black wool dress with long sleeves and a chaste white collar. *I'm too thin, but that's all right. The dress covers the bruises, and I look as if I'm surviving.*

Descending the stairs cautiously, fearful she'd break apart, she tried to breath normally, stop hyperventilating. She'd give herself away for sure to this plain man with the deep, kind eyes.

"Ona!" he said, standing when she entered the room. He'd been sitting in the ballroom, next to a roaring fire in the marble fireplace. It was too dark to see the stained glass Petras had made, but she felt it looming above her. "You look lovely but very ill," he said. "Are you all right?"

Tears stung her eyes. "Yes, and no. This is hard, living here, Danielius, I tell you the truth. But I am fed well enough. Tell Mamytè not to worry about me."

"I can tell her but she will still worry, Ona."

She lifted her head high and tried to laugh. "Yes, she's that way, isn't she?"

"A mother."

"Yes," she said, dragging the word out slowly as she stared into the fire. "Mothers sacrifice a lot for their children, don't they?"

"Yes. Please, come sit. I cannot stay long, for I know you're busy."

"Pavel knows you're here?"

He shook his head. "I saw no need to disturb him." He took her hand and led her to a settee by the fire. "I've come to pray with you. Marita and I have been praying for you for some time, and for your mother."

"And Petras?"

"Oh, yes, Petras too," he said in a dismissive voice.

She turned to look at him and said sternly, "Do not neglect to pray for him. He is a very special person, one who looks so tough, so strong, but he is good and gentle inside."

"Petras?"

"Yes. Don't be deceived. Whenever he is frustrated, he gets furious, but underneath he is kind and loving."

"This is not a side of Petras I've seen," he said gently.

"He needs your help and support." She stood and began pacing again. "Soon he'll need even more," she mused.

"What do you mean?"

She started, then turned to stare at him. "Nothing in particular. But please – I perhaps have no right to ask anything of you."

"No, anything."

"Please hold him in special regard, for me."

Danielius stood and led her back to sit beside him. "I will remember. Let me pray for you now." He held both of her hands in his – cold and trembling hands that she hoped would not give her away.

He prayed for a long time, and she felt a strange peace settle over her heart. If Danielius ministered to Mamytė and Petras in this way, they would be able to accept what she was going to do.

When he was through, Ona put her arms around him and hugged him. "Thank you," she whispered. "One more thing."

"What?"

"Will you wait here for me? I want to write Mamytė a short note. But you must promise not to give it to her before – oh – Tuesday."

"But why?"

"Just promise. Wait here, I'll be right back."

She dashed up the stairs to her room, where she hastily scribbled a note. Perhaps this would help Mamytė deal with the future.

Within minutes she was back in the ballroom. "Give this to her no earlier than Tuesday at noon. It will be clear why later. And, Danielius, you may read it after she has seen it. But not before."

"Of course not. I would never open someone else's mail."

"And that is why I'm entrusting it to you. Thank you." She leaned close and kissed him on the cheek. "You have done me a world of good with this visit. Blessings on you."

He smiled tentatively. "I hope so. And blessings on you."

"Good night," she said. She whirled and raced out of the room. She felt that tonight she could jump over the moon if she needed to, all because that quiet little man had come to visit. He would aid her plan, without knowing his part in it. And of course she appreciated his prayers, simple yet so heartfelt. He was a good man.

She'd planned to carry out her scheme this evening, but now she wondered if she should wait for morning. Surely that would be more dramatic, but she ran the risk of someone seeing her, stopping her. Soon, now, she should do it now.

She went to her closet to pick out an outfit to wear. Something white and flowing, something like Ophelia would wear. Something that would float on the water.

Looking over the dresses and suits and riding habits arrayed before her, she remembered a white wool robe. She was sure there was a nightgown that went with it, of the finest wool. She found them in the back of the wardrobe, and she put them on with trembling hands. There were tiny pink rosebuds embroidered in silk on the bodice of both garments: how dainty and pure she would look!

Like Ophelia! But no one had understood Ophelia's motives! Would they misinterpret hers? The note for Mamytė – she must write another, for whom? Who would be a safe guard for her secret?

Walther Funk? No. He was an honest man, but too silent, too conscious of his duties as Pavel's employee.

Vanya? No, Pavel would kill him, for sure this time.

Juodas, the priest? Perhaps. She examined Juodas's behaviors over the years. Was he trustworthy? Sometimes, merely sometimes.

Zeller, the Baptist minister! Yes, he would do, for he would have to tell the truth. His son was a Nazi, but the preacher wasn't. And he was German, therefore safe with a Nazi lover like Pavel.

Quickly she sat down to write him a note similar to the one she'd written her mother, without the endearments or requests for forgiveness and understanding. Halfway through, however, she stopped to think about what she was doing. What would happen to it? She decided a note was pointless, and she capped the pen, tore the note up, and stuck the fragments in her pocket.

Knowing how untidiness irritated Pavel, she strewed her clothes around the room and mussed the bed. A vase of hothouse roses, in dark crimson, sat on her dresser, and she picked them up and flung them and the water in the vase on the sheets.

Her hands trembling, she continued her final plans. She retrieved the rope and tied it to a leg of the bed. She turned off the light to let people think she was sleeping, and opened her window, so she could climb down the rope and escape the Castle. It was possible she would fall and break her neck, but she didn't fear that – as long as she died of it. If the fall didn't kill her, though, lying all night in the cold would, she was sure.

Truly, though, it was the thought of the cold that frightened her the most. She hated the cold. But surely she remembered reading somewhere that one just fell asleep while freezing to death. She could pray for that.

At that point, she heard a slight click at the door. The door opened. She could see Pavel silhouetted in the opening.

"What is it?" she asked, her heart in her throat. The room was dark; she could only hope he wouldn't notice what she'd done to the bed.

"I wanted to visit you, my pet, and talk about the day. Successful, don't you think?"

Ona quickly pulled up the covers on the bed and acted as if she were getting into bed. "I…I don't feel well, Pavel. Can we talk in the morning? I'm suffering from this horrendous headache." She kept her voice soft and smooth, a skill that surprised her, considering her fear. "I was just ready to climb in bed, you see. I'm in my nightclothes already.

"Ah, yes, that lovely, virginal gown." He hesitated. "All right. I'll come back. See how considerate I am when you are gentle and feminine?"

"Yes, Pavel, you are very considerate." Acid, sharp and cutting, rose in her throat. Where had she learned to lie so well?

"Come kiss me, then."

She obeyed and then closed the door softly in his face. Inhaling deeply, she set herself to wait a bit, until the house quieted down.

Then down the rope and out the window, into the cold.

The shock of the snow upon her slippered feet made her gasp. Could she really kill herself? She had to, she had to – she had to persevere!

"So," a quiet voice on her left said to her. "What is this?"

Ona nearly screamed, but controlled herself. She turned to look at the interloper. "Oh. It's you. What do you want?"

"You, of course."

She stared at him. "Why?"

He reached out and placed his open palm against her cheek, his thumb in the pit of her neck. "You know why," he said softly.

"Don't touch me. I have enough bruises already."

He grinned a vulpine grin. "But isn't it my turn?" He tightened his grip on her neck and chin and pulled her forward to kiss her. His mouth was wet and open.

She lunged forward to bite his lips and butted his nose with her forehead.

He yelped, snarled at her, and put both hands on her neck, squeezing, squeezing, until she could breathe no more. The thought ran her through her mind before she lost consciousness: *I didn't have to worry about freezing to death after all.*

CHAPTER 12

Danielius Martinaitis returned home and told his wife of his visit to Ona. "She was tender and kind, yet there was something… I don't know what it was."

Marita, small and slim and dark, with deep blue eyes, looked up at him. "Did you pray about it?"

He laughed. "No, I've only fretted about it all the way home."

She took his hand and led him to the old horsehair sofa in the front room. The charm of the room, with its cream-colored walls glowing in the lamplight, didn't touch Danielius tonight. Marita looked at his eyes intently, to get him to focus on the present. "Let's ask the Holy Spirit what it is."

They prayed together for a long time, Danielius begging for direction. "What should I do about her, Lord? Is praying enough?" Marita merely held his hands and prayed silently for her husband, the kind man who treated her so well.

At last he fell silent, stood up, and began to put his coat and gloves back on. His hand shook, and he dropped the gloves several times.

"What is it?" Marita asked, terrified by the look on his face.

"I must go back. I don't know, but I think she's in danger of some sort, but I can't see it. Pray for her as hard as you can!"

He ran until he got a stitch in his side, then walked as fast as he could the few blocks back to the Castle. *They'll think me a fool! Pavel will throw me out on my ear!* But he had to go, to learn whether his vision had been right. If he was wrong, no harm done, but if he was right, Ona was in danger.

He'd had a similar vision about three weeks before, and he'd increased his prayer vigils for her and her family. He got up an hour earlier each morning to beg God to spare her and her mother.

But this vision was worse, stronger. *What is it, dear God and Father? Why do You give a small, weak man such visions? I am not strong enough or good enough to handle this.*

He pounded on the door once he'd climbed the front stairs. He didn't dare be too cautious or well-mannered, not if his vision meant anything.

At last Walther Funk opened the door. His hair stood on end, and he wore a gray robe over his shirt and trousers, his suspenders dangling. "What is it, Danielius?"

"Ona! Please – is she all right?"

"Why do you ask? You saw her yourself just an hour ago!"

"I beg of you, let me check on her. I fear something terrible is about to happen to her."

Walther Funk shook his head. "If I didn't know you better, I'd say you're drunk. Or crazy." He opened the door. "Come."

Danielius tried not to step on Walther's heels as they went up the stairs and down the hall to Ona's room.

"I beg of you," Walther said, "don't make a sound. The Baron will have our hides for this. It is too late for a social visit!"

"Not a social visit, Walther."

They stopped before her door. "There's no light under the door. Usually I can see if her light is on at night. She was tired earlier today; I'm sure she's asleep already."

"Just let me peek inside the room."

The butler sighed. "Oh, goodness, this is preposterous. But go ahead – just don't go in, and don't make a sound."

As quietly as he could manage, Danielius pushed the door open and stuck his head in the room, to listen. Moonlight spilled across the bed, where he could see what looked like Ona sleeping there. One of the two French windows stood open a few inches: a healthful habit, he thought, but cold, too cold.

Once he was through looking, he pulled the door to. "Well. She seems to be asleep. But will you ask her to send for me tomorrow? Something is wrong."

Walther Funk snorted.

"What?"

"She lives here, doesn't she?" Walther scowled and ran his fingers through his thin hair. "Something's been wrong for several weeks. The Baron is a good master but a poor human being. And if you repeat that, I will deny I ever said it, or that I ever let you in tonight."

Danielius held Walther's gaze a long time. "Thank you. Everyone at the church says you are not like him."

"I should hope not."

Upon reaching the main floor, they heard someone on the steps. Looking up, they saw Pavel.

"What is he doing here, Walther?"

"Just a brief social call, sir. He's on his way out."

Pavel grunted. "Rather late, don't you think?"

"Yes, sir. I'll not allow this again."

When once more at the front door, Walther shooed him out into the cold night.

"I'll be praying for her – and you, too," Danielius whispered. "Blessings on you, Walther."

Walther bowed his head and closed the door behind the dull, unimpressive man known as Danielius.

Danielius trudged home, still feeling uneasy. What more could he do? He would pray tonight, then check on her tomorrow. And the note – what of the note? She'd seemed so happy at the end of his visit, happy to know he would carry her note to Donata. May God grant her happiness, he thought, tonight and tomorrow and a lifetime of tomorrows.

"Well?" Marita asked when he returned home.

"I guess she was asleep. Walther Funk let me in and we checked her room. The light was out, so I guess she was safely in bed." He shook his head.

"What?"

"I still feel uneasy." He shrugged out of his coat and handed it to her. Once she'd hung it up, she brought him a mug of hot tea. "There's not much I can do now but pray."

Once in bed, he couldn't sleep. He prayed as hard as he could, for her safety. At about midnight a headache began to grow, and he groaned. This would be a bad night. Once one of these headaches started, he knew it wouldn't go away until he vomited.

But this headache was different. The hours wore on, and he got no relief from the headache. He even got up to take aspirin, but that didn't help, nor did it help him vomit. The intensity of the headache grew until he thought a blood vessel in his brain would surely burst, and he would die. He remembered that only once before had he had such a terrible headache, when he was a young man.

Getting up at last, he stumbled to the kitchen to make tea. He didn't dare turn on a light: it would aggravate the pain, he knew. Once the tea was ready, he took it into the front room and sat in the old rocker that had once belonged to his grandmother. He sipped some tea, then laid his head back, eyes closed. An overwhelming vision, first of a man's hands on her in the dark, second of a frigid waterfall in a half-frozen river played itself out against the back of his eyes, until in it he saw Ona's body floating downstream. He cried out and stood up, spilling some of the hot tea on his hand.

Abruptly the headache cleared. Its departure was as rapid as its onset. He remembered: it was like the headache he'd had the night his father was killed in the mill in Joniškis. The authorities later said it was a matter of Papa's carelessness, but in his vision Danielius had seen another man kill his father. No one would listen to him, though, so the matter had been dropped.

Now Ona was dead. He dropped back down in the rocker and closed his eyes to feel what she was feeling now. He felt a release and a peace: she was with God.

But why? What had happened? In his mind's eye he saw she was scantily dressed, but why was she out at the river in nightclothes?

He shook his head to clear it and began to pray. *Almighty God, protect her and take her into your arms and love her, please. Protect Donata too; this will be so hard for her to accept, her beautiful child dead.* At that point, tears came, and he sagged in the chair, exhausted.

Could he tell anyone? No, only Marita.

No, not Marita. He couldn't burden her with his visions.

His feet were freezing. He got up to make more tea. Once he put the kettle on, he went into the bedroom to put wool socks and boots on, and a heavy sweater.

Marita stirred when he entered the room. "What is it, dear heart?"

"Oh, nothing. Just one of my headaches." He spoke nonchalantly, to ward off further questions.

She sat up and turned on the bedside lamp. "It's Ona, still? You're worried about her."

"Yes, I was, but I finally have peace about her."

Marita stood up and came to him. Putting her hands on his shoulders, she gazed into his eyes, which he tried to keep averted, for fear she'd see. "It's more than that, I know. Tell me, Danielius. I can share it with you."

He laughed weakly. "Oh, you don't want to."

"I want to share it with you."

So he told her about the long night and the vision. She sighed and shook her head. "Poor Ona. She must have suffered, for you to have suffered so." She reached up and kissed him. "Dear Danielius! Your heart is as big as the forest, isn't it?" She dressed rapidly. "Let me fix you some breakfast. I will get word to the school, that you cannot come in."

"No! I must go."

"You've had no sleep!"

"I'll be all right, sweetheart, I will. Just feed me. Perhaps this was all an overworked imagination."

He smiled, and she gave in. "All right," she whispered and kissed him again.

Dread washed over him: it wouldn't be all right, because he was sure Ona wasn't, and today would be endless.

Petras walked to Rima's house late the next afternoon, shadows already lengthening. The day had been so strange, with his work done on the stained glass window and no new jobs at the moment. Antanas had told him to take a few days off.

He thought about the strange encounter he had had with the two Communists the night before. They still pursued him to come over to their side. "You see what the Nazis are like, in our beloved Pavel," said one, Alexei, who was slim and fair, nearly as intense a personality as Petras himself.

He had snorted. "Such a prize he is."

The other one, Dmitri, was short and dark and muscular. He had eyebrows that grew across the bridge of his nose, and Petras wished the man would pluck them. On top of that, his hair was greasy. Everything about Dmitri made Petras itch all over, except for the money he spent freely on ale, bread, and cheese. "And you would rather seem to be allied with him? Soon the USSR will defeat Germany, and all like Pavel will die like the dogs they are. Join us now; don't wait too long, or you could be seen as a traitor, you know."

Petras turned and looked him in the eye, a dark eye under bushy brows. "But you'll speak up for me, won't you,

Dmitri?"

The other man laughed. "But of course, comrade, I will do the best I can for you. But still, you must take sides now, not later."

"I'll think about it," he'd replied, and he had, but while he believed nearly anything would be better than the Nazis, he wasn't so sure that Stalin's Soviet Union could be.

Today he'd seen no one but his mother, so he felt totally isolated and at loose ends. All his friends were somewhere else, except for Rima. He hoped she wasn't too busy to talk for a while. If she could get free, they'd go to the lake to watch the skaters who tended to gather at dusk, and later stop for hot chocolate at the café.

No political involvement for him any more. The rotten German sympathizers could do as they pleased – they would anyway. Let the Soviets fight them; he was too powerless.

He shrugged. No need for bitterness either. It wasn't worth the stomach churnings and the headaches.

Just a normal life. Court a pretty girl, get married, work day in and day out – well, that thought depressed him.

On the way to Rima's house, he passed elderly women bundled up against the cold, walking their cows home. Their bells rang dully in the air, muffled somewhat against the cows' bodies. At Rima's he knocked on the door. The curtain twitched aside, and she threw the door open and ran into his arms. "Oh, Petras! You're here! Come in! I'll finish the dishes quickly, and we can go. Papa is not well and is sleeping."

Drunk, that meant, but he didn't say.

When the dishes were washed, she handed him her coat, and he helped her put it on. "Do you want to skate this afternoon?"

"Do you want to?"

He shook his head. "Not really. I just want to watch people."

"Me too, then."

"Don't forget gloves and a muffler," he said. "It's very cold."

She laughed, her voice like a tinkling fountain. "Yes, I know, it's winter. You are so good to me, Petras." She stood on tiptoes and kissed him.

"You're like a child, Rima," he said. "I love you." He suddenly shivered, as if someone had walked over his grave. "May God grant you stay this way forever."

She laughed again. "Oh, but that isn't possible! Some day I will be fat, with gray hair and wrinkles on my face. Will you love me then?"

He sighed melodramatically. "Oh, if I must." He smiled, kissed her, and took her hand. "Let's go," he whispered.

They ran out of the house to catch a passing bus like young children off on an afternoon of fun.

CHAPTER 13

A good-sized crowd of young people skated on the lake, which was not far from the Castle. Fed by a stream that came down from the forest outside Šiauliai, the lake was frozen except for where the stream entered it, so everyone avoided that area.

Someone had lit smudge pots to illuminate the lake, and a few skaters carried torches. The little fires twinkled around them and in reflections on the pond. Sounds were muffled in the cold, snowy air, but Petras could hear the swish of skates on ice.

"It's lovely, isn't it?" Rima sighed, contented. "And all the bright colors, the mittens and mufflers and hats. I've always wanted a hat in red and blue, instead of this dull old brown thing I have. Oh, look!" She pointed off to the west edge of the lake. "The dogs!"

About a dozen guys that Petras recognized from school days had brought some large dogs along and were now tying ropes to their collars. The dogs barked and struggled to get away or started fights with each other. Two of the men noticed Petras and waved.

He grinned. "We'll see a few of those guys fall on the ice now, or perhaps even into the lake! They think they can get a good ride from the dogs, but the creatures will scatter every direction."

He was right: the attempts to use the dogs to pull them weren't successful. One large black dog with shaggy hair pulled free and headed for the open water where the stream entered the lake.

Everyone was laughing by this time, glad to see the dogs had foiled their owners.

One young man, Algirdas˙Tomas, who had played soccer with Petras at school, chased after the big black dog, his own. "Come back, Juozas!"˙Algirdas shouted. "You'll end up in the lake!"

The dog didn't listen but began barking wildly at something in the water. The rope still trailed behind him, so Algirdas tried to reach it before the dog could get too wet. Once he was close enough, he stopped, then turned and shouted. "You won't believe…" He looked for Petras and when he found him said. "Petras – I'm sorry! It's her."

Rima gasped. Petras blanched. He could guess just who was meant by *her*.

"No, no!" he whispered. "It can't be, not –" He couldn't bring himself to say her name. He began walking out across

---

Algirdas [al-GIR-dus]
Juozas [yoo-OH-zus]

the ice, toward the gathering group of people gawking at –
something. *A body*, he told himself.

Algirdas and the other men around him began untying
the dogs to use the ropes to get Ona out of the freezing
water. The dogs, Juozas in particular, were going crazy, trying to get at the thing in the water, the trailing fabric, the
dangling arms and legs.

Petras felt his rage growing out of his shock and grief,
and at last he began to shout at the dogs. "Get back, get
away, you curs! Get away!" He kicked fiercely at them, in
hopes that the heat of his anger would dry up the tears
burning his eyelids.

Time did odd things for the next hour or so. The men
succeeded in getting the body onto shore, and Rima sent
for a policeman. Petras thought he could hear people talking about Ona, but when he tried to listen, he heard nothing but a strange buzzing in his head.

The lake keepers arranged the smudge pots around her
body, and skaters brought their torches too, to stick in the
snow around her. She looked lovely. Her skin was blue, her
lips more so, but she was beautiful.

Petras noted something strange about the skin of her
neck. It was oddly colored, an angry purple over green and
yellow marks all around her neck. He pulled up her satu-
rated, frigid sleeves and saw more green and yellow marks
– old bruises. His stomach clenched, and his head pounded.
A beating, or several. She'd been beaten. Pavel – he killed
her?

The police arrived soon after and examined the lake
where she'd been found. They questioned everyone there,
leaving Petras for the last. First, he asked if Rima could be
sent home. "It's too cold out here to stand around."

Vidas' Tomas, Algirdas's father, was the chief of police and he agreed, sending one of his men to accompany her. Once she was gone, he decided to move the body to the police station and to take Petras along for questioning.

Petras followed dumbly, his mind in turmoil. What had happened? Where was Pavel right now? Would he look guilty if Petras could stare into his eyes?

Petras remembered his dream, of driving a truck that he didn't know how to drive, of making his way through heavy snow to deliver Ona's dead body to a well-lit house where Pavel and Juodas awaited him. This was too similar to that, too painfully familiar.

At the police station he was offered hot tea with milk. Vidas Tomas, a slim, dignified man, was gentle and concerned. He led Petras slowly through his schedule that day, then about the last time he'd seen Ona, and what had happened the last time he'd spoken with the Baron about her. Vidas wrote everything down in great detail, so the session took a long time. At last, he sighed and said, "You can go home, Petras. I am so sorry about this." He paused and spoke again. "Your mother – do you want me to go with you to tell her?"

At the man's kindness, Petras's tears were released. He shook his head to try to stave them off, but they burned as they filled his eyes.

"Are you sure? I've had experience with carrying sad news, and I can help a bit."

"No. I'll do this myself." He thanked Vidas for the hot tea and his consideration, then plunged out into the freezing night. He thought of how cold Ona must have been in the water; how long had she been in there? Would they

Vidas [VIH-dus]

ever know? Would the police even try to find her killer – for he was sure she'd been murdered – arrest him if it was the Baron? He didn't know. Vidas was known to be a fair man, but that didn't mean he could resist the power of someone like Pavel.

He trudged home slowly, in no hurry to tell his mother the news. This would kill her, he feared. His mind returned to the sight of Ona's poor, dead face. It had looked peaceful; should he be glad she didn't have to deal with her life anymore? Had she escaped untold pain at that man's hands? Even so, he believed life was preferable to death.

At that, his heart twisted in his chest, and a huge knot formed in his throat. *Ona, oh, Ona!*

Walking quickly up behind him, the American newspaper reporter Robert Branson called to him. "Petras!" he called, mispronouncing the name, making it a short *e* like in the English word *pet* instead of like *pat*.

"What is it?"

"I wanted to tell you I'm so sorry about your loss. That young woman was your sister, right?"

"Yes." Petras couldn't say more.

"What a shame – she was a beauty. I met her out at the Baron's once, at a *soirée* he put on."

Petras held his tongue. It wouldn't do, yet, to voice his suspicions that the Baron had killed her.

"Can we talk someplace?" Branson asked. "I'd like to ask you some questions about her. I know she was a very talented violinist."

Ready to refuse this request, Petras looked around him. He hadn't realized how close to home he was. In front of the house, the Baron's Mercedes pulled up, braking with a shower of gravel. Petras lost his grief, replaced it with utter fury. He stomped up to the back door of the car, where

Pavel Gerulaitis was exiting. "You!" he said. "You dare to show your face here, now?"

Pavel's face flushed purple. "Shut up, Petras. You're nothing but a hopped-up peasant, and I'm sick to death of you. I always feel as if I need to scrape dog feces off my shoes when I deal with you."

Petras walked up to him and made to hit him in the gut with his fist. Pavel grabbed his fist.

"Don't bother, Petras. You are such a nothing. Stay away."

Furious with Pavel's dismissive attitude, Petras spat out some swear words. "Who's less than nothing? Only you. You murdered her, and I'll get you for it, or die trying."

Pavel looked at him, cool amusement in his eyes. "Let me predict for you: you'll die trying." He turned to go inside Petras's house, but after a moment stopped and looked at him. "Murdered whom?"

"You have to check on the identity of your latest victim?"

Pavel dismissed him, as if he were a fly, with a wave of his hand. "You are so melodramatic. I'm constantly being told I have to consider your artistic nature and tolerate your moods, but I'm a busy man and I have work to do. Get out of my sight, will you?" He walked into the house ahead of Petras.

Petras, dumbfounded, watched him go. In spite of how much he hated the Baron, he thought his behavior was that of an innocent man, innocent of Ona's death at least. His brain buzzed, trying to figure the man out. At last he shook his head, then, leaving Branson alone out in the lane, followed Pavel into the house.

"Where is she?" The Baron was leaning over Donata and asking her this over and over. Petras could see the bewilderment in his mother's eyes.

"I don't know," she said. "I mean, surely at the Castle, certainly not here."

"Leave my mother alone, Pavel. You can dominate me outside, but not in my house. And you cannot browbeat her."

Pavel looked at Petras with hate in his eyes. "I am looking for my – wife, and I assume she's here."

Petras started to blurt out the truth, but he caught himself. This would not be the way for his mother to learn about Ona. "Will you come outside then, and we can talk. She isn't here," he said softly. "Come."

Pavel followed him outside. "Where is she?" he asked.

"She's – " At this he stumbled over his words. "Ona is dead. We found her at the lake this evening. She's dead." His voice cracked.

"But how? What did you do?"

Petras reared back and glared at him. "What did *I* do? Get out, just get off our land."

The man didn't move.

"I know you mistreated her, I saw the bruises. I won't let this die, Pavel. I'll hound you to your grave for this."

Pavel smiled, his face looking like some feral creature – a wolf. "You and what army?"

"The Soviet army perhaps?"

"The Germans will take over Lithuania within weeks, or even days. What will you do when that happens?"

"I don't believe you."

The Baron laughed. "Have it your way, Petras. You have to have all things your way, don't you? Let's see how you deal with the changes."

He left Petras and got into his car, which glided silently away.

Branson approached him. "Quite an arrogant beast, isn't he?"

"Sir, if you please," Petras said through clenched teeth, "we must deal with our grief, alone." He turned his back on the stranger and re-entered the house.

"What's wrong, Petras?" his mother asked. "Why is the Baron here looking for Ona?"

"I don't know, but Mamytė," – here his voice broke – "I have bad news, I fear. It's Ona."

"What, what!" Donata said, her voice rising hysterically. "What is wrong?"

"She –" He broke off. Taking his mother's arm, he led her to the sofa. "Please sit."

"No, no, I won't! Tell me what is wrong!" She grabbed at his hands and raked her fingernails across his skin.

"She's dead."

She flung his hands away; she covered her face with her own hands and began to sob great, heartbroken sobs.

"I don't know what happened. She was found where the stream enters the skating pond, Mamytė. Vidas has called for some men to bring her home. They'll be here soon. May I help you clear a place to lay her? Perhaps here on the sofa?"

"Drowned?"

"I...I don't know. It's likely." Petras steered his mother over to the sofa. "Let's get ready for her."

Her eyes looked wildly around the room, and she ran fingers through her sparse hair, making it stand on end. "She'll be wet, and cold. Let me find some blankets to warm her."

"Mamytė." He started to talk sense to her but dropped it. This wasn't the time to force her to accept the finality of Ona's death; that would come. "All right, let me go to the attic. I can find some special ones up there, I think – that beautiful woolen blanket Papa brought back from Lapland. Will that do?"

"Oh, yes. You know, Ona always begged for that one on her bed, because of the reds and greens in it, and I never…I never…" Her voice trailed off, and she began to cry. "Why wouldn't I let her have it? Why, Petras, why was I so selfish?"

"Not selfish, Mamytė, careful with things. You wanted to make it last."

"But I was saving it for her, for her wedding day. With the dress my mother made for my wedding day to your father. That is up there too; will you find it?" She shook her head and pulled him out of the way so she could get to the attic steps. "You'll never find it, you'll make a mess up there. I'll do it."

Petras raised his hands and dropped them, in surrender. "Of course, Mamytė, you do that." He sat in a chair and, placing his elbows on his knees, rested his head in his hands. He couldn't think.

He could hear her talking to herself as she shifted boxes and chests around in the attic. His head started to ache so much that he couldn't bear the touch of his hands on his forehead, so he rose and began pacing the room.

Footsteps up the front walk told him Vidas or someone else was here with Ona, returning home not in the way they'd prayed for. *Oh, Ona, how I wish you…* He stopped himself, for that was a fruitless path to wander down.

Crossing the room, Petras opened the door before the men could knock, and he motioned them to enter and pointed to the sofa. Several men, bundled against the weather, heads down, unable to face Petras, carried her in on a heavy board, which they laid on the sofa.

Mamytė scrambled down the stairs. "Is it Ona?"

"Yes, Mother."

"I couldn't find the dress," she said, breathless, "but I'll go up in the morning." She nodded greetings to the men and crossed the room slowly to see her daughter's body. "She must have been so cold. She always hated the cold, you know. I must take the wet things off her quickly and get her into dry clothes."

"Mamytė." Petras started to remonstrate with her, but stopped himself. It would be pointless. "I'll help you in a bit, Mother, once our guests are gone."

Vidas, who was in the back of the knot of men who'd brought Ona's body in, cleared his throat and approached Petras. "I'm sorry, I'll need to stay a bit and ask you some questions."

"Oh, but I thought you'd already —"

"The Baron has raised some questions about your whereabouts, Petras."

Blood left his face, and he felt lightheaded. He swayed and asked, "My whereabouts? But you know…"

"It won't take long. You men can go," he said. "I'll be down at the station house before long."

Once she'd seen the men out, Mamytė offered Vidas some tea. "You're probably cold." Before he could answer, she had bustled out of the room.

Petras looked at him and shrugged. "I'm not sure how she'll handle this."

"While she has precise duties to perform, she'll hold up. Now, can you tell me where you've been in the last twenty-four hours?"

"Vidas, you know I would never hurt my sister."

"I know that," he said, taking a small notebook from his jacket, "but the Baron wants me to conduct a full investigation. Once we're through, I'll find people who can corroborate what you say, and he'll have no complaints. I'll be able to say I treated you the same way I treat anyone else."

It took another hour. Vidas was certainly thorough: he very nearly made Petras give him an alibi for every visit to the toilet. At last he closed the notebook and returned it to his pocket. "*Ačiu,*" Donata, for your kind hospitality. You've always made the best filbert cakes in town, you know. And Petras," he said, putting a hand on Petras's shoulder, "don't worry about this. I know you're innocent – everyone does. This isn't the time to have to worry about proving it, but we cannot expect the milk of human kindness from – some types of people." He put his arms around Donata to hug her gently and said, "I'm so sorry about your loss. I'll find someone to help you lay her out in the morning. I hope you'll rest tonight."

Tears brimming in her eyes, she nodded. She'd played the proper hostess so far, but she would break down once he left. "Thank you," she whispered.

---

ačiu [AH-choo]: thank you

CHAPTER 14

Ona's funeral was small, which was to be expected, just the members of his mother's church, as well as a few close neighbors. Petras felt as if his heart would break, watching Mamytė, but he did his best to hide his watching. The news that Ona was pregnant when she died hurt his mother more than anything else, he thought, although he couldn't understand why.

Others stood outside the church and watched him, he felt sure, to see how he was taking it all. There was Pavel – why would such an important personage, at least in his own view, stand outside and watch a peasant's funeral, even if she had been his paramour? Pavel, wearing a well-cut cashmere overcoat in Prussian blue, hung around for a long time, shifting his weight from one foot to the other. After about an hour he went into a nearby café for a while. Once the funeral party had moved to the Simonaitis home, Pavel sat outside in his dark, heavy Mercedes for a long time. Mamytė asked Petras to go out and invite the man in, but Petras could not bring himself to do it.

Branson, the American journalist, came too. Was he planning a story for American readers about the poor in Lithuania and how they did funerals? He and Pavel kept about twenty feet between them and never looked at each other. Was the journalist so inexperienced that he didn't know Pavel was the story, not poor Ona?

And Kazys, underdressed for the cold, his face pinched in pain, stood about outside the church too, although he eventually came to the house later and found a seat in the corner of the parlor. "My feet are freezing," he said in apology, pointing to his thin dress shoes.

"You're welcome, one way or another," Petras said.

Mamytė made sure Kazys had tea and slim, trimmed sandwiches and left her other company from time to time to talk quietly with him, to tell him in her way that he was welcome there.

Petras tried to be a good host, but his stomach started to shake and his head to pound, and he was sure that, if he hadn't been so numb, he would be shouting the house down with his rage. What a strange sensation, to be so angry and so passive at the same time.

Rima came late to the house. She had come to the church service, but kept herself hidden in back, a dark scarf over her hair. Her father would have torn a patch off her hide if he'd known she was in a free church, sure as he was that no good Catholic could enter such a heathen place. At the house, she'd approached Petras shyly, like a deer, and slipped her hand into his. "I'm so sorry, Petras," she whispered. "I'm praying for you."

The day and evening wore on and on, and Petras feared this hell on earth would never end. It seemed not civilized that he couldn't be himself, day in and day out, but he ought to be used to it, after a lifetime of not being able to be himself.

The day finally ended. The next day Petras spent an hour at Ona's graveside fighting tears. That American reporter had followed him, had offered to keep him company, but Petras yelled at him. "What is it you're watching, you vulture? Can't you let a person grieve in peace?"

Petras didn't know why he thought Robert Branson was safe to yell at; no one else was, that was sure. But Branson didn't fight back, didn't take offense, but rather grew a deep sadness in his dark eyes that cut Petras's heart like a knife.

Danielius came to visit. He started by apologizing to Donata, who took his dark wool coat. Under it he wore an old Scandinavian sweater in blues and greens. "I'm so sorry to intrude, Donata. I can't begin to tell you how sorry I am about Ona's death." He nodded to Petras, who sat in a darkened corner seeming not to listen.

She nodded. "Thank you."

Danielius cleared his throat. "The night Ona died, I went to visit her at the Castle."

Donata stiffened and looked at him. "Oh? Why?"

He flushed. "I…it's hard to explain. I felt called to go."

"Oh?" she repeated.

He looked down at his hands. In the time it took him to speak, Donata asked him to sit down and offered to make him tea. He grasped at the delay; perhaps it would help him think.

Unfortunately, Petras sat staring at him the whole time, which made him even more nervous. How to explain the visions he got? Just outright?

Donata brought out the tea tray and started fussing over his cup.

"No, it's fine, Donata. Don't fuss." He took a sip of the boiling hot tea and grimaced.

"Too bitter?" she asked, sounding alarmed. "Take more sugar."

"No, hot. I didn't blow on it." He set the teacup down. "Well," he said. "How to explain?" He ran his fingers through his hair. "I sometimes get rather disturbing visions, and I did that night, about Ona."

Petras leaned forward and held his gaze. "Why?"

Danielius shrugged. "I'm sorry, I really don't know why. I got a terrible headache – this happened before, when my father died – and I knew she was in great danger."

"From whom?"

"I don't know. At the time I felt it was Pavel, but this is not a thing I can see. I went to see her, twice. The first time, to check on her. She looked fine, was glad to see me. Asked me to come and wait, that she wanted to write a note to you."

"Why?" Donata asked.

"I didn't ask. But she seemed to be very anxious that I deliver it to you, but not right away. Wait a few days, she said."

Petras glared at him, but didn't speak.

"I waited for the letter. Once she'd finished it, I went home. Once home I began praying for her, and I developed a severe, debilitating headache. I knew – well, believed – that she was in danger. I raced back to the Castle and roused Walther again, asking him to let me check on her. We both went up to her room, and it seemed she was safely asleep in bed."

"Did you see her?"

"We saw what looked like her asleep in her bed. I went back home, but stayed up and prayed into the night. Suddenly the headache ended and I felt relief for her. I didn't believe she was okay, just that she had been released from her pain."

"Oh, God," Petras moaned. "Oh, is there a good God?" He stood up and approached Danielius. "How much pain did she have?"

"I'd say considerable, Petras. I'm sorry."

Donata was crying silently. She asked, "The letter? Where is it?"

Danielius reached under his sweater and pulled a small cream envelope out of his shirt pocket; he handed it over to Donata without a word.

She opened it and read silently.

"What does it say, Mamytė?" Petras asked.

Without a word she handed it over to him.

"Dear Loved Ones," it said in Ona's rushed-looking handwriting. "I hope you can understand what I have done. I cannot stand the thought of bringing a child into this world and perhaps have it suffer from Pavel what I have suffered. Please forgive me and ask the good God to forgive me also. I love you both very much. Always, Ona."

"Did you know what it said?" Petras asked Danielius, hostility in his voice.

"No, of course not. I didn't open it."

"But," Donata said, "this sounds as if she killed herself. But how? Why?"

"I'm sorry, Donata, I don't know." Danielius felt as if his heart would break for her.

Petras shook his head. "Can't be. With all the bruises on her neck, and her not dressed for the cold? She hated being cold." He gripped his mother's shoulder. "I'll go talk to Vidas. He may know something he hasn't told us." He grabbed his coat and left.

Petras had to wait a while for Vidas to return to the station. He sat in the small cinder block house and counted the windowpanes in three small, high windows on the back wall of the station. He noted that the large panes in the two front windows were very old, for the glass had settled in the bottom corners. The building itself didn't seem that old; had someone used old windows to build it? He didn't like the yellowed whitewash on the walls; it made him feel bilious.

At last Vidas returned, with a warm smile and a handshake. His face quickly sobered when Petras told him about the note. "It does sound like a suicide note. The big anomaly, however, is the length of time she must have been outside before she died."

"What?"

"She was covered with bruises, old and new. Someone had to have choked her, but not enough to kill her. She was – I hate to say this, Petras, but I must – she was raped."

"Dear God."

"Her fingers and toes were frost-bitten, so she was outside in her robe and slippers for some time. Alive. Then she was drowned, not long before Algirdas and the dog found her." He looked at Petras. "I'm so sorry. She was a wonderful girl, I know."

"But the note. Why did she write a suicide note?"

"It's only possible to guess. She meant to kill herself,

but someone else did it for her."

"Did you check her bedroom?"

Vidas shook his head.

"Not at all?" Petras felt his anger rising. Once again Pavel escaped any fair judgment.

Vidas ran his hand up the back of his head and looked discomforted. "No. I'll go now. I can ask the servants what they may have seen."

"I'll go too."

"No," Vidas said softly, "that's not a good idea. Pavel will be bad enough to deal with as it is. I'll come to your house later, to talk to you and your mother."

Petras couldn't argue with him. His quiet authority left no room for arguments.

It took three hours for Vidas to get back with them. By that time Petras had chewed his nails to the quick, a habit he'd broken years before. He paced back and forth in the small house wishing he could smoke; surely that would help relieve the anxiety. But the pain on his mother's face stopped him from carrying out such a wish.

Vidas had a scowl on his face when he came. When he spoke, the irritation he felt was obvious. "I couldn't get much out of Pavel. He stonewalled me the whole time I talked to him. He wouldn't let me talk to his servants either, not even Walther. I went back toward the station house, but saw his car go past, so I went back. I was lucky enough to speak to Walther."

When he slowed down enough to take a breath, Donata spoke. "Please have a seat. May I take your coat?"

He looked at her as if he hadn't realized she was there. "Sorry. I wasn't thinking. Pavel is just so difficult…" He stopped. "I guess you know that."

Petras grunted.

"Walther told me there'd been fights for about a week earlier than the night Ona died. He said it was gruesome, but he felt helpless."

Petras started pacing again, but after a few turns up and down the room, he stopped at the doorway from the parlor into the back hall and drove his fist into it. There was a satisfying, to him, crunch in his bones. How he wished it was Pavel's bones he was breaking.

"Petras!" Donata screamed. "What are you doing?" She came to take his hand, but he pulled away.

"Leave it," he growled.

She shrank away from him, startled.

"I'll be fine," he said, trying to soften his tone. To Vidas he said, "Go on."

"Walther told me about Danielius's visits and the note Ona wrote for you. He told me that after her body was found, Pavel returned home in a rage, disappeared into her room for about an hour. When Walther tried to offer help, Pavel had raged at him to leave him alone."

"And then what happened?" Donata asked, her voice heavy with grief.

"He's not sure. Pavel tore out all the bedding and drapes in the bedroom and had it redecorated – again – he'd had it redone only weeks before. He wouldn't let any of the in-house servants enter the room until the decorator was done."

"But," Petras fumed, "doesn't that prove his guilt?"

"Who knows? Could be, could be just the way he does things."

"But he was hiding evidence!" Petras shouted.

Vidas shrugged. "Probably. But where is it? I've interrogated him over and over and haven't found a chink in his story. He's guilty of many things, I know, but I haven't found evidence for Ona's death. And now the note – well, it sounds like suicide."

"The bruises on her neck, the old ones and the new ones too! What about them?" Petras asked.

Vidas sighed. "Petras, I won't give up on this, but so far, I have no evidence. Pavel says if you're not guilty maybe Walther is, or even his brother. Vanya is missing, Pavel says out of guilt."

"Vanya? Vanya wouldn't hurt a flea! Why would he say that?"

"He says Vanya was in love with her."

That had a ring of truth to it, when Petras thought about it. "And?"

"She rebuffed him and he killed her." Vidas lifted his hands in a question. "Is that likely?"

"No. And Walther? What was his motive?"

Vidas shook his head. "I don't know."

"Pavel's trying to blame anyone else, just to exonerate himself."

"Could be. That makes sense, but I have no evidence." With those words Vidas took his leave, promising not to drop the case.

That day ended, and two more, while Petras spent hours walking to the forest and back, or making small repairs for his mother, or returning empty dishes to the church ladies.

They didn't even try to celebrate Christmas. Mamytė went to Sunday service, Petras did not. It all hurt too much. It was too hard to face life without Ona, her fierce will, and her music.

Mamytė got pneumonia in January and stayed sick for a long time. She was too grief-stricken to care, so Petras had to rouse himself enough to keep her warm and fed.

He spent more days, and weeks, at nothing more than

walking, visiting at the police station to see if there was any news about a case against Pavel. But no. Pavel, in fact, had left the country, during which time no one seemed to know anything about his possible guilt in Ona's death.

And Vanya was truly missing. No one knew where he'd gone. Even Walther Funk seemed to know nothing. Had Pavel killed Vanya too? Petras didn't know.

Petras missed Ona and her funny, dry humor. He couldn't go to work, too raw and too frozen to work or do anything practical, other than running errands for his mother, doing what she needed.

It took over a month for him to wake up to the reality that Rima was in trouble. It took a neighbor's low, hushed gossip to tell him so. "Petras," Mrs. Kazlauskienė whispered to him early one morning at the market, where he went to buy milk for his mother, "you have heard about Rima?"

He jerked around and stared at her. "What?"

"That man – he's tampered with her. Aren't you going to do something?"

His face flushed. "Tampered? Pavel, you mean?"

"Yes. She needs you."

Rage simmered in his head, but he kept it down. What could someone as helpless as he was do to help someone in Pavel's grasp? Even if the someone was the person he thought of as his Rima. But he hadn't even seen her, hadn't returned her kindness at the funeral. "I...I didn't know. I can't do much for her, though."

She clicked her tongue. "If you can't, no one can." She turned back to the counter and paid for her eggs and milk.

Petras picked up his milk can. Three mangy dogs followed him, licking up drops of milk dripping down the side of the can, as he carried the milk home to his mother and felt sickened by Rima's situation. Everything Pavel touched became begrimed with filth, and now he'd ruined even Rima. How had she handled his advances? Surely she hadn't welcomed him. But one way or another, Petras couldn't face her now.

When he was almost to the house, someone called his name. He turned to find Juodas, the priest, mincing after him.

"What is it?" he growled, and the dogs stiffened and growled also. They ran off a few feet when Juodas approached, their hackles raised with hostility that he had interrupted their access to the milk.

"Now, now," Juodas said, "don't be so cross. I'm trying to help you."

"Sure."

"I'm serious. It's about Rima. I warned you before, back in October. You'll have to spirit her off, marry her. Do it now while Pavel is gone."

"Where is he?"

"In Germany, I believe. He's waiting for the interest in Ona's – in Ona to die down."

Petras began to tremble. He ran a hand across his face; cold as it was, he'd suddenly begun to sweat. He examined Juodas's face. Did he know of Pavel's guilt in her death? He must.

Juodas went on. "I'll marry the two of you if you'll sign the papers to say you'll raise the child in the faith."

Petras's heart stopped. "She's pregnant?"

"Yes. She is too precious a creature to leave in Pavel's hands, although he may kill me for saying so."

Petras stared at the priest. "Why are you offering to go against him?"

"I just told you," he snapped. "She's worth too much to be wasted at his hands, and that is what will happen. She is showing signs of going mad, and I believe only someone as steady as you can save her." He stopped and stared at his hands. "Begging is hard for me, Petras. But please."

Petras's heart turned over. "She's going mad?"

"How can you be surprised? You saw what he did to Ana and her child. You know what he did to Una."

With one hand Petras grabbed the priest by the front of his cape. "Don't speak my sister's name. You knew what he was doing; you could have stopped him."

Juodas pulled back. "Take your hands off me, Petras. The sun is coming up and someone will see," he said softly.

"So?"

"I'm trying to help you. I can't stop him, don't you understand that? I cannot say the word no to him, ever. You'll have to do it."

"You have the power of the Church behind you and you can't stop him? I'm a nobody and I can?"

"Yes, and that's why. Representing the Church here as I do, working so closely with the propertied class, I cannot stand up to him. Why can't you understand something so simple?"

Petras looked into the man's dull, flat eyes. "It makes no sense to me!"

"That's why I always tried to get you into the Church, Petras. I've dropped the subject of your becoming my secretary for a bit, what with your troubles and all, but I still want you to work for me. You're a brilliant man, yet this is a huge gap in your thinking, that you don't understand how power works on us all. If you don't help Rima now, hide her away for a while, you'll have signed her death warrant."

"No one helped Ona!" A sob rose up from Petras's chest, and hot tears pricked his eyelids. He feared he was going to cry. If he cried, he would break down completely, his cries the howls of an abandoned wolf cub, wailing to the moon for his slaughtered sister. He would hate himself for such weakness in front of this man.

Juodas didn't move, merely watched Petras as he worked at pulling himself together. "Petras, I know you hate me, but I must tell you anyway that I'll pray for you. I'm not what you think I am, and you're not what you think you are. You're the only hope we have at this time."

Petras wiped his nose and laughed. "You must be joking. I'm no one's hope at all."

"Listen to my words and think about this. That's all I can say now. The sun is rising." Juodas turned his back on Petras and strode off, his black cassock flying behind him like some banner in battle.

Petras watched him go. *Almost as if he were some sort of hero*, Petras thought, *almost as if he were good and not the weak man I've always known.*

Why did anyone think he could save Rima? What could he have done? But the poor thing – think how she must be suffering.

The three dogs returned to Petras's side, licking at the cold edges of the can as he walked up the path to the house. He leaned down to pat each one. "You're starving, aren't you?" Using his foot to keep them away from the door, he entered the house with a heavy heart.

Antanas was there, sitting in the parlor drinking tea and visiting with Mamytė, who still looked pale and drawn from her pneumonia.

"Antanas," Petras said.

Antanas scowled, folded his hands over his belly, and blew a big breath out. He seemed to be cogitating about what to say.

Mamytė edged off to the doorway into the kitchen, rubbing her fingers over her apron, looking nervous.

"You don't ask why I'm here, I see," Antanas said in his high, squeaky voice.

Petras shook his head, wouldn't look at him, instead keeping his eyes on the milk he'd brought home for his mother.

"You need to come back to work. I need you. I'm swamped. You need to work, for many reasons."

"Yes, yes, of course. I'll come back."

"Today."

Mamytė re-entered the room to take the milk from Petras and disappeared into the kitchen. Petras stretched and rubbed his cold, cramped fingers, grateful that Mamytė had removed herself from the room.

Bright red spots flamed on Antanas's cheeks. Petras knew the round little man was angry, but he didn't know how to placate him.

Antanas spoke. "I can see you may need a few moments to gather your things, so I'll wait here." Petras didn't reply. "I don't want to fire you. But I'll let you go if I have to, if you don't come now."

Petras rubbed his chin as he thought. "Okay. Let me speak to my mother, then I'll come."

At that point Mamytė bustled into the parlor. "Let me feed you both some breakfast, hot cereal and ham. You'll need it for the day's work. Come into the kitchen, please."

Petras's stomach surprised him by growling. How could he feel any hunger, considering the life he faced? He didn't know, couldn't guess, but once he and Antanas had followed

Donata into the kitchen and sat before the heaping plates she put in front of them, he set to. He ate the food and was thankful for her and for it, for the first time in a long time.

Oddly, as much as he always fought against others' telling him what to do, at this point he felt relieved. No more need to make decisions. All he had to do was obey. Go to work, talk Rima into marrying him. Go off somewhere to hide her – he had his marching orders.

And Mamytė – well, he'd have to take her along, to protect her from Pavel. They'd go to Biržai* where they had relatives, near the health resort at Likėnai,* until Pavel's spawn was born – but how could he raise a child of that monster?

But it was also Rima's, and he would do his best by it. He would come into Šiauliai each day to work and keep his head down, praying he could become invisible to Pavel.

In the back of his mind he knew this wouldn't work. Pavel would never let him have Rima. Death, was that what he faced? He figured so, and almost welcomed it.

Biržai [ber-ZHAY]
Likėnai [Lick-EN-ay]

CHAPTER 15

Work was easy: Petras merely moved in time to an inner rhythm as he blew molten glass for an order of goblets for a wealthy man in Kaunas. Antanas kept congratulating himself on getting such a plum order, and Petras smiled at the rotund, cheery man.

The glass works had become cluttered while Petras was gone. Being orderly was hard for Antanas, easy for Petras, so he spent a couple of hours late in the day clearing out the clutter, organizing what needed to stay.

There was extra money in his pay packet. Antanas's business was improving, and he was passing on some of the profit to Petras. He could almost feel cheery. There were simply no more choices to be made.

"Mamytė," he said gently to his mother after work that evening, "we must pack up and leave for a bit, go to your cousin in Biržai."

Her eyes widened in fright. "But why? I can't leave my home."

"Listen. It's not forever." He paused to gather his thoughts, to force himself to overcome his reluctance to order his mother around. "I have to take Rima away from here for a bit. She is expecting a child – "

She gasped. "Petras, no! I raised you to be a good boy!"

"Mamytė, I cannot explain at the moment, but you must understand – you did raise me to be honorable and now I'm trying to do just that. She must be saved from Pavel."

Relief flooded her face. "Ah, Pavel's child!"

"It will be my child, once we marry. You understand, we have to avoid scandal for her. She is very delicate. Even if she weren't, she'd need protection from such a one as Pavel."

Mamytė's eyes filled with tears. "Yes. How long before we must leave?"

"Soon. A few days. I have to talk to Rima first." Distracted, he ran his hands through his hair. "I'm making these big plans and she doesn't even know what's in my mind. I need to go to her now. I can only pray –" He broke off. "Could you pray that her mind and heart be kept healthy and whole and that she can bear up under what's ahead?"

She took his hand. "Of course, and I'll pray the same for you." She put her hand on the top of his head. "Blessings, Petras."

He flushed, then turned away. Her gesture reminded him of how she'd blessed him every night when he was small, when she put him to bed.

He thought about his mother as he walked swiftly

through the night to Rima's house. Mamytė had always
believed he was special, yet had made him feel burdened
by his *specialness*, as if he carried the world on his shoulders.
Had she known what he'd face now, at this collision in
history between two giant countries eager to devour
Lithuania? Not possible, but he felt she'd tried to prepare
him in some supernatural way for a hero's role in history.
Hero, Petras Simonaitis? What a laugh, for he was just a
small-town poor man with a lot of rage inside.

He thought of Rembrandt's painting of Oginskis, a
mounted Lithuanian soldier, and wondered whether he
himself could have ridden a horse and fought in a war
hundreds of years ago. If he'd needed to, surely he could
have.

At Rima's house he had to run the gauntlet of first her
brother, who held him at the door, not letting him in, and
second her father. "What do you want with her, Petras?"
Mr. Baltrunas growled, suspicious.

"I need to see her, sir. I won't be long." *A lie, that – just
a lifetime as her husband*, he thought, *if she'll have me.*

Eugenijus Baltrunas glared at him, didn't move for a
long time. He spoke at last. "Okay, come in. But no funny
business. She's not leaving this house tonight."

Petras sucked in his gut. Who was this man to tell him
this, especially considering the dire situation Rima was in?
Or perhaps that was why he was so hostile now. "I would
like to take her out for a short walk. I'll bring her back
within thirty minutes, sir." He paused, seeing Eugenijus
waver. "I promise you."

"Where are you taking her?"

"Only for a walk up the street. I must speak with her at
least briefly, sir."

Eugenijus lifted one shoulder in surrender and left

Petras at the door while he went to get his daughter.

Petras nearly gasped when he saw Rima's face, for many reasons. One, he was truly glad to see her; two, he felt guilty for his neglect of her since Ona's death; three, her face was white and drawn, deep lines running down from her mouth, up from her nose from what – pain, distress, fear? She looked thinner even than usual. "Rima," he whispered.

"Petras," she said flatly, much like the tone he'd used in the morning to acknowledge Antanas's presence in the house.

He felt speechless; what to say in the face of such deep disillusionment? Her eyes and hair looked dull and lifeless, her hair tangled – *kaltunas,* sign of mental distress, Lithuanians believed. Why hadn't he done something before this?

At last he found his voice. "Will you come walk with me for a short distance? I need to talk to you."

She shrugged much like her father had. "Sure." She walked to the door as she was, in a thin gray dress, with tiny black triangles in it. Petras thought it was hideous.

"You'll need a coat," he said.

"Oh. Okay." She left the room briefly and returned carrying her coat, which she handed to him. He held it for her, helped her slip it on over flaccid arms. There seemed to be no life in her. Was this what Juodas meant about her mental state? He shivered. This wasn't good.

"Button up," he said kindly. "You'll freeze otherwise."

She lifted one shoulder. She didn't care about anything, it seemed.

He took her cold, thin hand and led her down the path from the house. "I owe you an apology, Rima."

---

kaltunas [kal-TOO-nas]: hair tangles from illness

"Oh? Why?"

"After Ona's death, I turned away from everything and everybody. Including you. I'm sorry."

Again that frightening lift of her shoulder.

"I know I can't make it up to you." He led her down the street toward the town centre. Why, he didn't know. To find lights and life, to revive her, warm her? Once they reached a street lamp at the edge of the centre, he stopped and turned her toward him. She didn't look at him, but rather over his shoulder, her eyes flat. "I've heard…" How could he bring himself to say it? But he had to. "I've heard that Pavel has…" What, how to say it? Old-fashioned words, like "he's had his way with you"; or modern words, like "he's raped you"?

She flinched. "Don't!"

He put his arms around her and pulled her thin, shivering body close to him. At least now she felt alive.

"I'm so sorry. I should have been able to protect you, and I didn't. I'm so sorry!" Again he heard in his voice the tones of a wolf cub's cry to the moon, but this time he didn't try to suppress it. "Now I'll do all I can." He held her tight, then pushed her away from him, held her at arm's length. "Please marry me, Rima."

She turned away from him, but not before he saw tears rising in her eyes "What? No! You can't want me," she moaned.

"I love you, Rima, although so far I haven't lived any love toward you. I'll make it up, or at least I'll try."

She seemed to melt against him, sobs washing away, he hoped, all her pain and bitterness. He'd always heard crying healed hurts, so he could be optimistic that she would heal from what she'd been through.

Tears stung his eyelids. Perhaps tears were what he needed too. But no – he hardened his heart: he'd have no time, no room to be soft in the future, that he knew.

It didn't take long for Juodas to learn that Petras and Rima were not going to be married in his church. He stormed over to Petras's house to find him and Donata feverishly packing their belongings. It was a Thursday, Petras's half-day off work.

"I told you to come to me, Petras, to marry in the Church. Now I hear you plan to marry in a Baptist church. What are you thinking of? How do you plan to protect yourself from Rima's family, the neighbors, the whole town?"

Petras straightened up from the trunk he was tying up and looked Juodas in the eye. "Yes, you told me what to do. That doesn't mean I have to do it."

Juodas snorted, speechless for a few moments. "You are the most self-destructive person I know," he said at last. "Where is your common sense?"

Petras shrugged and smiled. "Guess I don't have any." He returned to his packing, shoving the trunk out of the way to move another into its place. He thought of Juodas's favorite taunt in the face of stubborn students, back in school. "I guess I'll have to learn the hard way."

"Why? What is it that goes through your mind? You're not stupid, I know you're not!"

Again he smiled. "I can't explain. I just cannot bring myself to join the Church. Period." He gestured toward the door. "I'm really busy. Will you excuse me?" With those words, he slung one trunk up on his shoulder and carried it out of the house, to a shed in back where he had loaded other baggage while he and Donata packed up.

The blood drained out of Juodas's face at the insult, and he turned his back on Donata, who'd watched him being insulted, and left them.

Petras kept on working, eventually falling into whistling while he helped his mother empty the house so she could sweep it clean.

Chapter 16

By the end of February, Petras and Donata had moved all their belongings to Donata's cousin's house in Biržai. Petras felt tremendous pressure to move quickly, but everything took so long. What if Pavel returned before Petras could get Rima away?

Petras returned to Šiauliai daily for work; Antanas watched him closely to make sure he didn't shirk his duties, but he never once failed in his work.

He was exhausted, frequently falling asleep on the bus. One morning early, before the bus pulled into Šiauliai, he awoke to find Hans Zeller, now the regional Nazi Youth leader, sitting next to him and smiling like a Cheshire cat. His uniform was creased, his hair cropped close. He looked way too German for Petras.

The pit of Petras's stomach fell to his toes as he jerked

up to face the man. "What – !"

"It's good for you," Hans said through clenched teeth, "that you can trust me, Petras. You would be a dead man otherwise." Hans didn't pursue conversation with him, and Petras was relieved, but he wondered at the man's motives. Just playing at cat and mouse? He supposed so, but he was really too tired to care.

Hans had the bus driver stop at the next town and grinned widely as he left the bus. "Watch yourself, Petras. You never know…" He didn't finish the thought.

Sweat pouring down his back, Petras knew he had to get Rima safely away from Šiauliai, someplace where Hans would have no power over him, nor would Pavel, nor Juodas.

But there would be other such men, he feared, to take their places.

His biggest worry now was Rima's health. She looked like death, so thin a strong wind would carry her away and she wouldn't even notice. Her apathy ate away at her physical strength, and he didn't know what it would take to wake her up, to invigorate her.

He thought of their short meeting last night, when he took her to a small café for coffee. She hadn't been able to make decisions about the wedding.

"What will you wear, Rima?" he had asked, hoping to spark some interest in her.

"I don't know, I can't think." She looked at him, a trace of concern in her eyes. "Does it matter to you?"

"Yes, it does. Did your mother have a special dress? Can you find it?"

"Mama's dress," she said vaguely. "I wonder where it is."

"In the attic?"

"Maybe. I don't know." And with that she fell once again into a deep lethargy that was nearly sleep, and he couldn't shake her out of it.

He wanted to yell at her but didn't dare. He'd surely solidify the prison she was in if he did.

So he kept digging. "Is there a special trunk where she kept her things?"

She shrugged almost imperceptibly, never lifting her eyes from the cooling coffee in the cup before her, the coffee she didn't drink.

Petras shivered. She seemed half-dead. Her hair was dull, her skin sallow, her eyes focused somewhere other than on life. How would she survive a pregnancy? Would she be another woman lost to Pavel's desires and violence? He didn't think he could stand to see one more dead body. All because of Pavel's insane desire for an Aryan-looking child? *God, no!* he cried in his heart. *Help her, help us now!*

His dream the night before came back to him. He dreamed he was an oak tree, with all kinds of birds and animals nesting in his branches. The creatures raised their young, year after year; the snows and rains came, and sunlight, year after year. Someone cut him down, killing some of the creatures in his branches in the process, and used him as a Yule tree. The someone was a German who turned into Pavel. After the Yule season, Pavel threw the tree – him – out on the ash heap. He'd felt such a sense of loss, a deep heartache, a well of meaninglessness, that lasted for a long time after he'd awakened.

Now, holding Rima, Petras fought against that same feeling of loss and hopelessness. He'd have to fight hard to save her, make a difference for her and his mother, his friends and himself. He groaned at the thought of the pain ahead.

The next morning, he decided to spend the bus ride to town by adding a new ending to his dream. He closed his eyes and imagined that some peasant artist had come across him on the ash heap and dragged him home, where he spent the rest of the winter carving him into a suffering Christ figure on a cross. The pain of the knife would be somehow purifying, he thought. The artist put the cross on a horse-drawn cart, took it to the Hill of Crosses near Šiauliai, and raised it high on the old castle mound, for all to see the suffering face of our Lord.

Petras's eyes flew open. Such a Christian symbol, yet he had recently doubted in God and His providence. Did that make sense, when the face of a suffering Christ felt like his own, Jesus' wounded heart beat as his own?

Confusing, but comforting too. Maybe he hadn't lost his faith after all. That would please Mamytė.

The next week dragged by, mainly because of his worry over Rima. Would he get her away from Pavel's grasp before he returned from Germany?

Under his orders, Rima no longer went to work at the Castle. "Tell them you're ill – it's the truth. You must not, must not go back there, Rima." *He'll kill you*, he thought but didn't say.

Mamytė wanted Petras to be married at their church in Šiauliai, but he couldn't stand the notion of Herr Zeller's marrying them. "The man is a fraud, Mamytė!"

"No! He's not, Petras, he can't be. He's a man of God."

Petras snorted. "He'd better tell his son something about the nature of God, and his love."

She shook her head and thought for a minute. "What about Jona's church in Klaipėda?" she asked. The Kazlauskases had just moved to the western port and started a new church. "He's a good man, and you know them."

He stalled, pulling at his lower lip as he thought. "Okay, Jona Kazlauskas it is. I believe he's what he says he is. You'll go too, right, Mamytė?"

"I should say so. I couldn't miss your wedding." She smiled at him.

There was a brief contretemps when Rima nearly refused to get married. "In March? I can't! It'll be Lent, and you cannot marry in Lent! The Church…!"

"…is not my church, Rima. It's all right to marry in our church during Lent. You sound so superstitious!"

She argued a bit more, then, typical for her apathy, she gave in.

So on a sunny March day, the three of them, Rima as flat as a day-old fried egg, rode the train to Klaipėda. Mamytė sat on Rima's right side, held her hand, and talked to her the whole time. Petras recognized that she was trying to enliven Rima, to get her to act as if she cared, and at times it seemed as if Mamytė's sweet nature was winning.

Mamytė had taken over the issue of what Rima would wear. She took her shopping, on a small sum of money Petras gave her, and bought a new dress in rose linen and wool. It was very simple and very elegant. Petras told Mamytė to go back the next day and buy herself a dress too; she fought him on it, but ultimately gave in and bought a lovely dress in pale gray. "I will have the most beautiful women in Lithuania on my arms!" he said when he saw her purchases, and she blushed.

Rima smiled shyly whenever she looked at the dress he had bought her. "It's the most beautiful dress I've ever seen," she whispered when Mamytė made her try it on for Petras. Now on the train from time to time she rubbed her hands slowly over the fine fabric, as if it comforted her. He hoped it did.

He hoped too that she would slowly come out of her depression. For the most part, however, he felt a rising certainty of what marriage would be like to such a wooden block as Rima. Horrifying, like being married to a dead person.

Dear God, he prayed, *show me some sign that there is hope for her to come out of this.* No answer, nothing at all.

Until just before they reached the station in Klaipėda, when Mamytė pointed out some children playing soccer in the street. The setting sun slanted obliquely off the hair of the children, their young, healthy skin. "Look, aren't they precious? The big blond boy there, the one with the ball – he reminds me of Petras when a boy!" Mamytė said.

Rima smiled and looked out the window. "Yes," she said softly, "I see what you mean. He's quite handsome."

Mamytė strained past Rima to look at Petras's flushed face. Mamytė laughed out loud, happy, he guessed, to have roused Rima. "Oh, now we've embarrassed him," Mamytė said, "but, yes, very handsome."

Jona Kazlauskas and his wife Marija were at the station awaiting their arrival. "We have only an old farm wagon for you to ride in," Marija told them, "but we padded the bottom with quilts. We hope you will be comfortable."

She joined Mamytė and Rima in the back, covered them with extra blankets, and told Petras to join Jona on the seat. "You men will want to talk." Within moments it was the women, however, who were chatting away. Mamytė had brought letters from Marija's family in Šiauliai, and Marija wanted to know all the news from her old town.

Rima didn't speak, but when Petras glanced back from time to time, he thought her posture looked less defeated. He gave thanks for that and turned his attention to Jona's story of his new congregation, small but sincere, he said.

Jona was a tall, muscular man, fair with a long face and deep-set eyes. His manner was quiet and genial, open to others, a good listener. His voice was deep and full, a perfect preacher's voice, Petras thought, with no artificiality in it. His heart warmed to the man as they traveled along to the Kazlauskases' small home.

Marija was a small, bird-like woman with large brown eyes and a mobile face. Petras had known her some from before, as well as Jona and his mother, all good, humble folk. He listened as she chirped and Jona spoke slowly in his deep voice, and smiled to himself: normal people, well away here in Klaipėda, far from the frenzy of Šiauliai.

He corrected his thoughts. He knew that Klaipėda was no safer than Šiauliai, with the Nazis clustering in the town. He shook his head to clear it because Jona was still talking, of church things, not Nazi things, so Petras dismissed his gloomy thoughts and turned his mind to Jona's conversation. It was simple, uncomplicated, comfortable. He nearly sighed from the relief of being somewhere other than home, somewhere easy; someplace where he could expand, relax, breathe deeply.

Soon they arrived at the small church where Jona was pastor. From their conversation, Petras learned that Marija was an equal partner in their ministry. She knew five languages and spent much of her time, when she wasn't taking care of the children, translating inspirational literature from English and Latvian into Lithuanian. There'd been nearly no opportunity for any Christian literature in Lithuania, first because the Catholic Church used Latin, then because of Russian domination of Lithuania in the nineteenth and early twentieth centuries. There was still no Bible in Lithuanian, but fortunately, Protestant Latvia, under Sweden's influence, was fully literate scripturally, and

Latvians and Lithuanians understood each other's language
for the most part. There was a long tradition of Bible
smuggling, from Latvia to Lithuania, all the years the Lithuanian language had been outlawed.

Jona and Marija had studied at Andover Seminary in
the United States and were well suited to lead the Klaipėda
church. They were bright, lively, interesting, as well as
genuinely caring people.

About forty or so people came out of the church to
welcome them when they drew up. "Come in, come in,"
boomed a large, raw-boned elderly man. Grizzly gray hair
and eyebrows bristled as he spoke. "Jona and Marija told
us all about you lovebirds. Let's get this wedding started!"

A slim, elegant woman, obviously his wife, shook his
arm and said, "Settle down now, Steponas. You'll embarrass
them."

At that point Branson entered the church. Petras was
shocked. What was this American journalist doing, dogging
his path? Why was he so interested?

"It's Robert!" Marija exclaimed. "Come in!" To Petras
and Rima she said, "Do you know our friend Robert from
the US? We met him while there for seminary. He's a real
believer, you know."

Petras shook his head. "No, I didn't know. How did
you find out about our wedding?"

"Marija wrote me – she's a champion letter writer –
and mentioned it. I wanted to come see a true Lithuanian
wedding."

Marija laughed. "Well, this won't be typical, not being
a Catholic wedding, but it's Lithuanian through and
through. Come in, take a seat."

Petras couldn't understand why Branson was here. Why
was he always around? Were they in the middle of a play

with him as the Greek chorus, but they, the participants, didn't know they were merely acting?

Petras put the mystery of Robert Branson out of his head. This was a once-in-a-lifetime day, and no crazy American could spoil it.

The wedding began, with Rima in a daze. Petras, however, felt a rising joy in his chest. At last he was marrying his love! At last they would embark on a life of true adulthood, and he would no longer be considered a boy. It was time.

He did his best to pay attention to Jona's words, vows adapted from the American wedding service; he intended to take them all to heart and follow them to the best of his ability. *In sickness and in health*, yes; *for richer, for poorer*, yes, of course. He added his own vow: *to keep her safe from Pavel*, yes!

The wedding was soon over, too short for something so important, and the members of the church led the wedding couple and Petras's mother, Donata, who was crying and laughing at the same time, next door to the Kazlauskases' house. There Marija and the ladies of the church served a typical large wedding feast. "But no rue," Marija said, referring to the custom of replacing a bride's bridal wreath with a wreath of rue. "No sadness for you, my dear, just all God's blessings!"

Rima stared at Marija, then began to cry silently. "Yes," she whispered, "I pray so."

After the wedding Petras and Rima went to the town centre to sightsee and shop. On the square in front of the National Theatre, Petras noted that the statue of a young girl called Annika was missing. She had reminded Petras of Rima, small and slim and shy.

"Where is Annika?" he asked a women selling amber

on the square.

She laughed. "Oh, the little man from Germany visited – Adolph – and he was enraged that she had her back turned to him while he spoke from the balcony up there on the theatre. So he had her removed."

"So when will she be back?" Rima asked.

The woman shrugged eloquently.

Petras bought Rima some amber. "You want white amber, right?" he asked. There were over two hundred shades of amber, and white was the most prized, although golden-brown was the commonest shade.

"No, a golden one. I love the warmth of the gold shade. For some reason…" At this point she stopped talking and blushed.

"What?"

"It sounds silly."

He put his hand on her arm and drew her close. "Tell me," he asked gently, eager to learn more about his bride.

"I don't know – I love amber and sometimes pray that when I die I will be buried in an amber coffin."

He stared at her. "Why do you speak of dying? You're young and healthy."

"Amber is so warm, you know, and the golden color so warm. I don't want to be put into a cold grave without something there to warm me."

He thought back to Ana and her child, left unwrapped in a shallow grave, and of Mamytė's desire to be sure Ona was wrapped warmly before she was buried. He knew it wasn't logical: dead bodies didn't know whether they were warm or cold. Still, it was what she wanted, so even though white amber was the most prized on the Baltic, he would buy Rima only golden amber.

They walked all over town that day and learned how

much walking on high-rounded cobbles could hurt feet shod in thin shoes. They weren't accustomed to the sort of cobbles used in Klaipėda, which threatened to break the toes of their shoes.

For Rima the one disappointment with the wedding, or so she said, was the absence of a trip to the Hill of Crosses near Šiauliai, to place there a wedding cross and some of her bridal flowers. This hill, once a castle mound, held many memories for her. The hill was sparsely covered with hand-carved crosses placed there in memory of people who had died in Lithuania, the first crosses appearing to underscore the country's drive for independence under the domination of other countries, particularly Russia. It was there that she had taken a cross at the time of her mother's death some years before.

"We can't go now," Petras told her. "But some day, when Pavel is no longer a threat to you, we can do that."

"The crosses don't mean as much to you, do they, Petras? I think as a Catholic they mean more to me."

"You may be right, but if you want to do it, we will do it. Just not now. We've got to get to Biržai and set up house." His tone was harsh, but he didn't apologize. His sharpness with her nagged at him throughout the evening, but he eventually shrugged it off because she didn't seem to care much.

Peace quickly settled in and reigned at home in Biržai. The house was larger and sunnier, with high ceilings and many windows, than the one they'd had in Šiauliai. Mamytė patiently worked on Rima to draw out her opinions on decorations and placement of the furniture. When Rima decided on yellow for the kitchen, with a painted border of cherry blossoms and fruit, Mamytė praised her extravagantly. And when she decided on light blue with sailboats stenciled on the walls of the baby's room, which was upstairs next to her and Petras's room, even Petras got in on the act of cheering her choices.

So life was peaceful in their house, but Petras felt the tension rising in Šiauliai. From time to time Branson followed him to the bus stop after work, trying to grab a few minutes to talk with him. His persistence irritated Petras, but after a while he began to respect the man: at least he never gave up. He was like Petras's own personal newscaster, who kept Petras informed on the rest of the world.

Branson was beginning to look less American somehow, less sleek and well-fed, a bit more fretful. He usually wore workmen's clothes, but he still had his expensive wool overcoat. At times Petras could almost believe he was Lithuanian. His accent was still atrocious, but at least he was trying to learn the language.

Petras felt he owed Branson something, although he didn't know why. Maybe it was the puppy eyes trained on him, waiting for a pat from time to time.

One night, when he offered to stand Petras an ale at the tavern, he said, "There's rumor of a secret pact between Russia and Germany. They both want Lithuania, of course, so now they've decided to divide you up."

Petras flushed, anger rising. "How can they do that? Neither one owns us."

Branson shrugged, shook his head. "They think they do." He leaned back on the bench and looked off into the dark fug of the small, close tavern. "Really a beautiful country, as you know. Without the drama of Germany or the extremes of Russia, but just very lovely."

Petras examined his face. "So why do you care? Why an American, here?"

"My grandparents on my mother's side were Lithuanian. They left last century to escape Russia. Now it's happening again."

Tears stung Petras's eyes, but he blinked them back. *Yes, and it hurts so much, to think what the superpowers want to do with my homeland.* "Such a small country. Why don't they go pick on someone else?"

"Easy to overrun, don't you think?"

Just a few days later, it happened. Nazi tanks rumbled into Klaipėda, the Germans changing the name back to Memel. Petras and his family heard of atrocities beyond belief in the city. Mamytė couldn't get any mail to Marija and Jona, didn't dare try to phone them from a village shop. She stood at the kitchen window looking out, fingering the lace curtains, pleating them in her fingers.

Petras hated the grief in her eyes. He wanted to stomp around and wreck things. Instead he had to sit by the fire and wait with everyone else.

CHAPTER 17

Petras's life fell quickly into a routine. He had to ignore what was happening in Klaipėda because his responsibilities demanded his attention at work and at home.

His mother and Rima worked well together and quickly established a home for them in Biržai, near the beech and pine forest of the health resort at Likėnai. It was quite a large house, two stories, eight rooms, that had once belonged to Donata's grandfather but recently empty since her aunt Zoė died the year before. Solid and square, built of bricks, it looked as if it could withstand anything. Her cousin Jurgis was glad to have the house lived in. "It's not good," he'd said, his cheeks round and rosy above a white beard, "for a house to stay empty too long. The *aitvaras*˙

---

aitvaras [AIT-va-ras]: household demon of bad luck, brownie

would move in, and we would have to tear the place down." She'd scowled at him, and he'd laughed heartily, mainly because of Donata's disapproval of his referring to pagan spirits. "Oh, Donata, I'm only teasing. I'm a good Christian too."

The rent from the Šiauliai house increased their income, so they felt a little less strapped now than they had just a year before.

Rima stayed very silent, and every night Petras prayed for her to return to normal. He was gentle with her and at night in bed held her for a long while as she first trembled, then relaxed with a sigh, and finally fell asleep in his arms. He felt that it would take her a while to trust him completely, but it would come.

About five weeks later, one night in April, she pulled close to him in bed and whispered in his ear. "Petras, you are a good man, and I love you. Thank you for being so kind. Soon I'll be able to return your love." With those words she began to cry and sobbed into his shoulder for nearly an hour.

It broke his heart, but he knew he couldn't rush her return to normality. She accepted his love, returned it in her way. But he had abandoned her. The trusting, childlike love she'd had for him before that, before Pavel raped her, was gone.

His days were long. He came home to Biržai exhausted every night but learned to take catnaps on the bus. He figured if Hans Zeller wanted to take him with a gun, he could, whether Petras was awake or not. Being ultra-logical overcame his fears of the Nazi from the old neighborhood.

But Hans didn't bother him any more. Petras heard from Antanas that the Zellers were moving back to Germany, closing the church before they left. Somehow, the fact made him distrust their motives even more than he had before. Pastor Zeller had been so eager to befriend Petras's family when his father died, but he'd preached a gospel of wealth that Petras couldn't buy, and now he wouldn't take a public stand against Nazi incursions into Šiauliai. Some Lithuanians supported Nazi propaganda against the Jews because of envy of their financial successes. Forced to be money handlers from the Middle Ages on, because Christians weren't supposed to touch money, the Jews had become very competent in business. Placed in urban settings by Catherine the Great in the great Pale of Settlement, never allowed to own farmland, they'd become the financial wizards of the era. Now Gentiles hated them for the roles they'd been forced into.

Rising agitation against the Jews reminded him of Joelis. Where was he now – was he safe? Petras decided he'd do some cautious asking about for him, to learn whether anyone knew what had become of him since the melee at the gymnasium in the fall. Discretion being the better part of valor, he decided against asking at work. He'd go to the Jewish ghetto and ask for his parents; perhaps someone there would tell him where Joelis was.

So after work that evening, he sauntered along the markets at the town centre in Šiauliai, window shopping as he went, hoping he looked casual. When he reached the next-to-last shop, a bookstore, he entered it, walked through to the counter, and asked if he could step through to the back alley. The man at the counter was the father of his friend Saulis, and also a cousin to Jona Kazlauskas. Saul Kazlauskas, a tall, dark man with heavy jowls and a hound dog face, smiled at Petras's request and said, "Of course!" He took him aside a moment to ask how Donata was, how married life was, whether Rima was doing any better. Her father and brothers were presently in Kaunas, looking for work there. Petras chatted with the man a bit, asking how his family kept, how Mrs. Kazlauskienė was faring in particular, without saying, "since Saulis died," and at last said good bye. "I'll be back. I need to buy a magazine for my mother."

"Of course."

Then Petras darted out the back door of the shop, down the back alley and over a stone wall, into the Jewish ghetto.

It was silent in the ghetto. He could smell onions cooking, with cabbage too, but no meat. It hadn't gotten that bad, had it, that they could get no meat?

He threaded his way past small, neat houses of stone until he got to Joelis's house, a large house in pale yellow stone. He knocked carefully on the door, looking at the mezuzah on the doorframe as he waited. What did it say inside the little plaque – "Hear, o Israel"? Did God hear their prayers? He had to, just had to.

At last Joelis's mother came to the door. A small, slim woman, she didn't resemble her son at all, for she had wavy dark hair and soft brown eyes. Although her gray dress was old, it was very elegant, and he could imagine she was lovely and quite feminine in better days.

She looked at Petras and nearly fainted. "What is it?"

"I'm sorry. I didn't mean to frighten you. I used to be a – a friend of Joelis's, and I wanted to know how he's doing, where he is."

Three young girls who looked like Joelis peeked around the doorframe; they had the same large, luminous eyes as Joelis, the same triangle-shaped faces. The tall, thin woman shooed them away. She placed her hand along her neck, hesitated a long time, examining his face for something. At last she spoke. "Why do you want to know, Petras?"

She knew him, at least.

"Just how he is doing. And you?"

"We're alive. We don't know how long before the Nazis move us out. We've heard we'll be moved to villages in Germany for 'retraining,' whatever that means. All the young boys and men have already moved out of Šiauliai in hopes of escaping Nazi hands, but I don't know how successful they'll be at hiding away."

"And Joelis?"

"I guess I can tell you. He's in Joniškis with my brother, learning to be a tailor."

"I thought he was studying to be a rabbi!"

"Not now. Not while…"

"Not while the Nazis are here?"

"Yes. The school is closed for a time."

He looked at her, shame for what was happening in Lithuania mingling with his fear for her and her family. "I'm sorry." He looked down the street, then back at her. "He survived the beating that day at the gymnasium?"

She shrugged, shocking him with her similarity to Rima and her apathetic shrugs. "He'll never be the same. Something has affected his speech, and he can't speak at all now." She looked at her hands. "Or perhaps he chooses not to."

"No. It can't be." Petras thought of his own hearing loss, minor, really, but still frustrating. Not to be able to speak, for Joelis, would be dreadful. "Can I go visit him?"

"You can but try. I can't say whether my brother will allow it. But I will write him and ask. My brother hates all Gentiles now. Sad, but there it is."

He nodded. Could he blame the man? "Thank you. I'm so sorry about it all."

"Joelis told me you were different from the rest."

"I'm not the only one. Not all Lithuanians fall for

Hitler's talk."

"But too many."

Abashed, he nodded. "You're right, of course."

He took his leave and wended his way back through the ghetto, still eerily quiet. It had started to rain, hard, and he'd be soaked before long. He jumped over the stone wall and walked purposefully up the alley to the bookstore. From the end of the alley, through a stone archway, he heard a strange roar and a thudding that struck terror into his heart. Was it Nazi storm troopers at last goose-stepping through town, just as he'd always feared? Just before he reached the door, he saw a swift movement out of the corner of his eye, and the SS troops began to pass by. He feared his heart would stop when he saw a black hulk through the arch.

Pavel was back in town, his car parked on the street, and he was climbing out of it. Petras didn't know if the man had seen him, but he feared he had. He flattened himself inside a doorway and waited, barely able to breathe. He heard Pavel walk into the alley. Someone called the Baron's name, from farther away. Pavel replied, his voice muffled.

It was Juodas who was calling to Pavel. There was a younger priest with Juodas, a fresh-faced boy with ruddy cheeks and strawberry blond hair. What a contrast to the black-browed Juodas.

Juodas walked up to Pavel. Petras watched them talking, Juodas imploring, Pavel shaking his head. For the first time he noticed how much they looked alike. Their coloring was similar, but now he saw the similar bone structure in their faces, the way they stood and gestured as they talked. Pavel was younger than the priest, better fed, it seemed, sleeker; but they were very similar otherwise. Family? Was that why Juodas wouldn't stand up to him?

Then a commotion as a fourth person joined them: Hans Zeller. Pavel's body eased, and he straightened to welcome Hans. Petras wanted to groan; these two Nazi sympathizers made quite a pair. It became clear to him, however, that Hans was challenging Pavel in some way, arguing with him. Trying to establish who was top dog? Probably. Juodas was wringing his hands and saying, "You can't! You mustn't! Pavel, stop him!"

Pavel shook his head. "It's too late, Juodas. Wise up."

Then the unthinkable. Soldiers, their faces frozen, marched up to the entrance to the ghetto and shouldered their way past several men who stood there watching. Petras stopped breathing. What was going on?

The soldiers marched from house to house, pounding on the doors. The doors opened, the Brownshirts asked how many children lived inside, and demanded that they come to the door. Petras, frozen against the wall around the ghetto, unable to move, could hear a thin wail begin at the first house and growing as it spread, moving like the angel of death from door to door. The children were hustled out of their houses, with no coats, no shoes, some of them. Some little ones had obviously just wakened from sleep and were crying, rubbing at their eyes.

Mothers were dragged out of their houses and beaten, knocked to the cobbles, for refusing to give their children over. And the Brownshirts took the children away anyway, whether the mothers cooperated or not. It didn't matter at all. Although he was there, Petras felt totally removed by what he saw – it couldn't be real, this couldn't be happening.

Still Petras watched. He never saw Joelis's mother or little sisters come out.

With their rifle butts, the soldiers shoved the children into line. Petras saw Hans enter the courtyard of the ghetto, grinning at the mass of children.

The noise was deafening – mothers wailing, children crying and screaming, men shouting. Through it all the Nazis were silent, hardly saying a word, just moving the children inexorably out of their houses, out of the courtyard. Jackboots on the cobbles – thudding, slipping on wet cobbles, stepping on bare feet, which made the little ones cry even more. The slap of Hans's hand on one boy's face as he snapped, "Shut up, you devil's spawn."

Petras tried to count the children. By the time he got to three hundred, they had been moved out of the ghetto and into waiting cattle trucks. Their pale, small faces looked like Russian icons of the Holy Child, although they were stricken and not worshipped as He was. Once they'd been loaded in the trucks, they stuck their hands through the cracks in the walls, trying to reach for their parents, and their fingertips looked like pearls.

The sliding doors were closed, the trucks started, and the soldiers pulled away. It had all happened in about twenty minutes.

Petras felt he'd gone deaf, silence having fallen over the ghetto. He inched around the doorframe to determine whether they'd all left. No, still some people there.

Pavel climbed into his car and drove away, and Juodas and the young priest walked off. When they'd left, Petras dashed to Kazlauskas's shop and slipped in the back door, where he wiped his feet to avoid tracking into the shop. He leaned against the door for a moment, to catch his breath. His heart was thudding in his chest, and a cold sweat prickled in his hair.

"Petras." Mr. Kazlauskas stared at him, then reached

behind him for the magazine Mamytė liked, wrapped it, and slipped two bars of chocolate into Petras's package. "Tell your ladies hello from me."

Petras nodded but couldn't speak. He slippd out of the shop and searched around outside for any sign of Hans, but he seemed to have gone, all the soldiers along with him. Petras had to rush to catch the last bus out of town. The rain beat hard against his head and back; the streets were slippery, and in spite of his need to hurry, he had to be careful not to fall on the cobbles.

His heart racing when he got on the bus, he looked around on the street for Pavel's car, and inside for Hans Zeller, but he wasn't on the bus, nor were any other Brownshirts. Petras fell gratefully into a seat at the back and shivered in his wet clothes all the way to Biržai. He couldn't relax, not with Nazis in town and Pavel out and about; soon his muscles ached from the tension. The rage began to rise: why had he acted like such a coward? Why hadn't he tried to stop the Nazis? Why had he just watched as three hundred Jewish children were abducted? And where were they taken?

Why hadn't he jumped Pavel when he was first alone in the alley, pulled him back into shadow and killed him? The man was a killer; society was not going to bring him to justice. Why not do it himself?

He knew, though, that he couldn't kill anyone, not even someone like Pavel. Did that indicate good or weak character? He didn't know, and he fretted about it all the way home. Once the bus arrived in Biržai, however, he had to put it out of his mind.

After the long walk in pouring rain, he returned to a quiet, warm house, and he thanked God for that and for his mother's gentle way with Rima. Petras entered and

changed into dry shoes and joined Donata and Rima in
the kitchen, which was redolent of the meal cooking on
the stove, thick oxtail soup, kugelis, and hot bread and
honey. He hadn't known just how hungry he was until he
walked into the cloud of fragrances filling the cheerful room,
yellow and white, with cherry blossoms and leaves painted
in a border on the walls.

As usual, Mamytė made herself scarce with some excuse when he first came home, so the newlyweds would
have some time alone.

"You hungry?" Rima asked with a shy smile.

"Starving. I could eat a chisel."

"No chisels today, just ox," she said.

"I'll take it." He sat at the head of the table while she
filled a bowl of soup for him.

"Your hair is wet," she observed.

"I got caught in a downpour in town. I did a bit of
shopping, visited with Kazlauskas for a bit. In fact, he sent
you and Mamytė each a chocolate bar." Should he tell her
about visiting Joelis's mother? About the children
disappearing with the soldiers? He thought not.

"Oh!" she said, her face crumpling in compassion.
"How are they, with Saulis gone?"

"It's hard to say. You know he won't talk about it."

"No, silent like all Lithuanians."

"I talk a lot, don't I?" he said, teasing her.

"Only because I don't do my share," she said. "I know
that's hard on you. I promise to do better."

Petras grabbed her hand and kissed the palm. "I know
you're trying. All I can say, Rima, is that some day my love
for you will make a difference…"

"It does!"

"So you won't have any more sadness," he said,

completing his thought.

Tears rose in her eyes. "Some day, I think. I'm not trying to hoard my sadness. I just can't overcome it."

"But why? Aren't we kind to you?"

She flushed. "Oh, of course!" she said forcefully. "You and Mamytė are all gentleness and goodness to me. I may not seem grateful, but I am. Please don't forget that."

He looked into her eyes for a long time. "All right," he said at last. "I believe you."

"It's just that I feel I am wading through a bog and cannot move any faster."

He stood and took her into his arms, holding her close. "I can't imagine."

"No, I know. I couldn't have either, before."

He let her go and sat down at the table again.

Mamytė bustled in soon after, to join them in their supper. As usual, she was chipper, chatting about her day and asking about Petras's.

"Oh, you remembered!" she said, pleased when she saw the magazine he had bought for her, as well as the chocolate bars from Saul Kazlauskas. "I figured you wouldn't be able to buy it anymore, rushed as you are with travel."

"I'll do my best to remember, but I can't promise. There was a troop of Nazis marching through town today, and I saw… Pavel was watching them, in the alley by Kazlauskas's; I really don't want to run into him."

Rima's eyes widened and she cried out, "Oh, be careful. Don't let him see you!"

"I did my best, Rima. That's all I can do."

She flushed and looked away. "Of course. I'm sorry."

"No need to apologize," he said, his voice cool. "Mamytė, say the prayer, and let's eat."

CHAPTER 18

In May the weather began to warm, the sun stayed out longer, and the fruit trees blossomed. At times the small white and pink petals of the cherry and apple trees reminded him of the children's fingers thrust through the slats of the cattle trucks, but he did his best to banish such thoughts from his mind.

Petras forced himself to give thanks for the spring because winter had been so harsh. He'd felt a deep chill in his heart that he feared would never thaw.

And Rima's pregnancy was beginning to show. He looked at her and felt wildly different emotions warring in him. She was rake thin, and the growing curve of her abdomen looked incongruous. She was still depressed but more normal seeming, although not normal for her, the cheerful, bouncy young woman he'd known just last autumn. She had good color and her hair was less dull; still, she wasn't quite herself.

One night Petras took her by the hand after supper and led her outside. "Let's go walk in the forest for a bit."

She started to pull back but soon acquiesced. "Let me get a sweater first," she said. She came back wearing a new rose and ivory sweater he'd recently bought her in Šiauliai.

"It looks beautiful on you," he said. "Did I ever tell you I once dreamed of dressing you in clothes in just that shade of rose? It becomes you so."

She smiled shyly and put her hand in his. "Thank you."

They walked in silence for a while, until they entered the forest near the health resort at Likėnai. The birches, just coming into leaf, whispered in the night breeze.

On the way he asked, "Do you think we'll find any wild strawberries?"

"I hope so. That sounds delicious."

For most of the way into the forest they did not speak, but kept an eye out for strawberries.

At last Petras spoke. "I wanted to tell you, Rima…"

"Yes?"

"Well, I don't know what kind of a father I'll be to this child, but I'll do my best. I hate Pavel to an extreme. How will I love his child?"

She turned to look at him. "But I feel the same! How will I love this child, forced on me in such a hateful manner? I can't mistreat any child, I don't think I can, but what if I do?"

"Oh, Rima, I didn't know…"

"What if the child is born and I hate it from the first minute? It seems so large already, so violent in the womb. What if it's a male child, black-visaged like Pavel? What will I do?"

"There are people who will take in others' children," he said. "We could give him up."

Her eyes flashed and she pulled her hand away. She began to walk quickly ahead of him.

"Wait! I didn't mean to offend you."

She turned and looked at him with blazing eyes. "How can you suggest such a thing? You don't think I'm capable of taking care of a child, any child?" She ran away from him then, toward the lake at the resort.

"Rima, wait!" He raced after her and caught her by one arm, pulling her around to face him.

"What?" she asked through clenched teeth.

"How do I know whether you're capable? You still feel you're wading through a bog. Can you carry a child through it with you? How would I know?"

"I don't know either, but you can bet I'll try my very best! Can you really believe I'd mistreat a child?"

"How would I know? How do you know you won't hate the child on sight? It's Pavel's child!"

"I know that! I may hate it! What will I do?" Her voice ended on a wail that tore at his heart.

He grabbed her to him, holding her gently in his arms. "I didn't know. I'm so sorry! What can I do to help you, Rima?"

She began to cry, sobbing into his chest. He held her tight and let her cry it out.

At last she stepped back, pushed her hair out of swollen eyes. "I'm so afraid," she said.

One arm around her shoulder, he took her down the forest path to a bench by the lake. A pair of swans, nesting in some rushes, stretched their necks and hissed at the intruders. He knew how they felt.

His mind worked furiously: what to do, what to say?

They sat watching the swans for some time while the sun set. A chilly breeze rose as the sun descended, and she shivered in his arms. "Do you want to go back?"

"No, let's sit here. It's so beautiful."

"Mamytė will help you all she can. Do you want me to get the Widow Kazlauskienė? She is getting up in age but is so kind, I think, and has good sense."

She laughed a short, bitter laugh. "I don't have good sense."

"I didn't say that."

"No, I did. It's true. I am deviled by my feelings and can't get control of them."

"Give yourself time. What you've been through, it's been dreadful. You need to be gentle with yourself, as gentle as you would be with anyone else."

She shook her head. "I think that's what I can't do. He told me it was all my fault he treated me so cruelly." She turned to look at him with beseeching eyes. "Is it true?"

"Does anyone else treat you the way he did?"

Rima shook her head.

Now there was bitterness in his voice. "Has he treated anyone else as he treated you?"

"I don't know," she whispered.

"He killed two women and their babies."

"Two?"

"You didn't know about Ana and her child? Or that Ona was pregnant when he killed her?"

Shock registered on her face. "You know he killed her?"

"Was I there when she died? No, but as well as I can, yes, I know."

"I can't believe it. No, I do believe you, but how can a man kill other people?"

"I don't know. I have wanted to kill him several times

but can't bring myself to do it."

She gasped. "Don't, Petras, don't even say it. It's terrible to think of."

"But someone has to stop him! The police aren't going to!"

She raised shaking hands to her face. "Don't even think it. I couldn't live with you if you were a killer. You can't!"

"Okay, okay, I already told you I couldn't that time not long ago, and I couldn't today. I figured I was just a coward, but perhaps it's just as well."

She smiled and threw her arms around his neck. "Praise the good God!" She kissed his ear and made him laugh. "I love you, Petras."

He kissed her gently, then hard. "And I you, my pretty one. Please don't..."

"What?"

"Be afraid, or depressed or whatever. We'll face it all together."

"I can't promise, I can't!"

"Okay, okay."

Her face softened. "But I'll try."

CHAPTER 19

The summer was very difficult for Rima. Between the heat and her increasing bulk, she couldn't sleep. Everyone told her and Petras, over and over, that this baby was going to be a monster. Such a term did not put Rima's heart at ease.

Late one August night, Petras took her for a sunset walk in the forest. It was almost cool that night, a hint of fall in the air. "I was wondering – do you want to imagine what our next child will be like – just for fun?"

She flashed him a look that said, *If I could belt you one, I would.* "What next child?" she asked between clenched teeth. "If you think I will ever go through this again…"

"Now, now," he said, "no need to make such a choice now. You're young, I'm young. Surely you don't think there'll never be another pregnancy."

"Perhaps there will be, but I'm in no mood to think

about it now! This is not an interesting game."

He had learned that running his fingers up her neck and into her hair seemed to relax her, so he did that now. This time it didn't work.

"Don't you go trying that trick on me! I can't tell you, Petras, how miserable I am! If this baby doesn't come soon, I may jump into the lake."

He didn't take her seriously, and he didn't stop rubbing the back of her head either. Eventually it would work. At least she didn't pull away.

"What do you think? Will we have a boy or a girl after this one is born? This one will surely be a boy, as large and active as he is."

"We'd better have a girl. We wouldn't want a boy bullied by this monster," she said.

"Do we want a girl to be bullied?"

"No, of course not. See, we can't consider adding another child at all."

He pulled her off the path and helped seat her on a mound of moss. He began a slow, easy massage of her shoulders and back; when he reached her lower back, he could feel her muscles begin to unknot.

His own began to untense too, and he looked back over the past few months as an idyll, without immediate threats from the Nazis or from Pavel. The pastor on Sunday had cited a verse in Psalms about God being a lodge in the wilderness, and he realized that was where he'd been living since he married Rima. Not all easy, not all rosy, but still better than the months before, in Šiauliai – Ona's degradation and death, the violence at the gymnasium, Saulis's death and Joelis's disappearance, his own humiliations at Pavel's and Juodas's hands, the three hundred Jewish children taken from the Šiauliai ghetto.

His muscles tightened up: it wasn't over yet. He feared the birth of Pavel's child would signal a return to the pain and fear of the year before. The idyll would end, had to end.

Petras regularly read the newspapers on his ride to and from town, and he knew the Nazis were moving, but he did his best to ignore it. What could one man do in the face of the German juggernaut? Right now, his only concern was Rima's welfare, which included keeping himself as safe as he could from Pavel and his kind.

One evening, while they were all sitting in the parlor, Rima knitting, Petras listening to a program of jazz on the radio, Donata turned a stricken face to him, after she had read a letter from a cousin in Šiauliai. "Petras! Did you hear?"

"What?" he asked, wary.

"About the children from the Šiauliai ghetto."

He turned cold. "What about them?"

"Ruta tells me they were all taken away by the Nazis and murdered!"

He didn't speak. He couldn't.

Rima stared at him. "Petras. Answer your mother!"

He got up and, keeping his face turned away, said, "I have to go out." He ran a trembling hand over his head. "I… I hadn't heard, Mamytė," he whispered and rushed from the room before they could see his face.

Outside he raced to the water pump, turned it on, and washed his hands. Then he vomited all over his shoes. Sick as he felt, he took the time to clean them off, so Mamytė wouldn't have to later, or Rima. He walked off into the night, not returning for several hours. He couldn't face them, he couldn't answer their questions.

Rima took to weeping a lot the last four weeks of her pregnancy. "Look at me!" she sobbed to Petras one day. "I'm big as a cow! How will I ever be normal again?"

Mamytė, seated on a hard chair and knitting woolen socks, heard her and came over to pat her hair. "You will, never fear. It takes a few weeks, but you are so thin."

"No, I'm huge!"

"It won't take you long to feel slim again. You'll see."

Rima looked at her through tear-filled eyes, but Petras could see a trace of hope in her face. Mamytė tended to be so optimistic that it affected others; still, at times it made people suspicious too – how could things go as well as she always predicted?

"Really?" Rima whispered.

Mamytė nodded her head, a broad smile on her face. "Would you like to learn to make baby socks? I don't mind making them for your baby, but perhaps you need to know how too?"

"I know how to knit, of course."

"Of course. The socks take just a bit of a trick, though, to turn them at the heel. Come with me, we'll sit by the window."

Once again Petras was thankful for his mother's kindness and good sense. He believed, however, that she hid her negative thoughts. He was sure that she cried at night for Ona, for some mornings she awoke with swollen eyes. He wished he could help her in meaningful ways, but he doubted there was much he could do but give her a home – where she gave as much as she got. And treat her decently, better than he used to, just a year ago, when he often got so irritable with her.

For Petras the last weeks went quickly, but he knew they dragged for Rima. Soon they'd see, face to face, the child Pavel had got on Rima. Petras preferred to put that moment off because he feared it.

Antanas had three big jobs for him in September; they helped the time fly past. One was in Biržai at the health spa, some stained glass windows for the indoor pool, so he carried them home on the bus with him in a canvas carrier. He was well known by now among the regular passengers, and they liked to tease him about his precious cargo. "What if the glass gets broken? What if drunken Gintis over there drops a boot on it? What if the SS stop us and confiscate it?" The threats were not light, but the tone was. He did his best to take the teasing as it was meant. That was better than the jokes about his pregnant wife. He couldn't explain to anyone that they weren't happy about this baby, so he didn't try; he merely smiled, weakly, he feared, but the other riders were used to his taciturnity.

At last Rima's time came. On September 28, she woke up in the middle of the night gasping. Her eyes wide and her face pale, she shook Petras awake. "I can't breathe," she told him. "I'm so sorry to wake you, but can you run for the doctor?"

"But of course," he said, pulling on his trousers and boots. "I'll get Mamytė to come sit with you."

"Oh, don't wake her!"

"I'm up already," Mamytė called through the door. "There's a bit of hot tea for you, Petras, and a slice of bread. There's a cold wind from the north."

He snorted but ate the bread, drank the tea. He should

have known Mamytė wouldn't let him get out without a bite of breakfast, not even with Rima in labor.

"Maybe I should stay home today," he offered.

"Oh, no," Mamytė said. "You'll only be in the way."

Somehow that wasn't a comforting thing to hear, but he felt relief anyway. He didn't really want to be here during the labor.

"Before you go," Mamytė said, shyly, "I want to offer a prayer."

"Oh, not now!" Petras said.

"Yes, now. Please." She pushed him toward the bed. "Kneel next to Rima, and place your hand on the baby."

Petras put his hand on Rima's stomach. Mamytė put her hands on Petras's and Rima's heads to bless them, prayed for safe delivery, and added, "Father God, I pray you give us all a deep love for this child. He was conceived in pain and hatred, but he is just a child. Help us love him and care for him as well as we humanly can. I pray for an extra dose of the love of the Spirit in this household."

Petras felt shaken after the prayer. It was what they needed, but would it work? Rima was staring wide-mouthed at Mamytė. "Thank you," she whispered, tears in her eyes. "This is what I hope for."

"Don't just hope," Mamytė said, "ask too. He will give it."

When Petras returned about thirty minutes later with the doctor, Mamytė fed him a more substantial breakfast and at last shooed him out the door. "A first child can take a long time to come. Go to work, but come straight home. Don't dally in town. And pray!" she called after his retreating figure.

Petras felt sick to his stomach. This was so frightening. The baby was so large, Rima so small. Childbirth was dangerous! What if…? But no, he put that from his mind, tried to pray on the bus to Šiauliai but instead fell asleep for most of the ride.

He was preoccupied at work, which unfortunately that day was at the glass works under Antanas's eye. Antanas accused him of laziness, but Petras didn't try to explain or defend himself. He kept on working at the furnace but at a maddeningly slow pace. He could not make himself go faster, as if he were in the bog of Rima's depression. He didn't feel depressed, however; he felt completely, totally terrified. Would the baby be a monster? Would Rima survive? Would they all survive adding an unwanted child to their "lodge in the wilderness"?

A few moments later he realized he had high hopes for this child. Even though it was biologically Rima's and Pavel's, he felt the child was his too, would be his own; hadn't he already put hours and hours of energy and worry into its life? Yes, it would be his child too.

After work Kazys caught him as he was running for the bus. "Do you have time for a drink?" Kazys called from across the street by the bus stop.

"What are you doing here?" Petras called back. "It's been so long since you've been in town."

They joined each other in the middle of the street. Kazys clapped him on the back, and Petras could smell alcohol on his breath. He'd been drinking more and more lately, Petras knew.

They chatted as they made their way to an inn. Petras noted Kazys's worn jacket and scuffed shoes. He was looking poorly cared for. No wife to take care of him. "So how are you doing?" he asked.

"Too busy," Kazys said, "and worried about the Nazis. You were right, about the threat they are, but I was, too –

there's nothing we can do. Have you heard the latest?"

"What now?"

They settled in the taproom and ordered ale. "You heard of the Ribbentrop agreement, which signed Lithuania over to the Nazis in the spring."

"I didn't know it was called that, but I'd heard of something, yes."

"Well, now the Germans need money more than they need us, so they've sold us to the Soviets for seven and a half million dollars."

Petras brought his fist down on the table, and their glasses of ale jumped. "How can they sell us if they don't own us? How can these foreigners own us?"

Kazys shook his head. "I don't know, Petras. You remember, I said you were right, but I was too. Just think – what can we poor plebeians do about it? So why shout and beat the furniture?"

"Why not? You want us to feel nothing?"

"No, of course not, but at least the Soviets have to be better than the Nazis!"

Petras picked up his glass and stared into it. He thought of how the Jews were treated. "It seems so. No one can be more vicious than the Nazis." He drank deeply. "How can they make decisions about us without our being part of the process?"

Kazys snorted. "You're a bit naïve, Petras."

He flushed. "You've said so before. So what's happening now that the Soviets own us?"

"We'll see fewer Brownshirts in the streets. That's worth something."

"But we'll see another kind of soldier, surely."

"Yes. Already they're in the streets of Vilnius. We've

handed the city over to the Russians." His voice was heavy and flat.

"It's senseless!"

Kazys shrugged. "From our viewpoint. I'm here in town to pack up everything I own. It may not be possible for me to get back for a while. At least I haven't lost my position at the university."

"Do you pray?"

Kazys glared at him. "You know better than that. Who should I pray to? That's one good thing about the Soviets – no phony religious stuff. I look at the stars, up close, through the university telescope, and I don't see a god out there. Another good thing – they'll never massacre Jews the way the Nazis have, with their exploitation of medieval beliefs in Jews as Christ killers, using Christians to do their dirty work."

"Not Christians. Maybe pseudo-Christians. No true believer could…"

"Aren't they all fake, or just so painfully ignorant and superstitious? No real scholar can believe that myth."

Petras stiffened. "I know some who are not fake, and who are not superstitious. My faith isn't the strongest, but there are real, living believers who live as Christ would command them to."

"You wait and see. When the Soviets force their atheistic, materialistic beliefs on all your friends and family, you'll see how real they are."

Petras pushed his glass aside and stood. "Thank you for your news, Kazys. I wish you safe return to Vilnius." With that, he turned on his heel and left the taproom.

His mother wasn't fake, nor the Kazlauskases, nor was Danielius Martinaitis.

But Herr Zeller had been, and his son, Hans, with his starched uniform and his shiny pistol. What would happen to them now, he wondered.

CHAPTER 20

With fall now here, dark had fallen well before Petras left town, so he rode back to Biržai with only his reflection in the windows to look at. That wasn't an interesting prospect, the reflected eyes large and fearful, mouth turned down, but he couldn't relax enough to fall asleep on the ride the way he usually did.

Returning home later than he expected, he felt sweat pouring down his back. Wanting to be home but afraid too, he hoped he'd return to a quiet family scene, but he figured he wouldn't.

Rapidly he walked home from the bus stop. When he entered the house, his heart constricted: Mamytė's face was drawn and pale.

"No baby yet," she whispered. "She is having a difficult time."

He nodded dumbly.

Mamytė took his coat and lunch box. "Come say hello to her, then come to the kitchen. I've tea fixed for you."

Petras dreaded going into the bedroom. He felt nothing good, at this point, could come out of Rima's labor. He poked his head around the doorframe and saw a nurse holding Rima's hand and wiping her brow with a damp cloth. The woman, whom Petras did not know, looked up and grunted. "Come over here and help this poor thing. I thought you'd never get here."

"I…I," Petras stammered. "I don't know what…"

"Aren't you the doctor?"

"No, I'm her husband."

"So you're the one got her this way. Men!" she spat. "Beasts, all of them."

Petras didn't know what to say, so wisely said nothing.

Rima looked dully at him, her sad eyes tugging at his heart, so he walked over to the other side of the bed from the midwife and took her hand. "It's very bad, huh?" he asked.

She scowled and shook her head. "It's just that I'm so tired."

"She's worn out, near to death," the midwife said.

Again Rima shook her head. "Not true, Petras, don't worry now. Have you eaten?"

"I will. Don't worry about me, I'm fine." He leaned over and kissed her forehead. "I'm sorry this is so hard."

"I'll be fine," she said.

He sat by her a few moments. When she was shaken by labor pains so intense he thought she'd rip open, he cried out, "Oh, Rima!"

"Go on, get out," the midwife snapped. "You'll just worry her."

He left, joined his mother in the kitchen. "It's been like this all day?"

She nodded.

"And who is that woman?"

She began kneading her hands in her apron, and he saw the fatigue and concern under her calm exterior. "A nurse recommended by a lady in town. The doctor has been called to come back, though. We can only pray he gets here soon."

"It's bad."

"Perhaps." She gestured to the food on the scrubbed pine table. "Eat up. Once you're done, I'll send you for the doctor if he hasn't come yet."

Within thirty minutes, the doctor arrived, apologetic, especially when he saw Olga Vanevičienė, the nurse, there at the birth. Olga snarled at him; he snapped at her to get out of his way. Petras wondered what reasons they had for such animosity toward each other; surely that wasn't good news for Rima. Olga withdrew to the kitchen where she fussed over boiling water and clean linens and such; Dr. Rudminas thought that was the best job for her, it seemed.

A man of medium height and weight, of fair hair and ruddy complexion, the doctor exuded confidence and purpose. To Rima he was gentle and kind. "We'll have this baby here before long, Mrs. Simonaitienė."

Unable to open her eyes, Rima merely nodded.

The alarm that arose in Petras was worse than that caused by seeing Pavel or storm troopers on the streets from time to time; this was a life-threatening situation for Rima now, and he felt helpless to do anything for her.

"Now!" the doctor said. "It's coming. You see the head?"

Petras didn't look; he didn't think he could.

"It's coming. Oh, my, so small."

"What?" Rima whispered.

"Oh, my," the doctor said sadly. "She didn't make it." A tiny little female baby, with dark red hair and very white skin. He shook his head. To Petras he whispered, "This is a full-term pregnancy, right?"

"Yes, sir."

He tsked. "This little one stopped growing long ago."

"What did you say?" Rima asked, weak now, defeated, Petras thought. Tears began to stream from her eyes.

"But Rima grew so large!" Petras whispered furiously to the doctor. "How can this be?"

Dr. Rudminas shrugged, laid the dead baby aside, uninterested in one that wasn't alive. Within moments, however, he smiled. "Ah, here's another, and I can see the heart beat strongly in the skull. Look, Simonaitis, come see! This is a big one!"

Still Petras didn't leave Rima's side. He felt sure she wouldn't want him to see the birth area, although she'd never said so.

At that moment Mamytė, with Olga behind her, entered the bedroom. "A baby?"

"Yes, Mamytė," Petras said, "the first one was dead, but this one looks alive."

Her face crumpled. "One dead?"

Rima squeezed Petras's hand hard. "Don't speak of it!"

He picked up the wet cloth Olga handed him and began to wipe Rima's face. "Hang on, it'll be over before long, dear one."

She managed a weak smile.

Then the birth cry!

"What a lusty one," the doctor said as he held up above Rima's head a large boy with a full head of black hair. "At least ten pounds, I'd say!"

The baby screamed and screamed, until the doctor handed him to Olga, who wiped the baby off and wrapped him in a dry cloth before laying him beside Rima.

Petras held his breath as he watched her face. She turned toward the large baby, with wide Slavic cheekbones and a rounded skull covered with long black hair, and smiled. "Hello, little one. At last I meet you."

His withheld breath whooshed out of him, and he fought back tears. She would be all right now, he felt sure.

"Petras," she said firmly, eyes still riveted on her son, "I want to call him Gintaras, for amber." There was no question, no hesitation in her voice. Just a firm, strong naming: Gintaras.

CHAPTER 21

Rima recuperated quickly from the birth, which amazed everyone. She showed nearly no interest in the poor, small, undeveloped fetus that had been born first. She let Donata name her Ina, let Petras handle all the details of the funeral. The baby was buried in a Protestant cemetery across the border in Latvia, where Petras's father was buried.

And that was the sum total of the little girl's life.

For Gintaras Rima had something akin to adoration. He was the biggest, strongest, brightest child anyone could ever imagine.

Certainly Petras could not have foretold her attachment to the child, Pavel's child, but he preferred it to the mental derangement and *kaltunas*, the tangled hair, that he had expected. Having finished a big job for Antanas the day the child was born, he stayed home for five days to keep an eye out for Rima's stability and health, but soon he laughed at himself for his anxiety.

And Donata went about the house singing, happy to have a baby in the house. Petras couldn't believe the number of diapers she boiled and hung out to dry; how could one small child, brute that he was, soil so many?

Gintaras ate voraciously, and Rima winced in pain at his vigorous nursing and laughed in relief that he was thriving so.

"He's a little pig," Petras said one night.

"Yes." She smiled proudly.

Petras couldn't quite figure out the child's look. He did remind him a bit of Pavel, but more so of Vanya. By the time Gintaras was two weeks old, he was smiling, which both Donata and Rima assured Petras meant he was very advanced, and his toothless grin was sweet and innocent. Petras's fear about Pavel's character coming through in the child began to fade. Perhaps life would be simpler than they feared, with this child added to the household.

Gintaras slept well, for the most part. From time to time, inexplicably, he'd scream for two or three hours, usually at supper time and early evening. Either Donata or Petras would take him out for a walk in the forest, to let Rima rest some from the care of the very large, demanding boy she was nursing.

Autumn was shortening the days and chilling them with lack of sunlight, and still Gintaras seemed to thrive. "He ought to," Donata said proudly, "as much as he eats."

"Demanding babies grow well," the doctor said when he came to visit his patients. He wanted to claim some credit for the baby's size and obvious brightness and enjoyed coming to see how he was faring. The child was the talk of the village, at least partly because of his dark coloring and his parents' fairness. But the Simonaitises did not address the issue with anyone.

It happened to be Petras's birthday one afternoon when Dr. Rudminas arrived, and Donata bustled around serving tea and a cake she'd made.

The doctor teased her, she blushed, and Petras wondered whether there was a romance budding between them. It would be all right with him; the doctor seemed a good man, and Tėvelis* was long dead now. Mamytė didn't need to stay single for him.

His wilderness retreat, in the forests of Biržai, contrasted sharply with the tensions in Šiauliai. Rotund, affable Antanas even felt the tension and snapped at Petras several times a day. He would apologize later for his sharp tongue. "I'm not able to collect payments for some of the work we've done the past few months, lad. Don't take it personal."

"Did Pavel ever pay you for the window we did for him last fall?"

"Only some of it. That's the biggest concern. And now with the Nazis gone, things are less stable for him, and he's less likely to pay. He owes me thousands of *litai*, but he says he wants to see how the window holds up under bad weather."

"He's had a whole winter and a spring, nearly a year. What more does he want?"

Antanas ran his hand over his sweaty face and shrugged. "Just what I asked him. I don't suppose..."

"What?"

"Could you go look it over, talk to him?"

Tėvelis [teh-VEH-lis]: Papa

Petras snorted. "You think he'd pay me over you?"

Antanas, of course, knew Pavel had raped Rima, so he spoke hesitantly, careful not to offend. "He wants you to inspect it. Says you built it, so why haven't you been back to check it out?"

Petras groaned. "I can't face that man. Most often, when I think of him, I want to kill him, but I also wonder why I'm such a coward not to have done it already."

Antanas shook his head. "Never, Petras. You couldn't live with yourself."

"And Rima would hate me for it."

"Killing changes a person."

Anger rising in him, Petras turned to the ovens and began to jab at the coals with a poker, to stoke the fire. "How many has he killed?"

"None, that he's been found guilty for."

Petras glared at him. "You know better than that," he growled.

Antanas held up his hand. "None, that you know for sure, Petras. Remember that. You believe he's guilty; it hasn't been proven."

"That's a defense of the odious man? His crimes haven't been proven?" He was shouting now as he jabbed at the coals.

Antanas shook his head. "No. But listen, I'm sorry. Forget I mentioned it." He took the long poker out of Petras's hand. "Give over. You're spilling sparks out on the floor."

Petras stepped back from the ovens, went to a dark corner of the room, and sat on a bench against the wall. He held his head in his hands.

"Look, I said I was sorry. I shouldn't have brought it

up," Antanas said. "I don't blame you for hating the man, but what can you do? He's too powerful, and ensconced up in that castle of his, what can we normal folk do? Nothing. So do your work and forget him."

Petras dropped his hands to his knees. "Forget him? You realize I see his son every day of my life? I see my wife feeding the boy, see him taking the very life out of her, and you say I should forget him?" He stopped himself. He could hear in his words a resentment of that sunny baby at home, and it shocked him. Yet it comforted him too in an odd way: of course any real man would hate a cuckoo in his nest.

Antanas stared at him. "I hope for your sake and the child's you get over it. This isn't sound thinking."

He exploded. "It isn't thinking at all, it's just gut-level feeling! I can't help what I feel, which is rage, black, poisonous rage!"

"Poisonous is right," Antanas said wearily. "Forget I brought it up. Get back to work."

"Sure," Petras growled. He stood up and returned to his work at the ovens. Work was always Antanas's solution to problems; perhaps it was a good one. That didn't mean, however, that it made welcome advice.

On the way home that night, Petras fell asleep on the bus and dreamed about Ina, the poor dead baby no one had paid any attention to. He saw how she looked like him, and he knew in the dream that the child was his, overwhelmed, overtaken, defeated, starved out by Pavel's child. He awoke to a tight, acid feeling in his mouth and a dull headache. He knew it had been only a dream, but the feeling stayed with him.

Ultimately Antanas won out – and Pavel. Petras had to go inspect the window. Antanas agreed to accompany him, in fact, drove them both there in his beloved rusty, old truck. It was rare that Petras got a chance to ride in a private vehicle. The heater didn't work, and inside the truck was frigid, but at least there was no wind.

"This is so wasteful, for us both to be gone for who-knows-how-long on a busy day," Antanas groused.

"So I'll stay here and you can go." Petras was getting bolder in his tone to Antanas since the day Petras had yelled at him and Antanas hadn't held it against him.

"No. Pavel says you inspect it, or he doesn't pay."

"The toad. He always gets what he wants, doesn't he?"

"If you get what you want on this – my going along, I mean – does that mean you're a toad too?"

Petras's anger flared up. "You know better! I am not anything like that scum Pavel!"

Antanas hid a grin. "Sorry. I thought you were equating getting your way with being a toad."

"You didn't think any such thing."

Soon Antanas was talking away normally as they drove to the Castle. The sun shone bright on that chilly October day, and it set the fine lines of the small castle off like a rich setting for a precious gem. "Nice specimen for a Russian castle, huh?"

Petras grunted. But even he could appreciate its architecture.

"Perhaps some day you'll live in that castle, Petras. Imagine! Now that you are raising Pavel's only son…"

"As far as you know. Who knows how many other women he's raped?"

"Now that you're raising his son, you may end up here, with Gintaras in charge. How does that sound?"

Petras remembered the dream he'd had the day he began working on the rose window, of the widows and orphans upon whose backs the Castle must have been built. "It would sicken me."

Antanas turned to stare at him. "Really? Why? It's so lovely."

"You wouldn't understand."

"Try me."

Petras ran a hand over his face, then straightened in the seat and told Antanas about the dream he'd had. "How could I live somewhere built on their blood and bones and teeth?"

"Such an imagination. You're a true artist, with your fanciful dreams." Antanas slowed to negotiate the circular drive in front of the Castle. "Perhaps you could dedicate it, purify it some way. You know, have the priest come pray over it or something."

Petras gave a harsh bark of laughter. "Juodas? Purify anything?"

"Another priest perhaps. There's a new young one, here to help Juodas, idealistic, a true Lith. Perhaps he's the right one."

He shook his head. "I can't imagine anything cleansing it."

"It's possible," Antanas persisted, his natural optimism bubbling to the surface.

"*Taip*, *taip*, it's possible." Petras looked glumly up at the large front doors to the hated building. "But not likely."

Chapter 22

Walther Funk let Antanas and Petras in, then held Petras's eyes for a second too long. Petras felt as if the man wanted to tell him something.

He gestured to several chairs along the wall. "Please wait here," Funk said. "I'll let the Baron know you've arrived."

Petras looked around the large, open foyer, and felt once again the old sickness he always felt in this building and his old rage with Pavel Gerulaitis. He sat in the chair, looked down at his hands, with their glass cuts and burns from the ovens, and wondered how a person could use his hands to harm and kill another human being.

He remembered the first time he'd come here and waited in the ballroom for Vanya to turn up and help him build a scaffold. Where was Vanya now?

This time they waited about ten minutes, not long enough to enrage Antanas, but long enough to irritate him. "I need to be back at the foundry, Petras!"

"Why are you telling me?" Petras asked, trying to stay cool and rational, two characteristics he had only in minuscule doses, which were now depleted by having to face Pavel. "I didn't think we should come at all."

Antanas snorted. "Hmph! I should have ordered you to come alone!"

When Walther returned, he led them to Pavel's study, where the Baron stood looking out at the view of the lake, his hands tucked under the tails of a black morning coat. After what seemed to be a very long while, he turned to look at them and said, "Well, at last. I didn't think we'd ever get this job finished."

"Finished?" Petras spat out. "It was finished months ago."

"No, I think not. There's a leak around one of the lead seals that you need to fix. There's also one piece of glass that isn't quite the right color, in the row of wolf images."

Petras nearly laughed. One pane out of hundreds this man didn't like the color of? But he said nothing.

He and Antanas followed Pavel to the ballroom. Pavel had a hint of a limp.

"You injured yourself, Baron?" Antanas asked solicitously.

"It's nothing."

Antanas persisted. "Nothing?"

"A slight wound, when I was working in the cellars."

The cellars. Where Petras had dreamed of widows and orphans holding the Castle up on their backs.

"Vanya," Petras said. "Where is Vanya these days?"

"Why do you care?" Pavel asked.

Petras swallowed, taking a moment to frame his reply. He didn't dare mention Vanya's caring for him the two times when he was injured. "He helped me build the scaffolding for the window, and I enjoyed his company."

"He's gone, off getting military training."

"Vanya?"

"Why not? He may be pathetic, but he has to be useful in some respect. He's not completely stupid, you know."

Petras's eyes widened in surprise. "I never thought he was." He let the subject drop. It was likely to be an unpromising conversation.

The halls they walked through were lined with different art objects that looked new to Petras. They didn't appeal to him: they all seemed very Germanic and muscular, very puffed up. At last they reached the ballroom, where a young woman sat at a grand piano playing some Chopin etudes. Petras started: she reminded him of Ona. She was lovely, fair, tall – slim and blond, of course. In an ivory wool dress, her hair golden, she matched the gold and ivory of the room.

Pavel smiled a tight smile when he noted Petras's reaction. "My wife," he said in an oily voice. He didn't give her name, and she didn't speak. "She's German. Isn't she lovely?"

Antanas stammered in his haste to respond, because he knew Petras wasn't going to, at least not in a socially acceptable way. "Yes, she is. Nice to meet you, madam," he said with a slight bow.

Petras, keeping his emotions in check, felt the muscles in his jaw tighten. He didn't say a word, although Pavel was waiting for something, staring at Petras.

At last he lost interest and pointed to the rose window. Petras nearly gasped, for he had forgotten how beautiful it was.

Antanas beamed. "Oh, it's a real work of art, isn't it? Petras, you outdid yourself."

"My design, of course," Pavel said.

"Of course," Antanas said. He rubbed his hands together. "Well, let's get busy. Where's this leak and the one wrong piece of glass?"

Pavel pulled a library ladder out from behind some gold drapes and positioned it under the window. "Let the 'artist' climb up and inspect it. He'll find it, right enough!"

Petras glared at the man but didn't reply. He climbed the ladder carefully and began running his fingers over the lead solder between the myriad colors and shapes of glass. At last he found a small air leak at the far right side of the window. "Here it is, surely easy to fix. You have leading in the truck, Antanas?"

"Yes, I'll get it."

"Before you go, though, let's see about the wrong colored piece. Where is it, Pavel?"

"*Baron* to you, Petras," he said, his voice heavy with sarcasm. "It's there, the bottom right quadrant of the wolf ring. It ought to be obvious to someone with such an artist's eye."

Petras began searching for the offending piece of glass, but nothing leapt to his eye. He told himself to slow down, take his time, that pleasing this man was necessary if Antanas was going to be paid. He went over the pieces, one by one, over and over.

By the time he'd checked every piece of glass seven times, Antanas was extremely anxious. "Come down from there and let me look!" he snapped.

"Certainly," Petras replied, holding on to his temper. He was beginning to believe the tale of an offending piece of glass was a ruse.

"Hold this ladder for me!" Antanas barked at Petras. "I'm not as young and lithe as you are."

Petras held the ladder while Antanas climbed, slowly, laboriously. He began the search for the piece of glass that was the wrong color. He spent nearly a quarter of an hour, but did not find anything.

The whole time, Pavel leaned against a gilt-painted chair and smirked, obviously enjoying their discomfiture.

At last Antanas, his face red from the effort to hold his temper, turned and looked at the Baron. "Okay, where is it? I can't believe…"

"You couldn't find it? It isn't obvious to your trained eye?"

"No, it isn't!"

"Come down, then, and I'll show you."

They switched places, and the Baron began to look for the odd piece of glass. Petras could tell he was beginning to sweat because he couldn't find it either. "It's here, and when I find it, you'll see it's a gross mistake."

Petras began to enjoy the spectacle of the Baron hunting for something that didn't exist. He glanced at Antanas and was going to wink when he realized Antanas was steaming. He didn't see the humor in the situation.

Petras sobered immediately; he shouldn't see it either, for soon they'd be paying some consequence for the Baron's having humiliated himself. But what?

"So," Pavel said at last, "did you cover it with something while you were up here? A thin piece of glass or something similar? It's gone."

Petras and Antanas both shook their heads. "No," Petras said.

"Maybe someone else did."

"No," Petras said. "We would have felt something like that."

"Well, you're so smart, you explain it!" Pavel snapped.

Petras looked down at the floor to compose his words. "I'm sorry, sir, I can't. It looks perfect to me. Except for the small air hole in the lead. I'll repair that for you right now." With that, he turned his back on the man and walked as slowly as he could from the room, the Baron's eyes – and those of his wife – boring into his back.

Once he returned with the softened lead, he clambered up the ladder and repaired the hole smoothly, as unobtrusively as possible. He didn't want a return engagement at the Castle. "There," Petras said softly, "it's done. You can pay Antanas what he's owed now." He cleaned up after himself, pushed the library ladder back behind the drape where it had come from, and bowing slightly to the Baroness and to Pavel, exited the room, leaving Antanas to deal with the man who had nearly ruined his life.

Pavel dashed to the door and called him back. "Wait, Petras," he said, his oily voice back. "How is Rima? And her son? I understand he is dark like me." His eyes bored into Petras's, waiting for an explosion. "Not your child, surely."

This man had an atavistic drive to father many children, did he? To use as many young virgins as he could? Petras didn't feel he himself had such an urge, but perhaps he was wrong.

Petras smiled. "Yes, my child, Pavel – Baron. He calls me Tėvelis."

"He speaks, so young? A brighter than average child, you say?"

"My mother assures me I did the same."

Pavel flinched, but waved his hand in dismissal. "Get

out. You are a thorn in my flesh."

Petras grimaced at this evil man's reference to Scripture. "Like Saint Povilas?* You don't resemble him at all." He could tell the barb had hit home. He bowed and excused himself, went out to the truck to wait for Antanas, who came beaming, clutching his wallet into which he was stuffing some large bills.

"At last, we've been paid, at least most of it. I really couldn't carry him on the books much longer." In his excitement his voice was higher than normal and sounded like a small child's.

"Only part? Do you think you'll get it all from him?"

Antanas shrugged. "Perhaps not. But we got the lion's share." He climbed into the truck and started the engine. "I'm surprised, if he's the devil you think he is, that he didn't kill you on the spot for the way you treated him. Challenging his authority in that way! Don't you know any better?"

"Don't ask me to treat him the way I would a normal person. I can't. He's too odious."

Antanas sighed and dropped the subject. "What do you think was the story on the wrong color glass?"

"I don't know. I do think he sincerely felt there was a problem in the wolf ring. I can't imagine his putting on an act that would make him look a fool."

"No, but perhaps he'd do anything to get out of paying such a large amount."

"I think it was a good thing you went along, Antanas. He'd have done his best to put me in the wrong if you hadn't."

Antanas stuck his lower lip out as he thought. "Yes,

Povilas [PAH-vi-las]: Lithuanian for Paul (Pavel is Russian for Paul) you're probably right. So it wasn't a waste of my time."

"No."

Antanas was so jubilant when they returned to the shop that he let Petras go early, with a bonus payment for having helped collect from Pavel. "Buy something pretty for your wife and your mother. And a toy for the boy. He's smart, huh?"

"Mamytė thinks so."

"Sweet?"

"Very, like his mother and my mother."

"Good. I've been praying for you all. Rima's father is my cousin, you know, and I've always taken an interest in the family. Eugenijus is drinking himself to death, unfortunately."

"I'm sorry to hear that."

Antanas shrugged. "He won't listen to anyone who tells him to stop."

"Do you think his time is short? Should Rima go see him?"

"Yes, his time is short; no, she shouldn't go see him. He'll curse her and revile her for marrying outside the Church."

"But she's his child, and Gintaras his grandchild!"

Antanas scowled at Petras, all joviality gone from his round face, as he paused a moment to think. "No, she must not open herself to his hatred, believe me."

So Petras left early and went shopping for his family. He bought chocolate as well as sweaters for the winter – blue with red sailboats for Gintaras, a warm brown for Mamytė, and a soft rose, of course, for Rima.

He worried about what to tell Rima, whether he should even mention her father. On the way to his bus, however, he saw Soviet soldiers marching toward the high school gymnasium and the sight drove from his mind all thought of Eugenijus and his anger and his dying.

Petras didn't sleep on the bus that night. Instead he worried about the safety of his family and his friends. The future did not look rosy.

CHAPTER 23

November. A year after the horrific Nazi storm troopers had come to Šiauliai under the guise of a sporting event and attacked the Jews and Lithuanians in the Gymnasium and killed Saulis, got Joelis exiled from his home, damaged Petras's hearing. The hearing loss didn't bother him much, only on some quiet evenings when he and his family sat in the parlor and listened to a radio broadcast of classical music. And those were the times he missed Ona the most, and her music. She had loved to play her violin – classical pieces – and have him and Mamytė sit and be her audience. Those happy evenings seemed a long time ago now.

Gintaras nearly grew by the hour. He was a cheery child, almost always smiling, unless he was howling for something, usually his mother's undivided attention. He'd given up saying *Papa* already, but Rima and Mamytė assured Petras he'd say it again later, when he was a bit older.

He was extreme in all he did, Petras noted – either wildly happy or sad, either eating voraciously or sleeping deeply. His hair was thick and long and black, falling over his forehead, his black eyes merry. Fortunately, he still reminded Petras more of Vanya than of Pavel, and for that he was thankful. He couldn't hate the child, and he did believe what he'd told Pavel, that Gintaras was his own, even if Pavel's blood ran in the baby.

Dr. Rudminas came by frequently to visit Rima and Gintaras, but Petras was sure he came primarily to see Donata. She certainly didn't discourage him at all. Petras was amazed to see his mother blush and look so young when Gerardas dropped by; he realized that at forty-five, she wasn't really all that old. Her hard life since his father died, and then Ona, had aged her, put lines between her eyes and gray in her hair. But now, she seemed to have grown younger, with Gintaras to watch over, Rima to work with, and Gerardas to talk to. Her dresses were still of somber shades but of a better cut, and Petras saw that his mother was pretty.

She and Gerardas visited at the house, or he took her along on some visits to patients, usually the elderly ones, who appreciated her company. She talked to them of gardening and cooking, usually taking the time to cook up a pot of soup or to put together some rye bread to rise, for them to bake later. She was a good listener, so welcome everywhere.

"I don't ever want to take you somewhere with sick children, however," Gerardas said to Rima on one of his visits. "You keep Gintaras healthy, well away from sick little ones. He's such a gem, we don't want to risk his health."

Rima laughed. "This one? I don't believe he'll ever get

sick, strong as he is. Oh, maybe a cold from time to time, but that's all."

Gerardas shook his head. "Don't tempt the *velnias*, you never know when he might decide to make you a liar."

"Oh, tell me you're not superstitious!" Rima said. "This is a strong child with the best of care. He'll never have any problems."

Petras watched the doctor's face. Somehow he feared what he saw there, for he knew the doctor had wide experience with children and illness. "Let's humor our friend," he said softly to Rima. "He is only thinking of the child's best interests."

She smiled at him. "All right. I'll go along with him. It can't hurt." She picked Gintaras up from his cradle, kissed him on the head, and bundled him up for a walk before bedtime. "Will you come with us, Petras? It's mild tonight."

He got their coats – as usual, she was ready to leave the house without enough warm clothing on, but at least she was no longer depressed, as she had been before the child was born. She smiled now, laughed and talked, although not much. She was a quiet person, which she hadn't been before her trials with Pavel, but content and warm with her family. Petras's heart filled: this was what he'd hoped and prayed for, his own home, his wife and child in it. The Nazis were gone, the Soviets didn't threaten them, and they could get on with their lives.

Still, Petras was aware of the tension in his life, in his country, between the peace of Biržai and home, and the strife in Vilnius and Klaipėda. The Germans still claimed Klaipėda as a German city and were poised to renege on their latest agreement with the Soviet Union.

His income from working for Antanas was quite good; Antanas valued his artistic ability and his sober, hardworking

ways. "One good thing about having a Baptist work for
you – rarely a drinking problem," Antanas said.

And Donata now had some income from a small farm
she owned with her brother, so they didn't feel strapped. In
fact, Petras felt as if life for his family was about the best it
had been since his father died.

A lovely life, in spite of all their losses, but oh-so
precarious.

Soon after the beginning of the year, Pavel sent Walther
Funk to the glass factory to fetch Petras. "What now?" Petras
said, cross from the heat of the furnace and the finicky job
he was working on.

"Sorry, he didn't say, Petras." Walther Funk spoke in
his usual slow, gracious way. "I suspect, however, that he
fears the imminent arrival of the Soviets and wants your
help." A hint of humor flicked across his face.

Petras stared at him, wondered if he dared to ask him
what he felt about the Baron. Or the Soviets. "How does
this affect you, Walther, a German and all?"

He shook his head. "I'm as Lithuanian as you are. My
mother was Lithuanian, and we've lived here for many years.
I have no empathy for the Nazis, you know."

"Does Pavel know that?"

"Do you think he's ever asked me? No. He just wants
the veneer of the orderly German. I can provide that." He
gestured toward the door. "I have the car, if you'd like a
ride."

Petras nodded. "Let me finish this up. Antanas is out
for the afternoon, so I can't just leave this job. Won't you
have a seat on a bench? I'll be with you in just a few minutes."

The trip to the Castle was a pleasant interlude, in spite of Petras's natural hesitation to be near Pavel. Weak winter sun shone a pinkish gold on fresh snowfall, and his spirits rose. He found in Walther a person who could be a friend, he thought, if things were different.

"How's Vanya doing? I haven't seen him in a long time."

Walther didn't answer but kept his eyes on the road for several blocks. At last he said, "He's fine."

"He's fine? That's all?"

"He's fine, count on it."

Petras shook his head but dropped the subject. "How did you end up working for Pavel?" he asked at last.

"It's hard to say. I often ask myself why I'm here. My father was Mennonite, you know," Walther said, "a member of a peace church. All of Pavel's military posturing is abhorrent to me, but what am I to do? I can't change the man."

Petras stared out the window beside him before he could bring himself to speak. "Tell me, does the Baron have any redeeming qualities?"

Walther laughed, a short, barking sound. "Oh, my, you want me to criticize my employer? I don't think I can do that. But he has some good qualities, beginning with a love of beauty."

"Ha! To impress others, only."

"No, I think it's a sincere, deep love. It's tainted, of course, with his Germanic mania, but it's genuine enough. He respects the work you did on the stained glass, you know."

"So what was the story on the so-called wrong color glass in the wolf row?"

"I really don't know. I do know he believed there was a flaw in the color selection, and now he thinks it's fine. And he's good enough to this new wife, I think, but she looks down on him as a boor. Not easy for him. He's never had a woman who appreciated him for himself."

"What a surprise."

Walther shook his head. "Be careful. You don't want this attitude to come through while you're with him. He'll make your life miserable."

"He already has, you know."

"But he could damage you still more, believe me, Petras."

A chill ran up his spine. The quiet certitude in Walther's voice filled him with dread.

Chapter 24

When Walther Funk and Petras arrived at the Castle, everything was in an uproar. Pavel ran to the door when he heard them enter and grabbed Petras by the arm to pull him into the front hall. "Come, there's no time to waste!"

"What's going on?"

"What do you think, the Russians are coming! You must help me save the window."

Petras felt confused. What did the Russians have to do with the window? "But why?"

"They'll destroy it! Don't you know – they despise beauty and lovely things. To the Soviets, everything has to be *utilitarian*," he said, scorn in his voice, "*useful,* and *practical.* I detest all the Communists stand for!"

"But you like what the Nazis stand for?"

"Oh, stop being such an adolescent idiot, Petras, and

get the window out!"

"You brought me here but didn't tell me I needed tools. I'll have to go back and…"

"Of course. Run back – no, I'll have Walther take you. But hurry! There's no time to waste!"

At that point his wife came into the wide hall. She wore a traveling suit in gray wool with a fur stole over her shoulders and carried two leather cases, which she set by the front door. She spoke to him in German. Petras knew enough German to understand her, and the expression on her face underscored what she was saying; she was sneering at Pavel for wanting to save the window. "You fool, don't you know they'll kill you if they find you? You're on their list!"

"Where are you going?" Pavel asked her, panic in his voice and eyes.

"Out of here, Pavel, back to Germany. Conrad is picking me up. Hans called just a few moments ago."

Conrad? Hans? The Zellers?

She must have seen the question in Petras's eyes. "Yes, the Zellers, your old pastor; they're my cousins."

Her mention of Conrad Zeller brought back to Petras old memories of the man's sermons, more about being successful and hardworking than about the Kingdom of God.

"Conrad can hardly wait to get out of this godforsaken, backward place for good." She turned to Pavel. "You'd better come now; I doubt if there's even an hour left before the Soviets arrive, and you know where they'll come first! You and your big talk!"

She brushed by her husband and out the door. Over her shoulder she called, "If you're out here when Conrad drives up, he'll give you a ride too. If you're not, well, too bad."

Pavel stood speechless and gazed after her. The blood had drained from his face. When he could take a breath, he turned to Petras. "You see, you must help me! I'll lose her if I don't rush."

Petras shook his head. "I can't remove that glass in an hour, and I can't even start without some tools and somebody to help. If you want to save your skin, go, man, but you'll have to leave the window. All I can suggest is that you leave an address with Walther, and some money, and I'll ship it to you."

"No, no, that won't work. You'll have to bury it somewhere, and I'll come back. Call Juodas, ask him for a plot in the cemetery. There's one there…"

"Where you buried and dug up Ana and her child?"

Pavel's face turned purple. "Who told you that?"

"No one. I found them, tried to save the baby, who wasn't dead when she was left there in the cold." Petras's eyes narrowed, and his hands itched to surround Pavel's throat and strangle him.

Pavel raised a hand to stop him. "Enough. I don't have the time."

"You killed them, and you killed Ona."

Pavel's face went pale, then he smiled. The effect was ghastly. "What nonsense." He waved the subject away with one hand. "Listen, Petras, I've got to go. You talk to Juodas; he'll pay you well – he's my brother, you know – he'll do anything for me, and he'll know where to reach me. Just protect the window."

"Your brother? That explains…" Why hadn't he known that? Surely everyone in town did.

"What are you mooning about? Get to work!"

Petras sighed and gave up trying to reason with him.

"Sure, Pavel, just go ahead, get out."

"I'll leave the car for Walther to help you." He yelled for Walther, who came so quickly he must have been hiding behind a door in the hall. "Run tell Luisa to wait; I'll be right out." Pavel turned, ready to dash up the winding stairs to his room above. "Take Petras back to the glass works to get whatever he needs, do whatever he tells you to do. But hurry!"

"Certainly, sir." Walther didn't rush, he walked slowly, with great dignity. Once he'd conveyed Pavel's message to Luisa, he bowed to Petras to precede him out the front door and to the car. "My, my, what unseemly goings-on."

Petras grinned. "Yes, Walther." He sat back in the cushy leather of the car and planned to enjoy the ride, for the time being at least.

On the way to the glass works, however, Petras realized the straits Walther would find himself in. "But what about you? Surely you're in danger from the Russians."

"No, I don't think so. As I told you, my mother is Lithuanian. I've papers in her family name, you see. I've known this would likely happen for some time. I'll hide my German identity card, which I needed for Pavel to employ me, and dig out the Lithuanian one. I'll be fine." He kept his eyes on the road, and Petras watched as they hardened and his hands tightened on the steering wheel. "Once we return to the Castle, I will help you, but first I must free Vanya."

Petras straightened in his seat and turned to look at Walther. "Free him? What do you mean?"

"Didn't you know?"

"Know what!"

"No need to shout," he said coolly. "I can hear fine. He's down in the dungeon. Has been for months. Walled in, although I opened an old secret tunnel from the back of the cellar, to get him in the fresh air from time to time. The man hardly sees the light of day, except when Pavel is off on some trip or another. This time, he won't have to go back, ever."

"In the...? But why?"

"Pavel is not a nice man. I thought you knew that," Walther said coolly.

"But he said Vanya was in military training! How did you live with such a horrendous thing, your boss keeping a man in a dungeon?"

He shrugged. "I had no choice. I just did the best I could for Vanya, when Pavel wasn't looking. If I'd protested, I would have lost my position and with it the chance to wait on Vanya. I feared he'd go crazy, you know, but he hasn't, he's only grown sweeter. You'll see."

Petras put his head down in his hands. "Oh, dear God! How could he?"

The rest of the ride was silent and strained. Petras didn't know what to say. He told Walther to wait in the car for him while he fetched his tools. He wanted to kick something, shout and swear, and he didn't want an audience. Antanas's truck was not there, so Petras figured he would be alone for a few moments.

He gathered his tools quickly, not eager to get back to save the window but to get back to help Walther get Vanya out of the dungeon. *Oh, dear God, oh, dear God*, he prayed over and over. How could he not have known?

How to face him, that man-child who'd been mistreated by his own brother! And Juodas! Another brother. Was he in on this hateful thing too? Where had they come from? Suddenly Petras realized he knew nothing of their background, other than the fact that their mother had loved all

things Russian. Yet Juodas wasn't a Russian name. It wasn't
a Lithuanian proper name either, for that matter; it just fit
him: *black*, like a large, black bat. He seemed much older
than Pavel, but they had similar facial structure and
coloring. And both seemed to Petras to ooze evil, evil that
came from too much power.

And then there was sweet, gentle, slow Vanya. The one
without any power.

Petras felt his skin crawl. He had to get back in that
car, go back to that castle. He didn't have to save the stained
glass, but he'd do his best.

Only after Vanya was out, though, and safe somewhere,
in Biržai, perhaps. Or likely, someplace Walther had already
planned to take him. The man's coolness was an affront to
Petras. How could he live with it all?

Yet, to be fair, he realized no one could have helped
Vanya in the cellar, except someone like Walther Funk.

The next hour was a nightmare. At least Pavel and Luisa
were gone, and there was no sign of the odious Zellers.
How could the church have been fooled by that pastor?
How could Petras himself be fooled by the man?

Walther took time to change into comfortable clothes,
out of his butlering costume, for that was what he called it
– "Like playacting, you know?" He led Petras around the
back of the Castle to a closed-up coal chute. "This is how
we get in and out," he said as he removed false nail heads
and opened the wooden door to the chute. Walther sat in
the opening and slid under the wall, motioning to Petras
to follow him.

There was a small, low-ceilinged subterranean room,
dark and cold. At one end stood a wall, made of stacked,

flat stones, each stone about a foot long and two inches thick. There was no mortar to hold the stones above the bottom two feet, so it was clear how Walther had been able to get to Vanya.

But why hadn't Vanya gotten out on his own? When Petras asked Walther that, the man said, "Oh, he does his best to obey Pavel when he can. Besides, he feels this is perhaps a religious duty."

How had Pavel not suspected his servant at all? Had he ever tried to spy on Walther to see what he was up to? Did he never check on his brother once he'd been walled up?

Across from that wall was the narrow door, with a slit in it for handing food through to Vanya, just like in the old Russian Orthodox hermit holes. Did Pavel think having his servants hand food in to Vanya was sufficient to keep him alive?

"Pavel thought this would help cure Vanya of his religious 'superstition,' he called it. Let him be walled up like the crazy Russian hermits and see how he liked it," Walther said.

"So did he ever check to see how Vanya was doing?"

"From time to time, and he was always surprised at how Vanya seemed to prosper. 'It's my faith,' he'd tell Pavel. 'It's like the Hebrew boys in the fiery furnace.' That infuriated Pavel, so it wasn't such a good thing for Vanya to say. Pavel certainly grew enraged by his placid acceptance of the situation," Walther said. He began to whistle as he removed stones from the top of the wall.

He seemed to be enjoying himself, and Petras began to wonder just how sane Walther was at that moment. A bitter taste rose in his throat as he waited for Walther to reach Vanya. He was afraid of what he'd see when Vanya emerged from the hole.

The air in the hole was dank and moldy, but strangely, not unclean. He could smell water and sulfur from the sunken baths at the other end of the Castle cellar. At that point Petras imagined how much work Walther had gone through to keep Vanya safe and clean, carrying out wastes, carrying in bath water and clean clothes. He shuddered at the thought.

Somehow, however, it made him lose his fear of seeing Vanya. Surely, considering how much he and Walther had gone through, Petras could stand to be a witness.

"Walther!" A voice whispered out of the depth of the walled-in chamber under the Castle, and Petras shivered.

"We're coming, Vanya, hold on," Walther said in a normal voice as he carefully removed flat, gray stones that formed the wall. "He's gone, perhaps for good."

"For good? How can that be?" asked the disembodied voice behind the wall. "No need to be careful, huh? I'll help. Step back." With that, the remaining stones caved out into the open area, and Vanya, thin and pale but smiling broadly, emerged from his hole. "This is a sad day. I was almost beginning to like it in there."

There was something in his face that reminded Petras of Gintaras and made him want to protect Vanya. "Oh, Vanya!" Petras said. "You don't mean it."

"Petras, old pal! Long time since I saw you!" With those words he stumbled and nearly fell, giggling as he struggled to stand. "Oh, give me a hand, I'm weaker than I expected. So, how are you doing?" He patted at his tattered clothing, raising a cloud of dust.

Petras laughed. "I'm fine. You're the one who's been sealed up in a dungeon."

"Oh, it wasn't so bad. Walther took good care of me." He turned to Walther and hugged him. "Thanks for all you've done. And he never caught on?"

Walther smiled. "Never." He put an arm around Vanya's shoulder. "Let's go get you fed."

"And bathed. I really have missed having a good, hot bath, although what water you provided helped."

"How long has he kept you down here?" Petras asked.

"I don't know." Vanya looked at Walther. "How long?"

"Over eight months, perhaps nine. Too long."

"But why?" Petras persisted.

"He was afraid I'd tell," Vanya said simply.

"Tell what?" Petras asked.

"About the deaths."

Petras froze. "Deaths? Like Ana?"

"Oh, yes."

"And Ona?" he whispered, afraid to hear.

Vanya hesitated, then nodded. "Yes, like Ona. He was afraid I'd tell. You know, the one policeman, Vidas, kept coming around, kept asking him the same questions over and over. I thought it would be easier for Pavel if he just told and got it over with." He shrugged. "He thought I was stupid." He looked at Petras and tears sprang to his eyes. "I'm sorry about Ona; she was good to me. And Rima too – he misused her, you know. I tried to help her…" His voice trailed off.

"I understand," Petras whispered, unable to speak. He knew what it was like to want to make a difference, to save the people you loved and not be able to.

Walther spoke up. "Let's get you fed, Vanya. You need some good hot soup and some tea. I'm sure you're hungry. It's way past lunch now."

"Now don't fuss, Walther," Vanya said. "This was good for me, in its way. It was hard on you, though."

Walther waved his words away. "Let's get you out of

here. We've heard the Russians are coming, and we mustn't
waste time. I have identity papers for us both, and a place
to go. We need to get you out in the sunlight, though, and
fattened up a bit. May it please God that we have a few
days, rather than the hours Luisa feared."

Once they got out of the cellar, climbing up the narrow
strips of wood Walther had nailed into the side of the coal
chute, Petras began to fret. He didn't feel he had to obey
Pavel about the window, but he wanted to preserve the
stained glass if he could. Yet he wanted to watch Vanya
recuperate too. At last he said to Walther, "You won't pack
up and leave within the next few hours, will you? I don't
want to lose track of you and Vanya."

"No, no. It'll take some time for his strength to return,
I'm sure."

"I feel…"

"What?"

"An obligation to him, and to you. Wait for me."

"Why are you saving the Baron's glass? He won't be
back, I'm sure."

"Why do you say that?"

"I know the Zellers a bit better than most people do in
Šiauliai. I could tell you… But that must wait."

CHAPTER 25

At Walther's words about the Zellers, Petras felt an electric shock run through him. He grabbed Walther by the shoulder and shook him lightly. "I want to know! Save the story for me – I've got to get to work on the window. Not for Pavel, but for me."

Walther nodded. "Whatever you say. You'll need help. Let me take care of Vanya; I'll come after that. I'll call for some other men to come help."

"Thanks. I'd appreciate it."

As it worked out, Vanya came too, and it was like a replay of the days when Petras had installed the glass. Vanya was quieter and less ebullient, but still kind and innocent. A holy fool, Petras thought, like many before him. He couldn't reconcile in his mind how much Vanya resembled Gintaras; he wanted them to meet, to see if they recognized each other.

Petras really didn't know how to disassemble a stained glass window, so he just took it apart in reverse order of the way he'd put it up, but without removing the frame from the wall. He carefully pulled out the leading, removing each piece of glass one by one. It was a faster process than putting it together had been.

Vanya was good help, although slow. He meticulously wrapped the pieces of glass in strips of canvas Walther had found in the cellar. Walther floated in and out of the room, busy directing all the house staff on packing up and preparing the Castle for closure.

Well after dark, with perhaps half of the work of removing the window completed, Petras stopped with a cry of alarm. "Oh, no! I forgot! I'm supposed to be home for dinner. They'll be worried, what with the troop movements!"

"Do you have a phone?" Walther asked.

Petras shook his head.

"Someone close by?"

"The doctor – but he may be at the house already. He and my mother…"

"A romantic story?" Walther asked.

"I think so."

"Come to the study and use the phone. I'm sure it hasn't been disconnected yet; I tried it not long ago."

Petras had used a phone only a handful of times in his life, so he felt strange. Gerardas answered rather quickly, said he was on the way to visit the family anyway and was glad to carry Petras's message. Petras asked him whether things were quiet in Biržai.

"Yes, as far as I know. Why do you ask?"

Petras filled him in on the change of power in Šiauliai

and told the doctor what he was doing with the stained glass window.

Gerardas got very quiet. "This isn't good news."

"No. But I'll never understand why either Germany or Russia thinks she can run us."

When he hung up, Petras stared at the phone and thought how easy a phone made things. Perhaps they needed one at home. He shook his head. Trivialities, when they were facing death.

He returned to the large hall to complete work on the window. Soon after, Walther bustled in supervising three kitchen maids with trays of food. There looked to be enough there to feed an army.

Petras shook his head. "No time for me to eat now, Walther."

"It's possible we may not get to later – who knows? Fill up now, at least. And it's good food, only the best, you know."

Petras stared at him, decided not to argue. "If you'll sit with me and tell me about the Zellers."

A ghost of a smile flitted across Walther's face. "You're very curious, huh?"

"Yes, and you know it. So tell the story."

"Stories, actually. And some are Vanya's to tell, not mine."

They looked across the room to where Vanya had curled up in a pile of padded cloths, there for the workers to wrap the ballroom furniture.

"He's surely worn out. He never knew, down there, whether it was day or night. It confused him a bit."

"But you thought of something to help him?" Petras asked.

"Yes, I did my best to go down there for an hour a day,

or sometimes every other day, to get him out in the sun for a bit. Gave him a piece of paper and pen to make marks on, to count the days. Minor things, but they helped him pass the time."

Petras shook his head. "I can't imagine. But the story about Herr Zeller."

Walther gestured to Petras to serve himself. He helped himself to some fish, borscht, and fresh bread with cheese; it was simple stuff but well prepared. Petras sat down gingerly. He felt funny about sitting on the brocaded chairs in the room, but he obeyed, groaning a bit when he sat. "I didn't know how sore I was."

Walther sat down too and leaned back in a flimsy gilt chair. He sighed. "Where to start?"

"Are you going to eat?"

"What? Oh, yes, a little." Walther filled a plate for himself and ate a few bites, gathering his thoughts, Petras figured. "It started several years ago, you know, before the Zellers moved here. The Baron was raised Catholic – Juodas is his brother, you know."

"I just learned that."

"But the Baron felt Juodas and the Church weren't moving fast enough to please him. So he decided to punish Juodas, knowing how much your family stuck in his craw."

"My family! But why?"

"Because you were the best student he ever had, and you weren't a member of the flock. It galled him. Yet he always respected you and your family. What was there to fault? Nothing, of course."

"You mean that big black bat ever thought of me? I can't believe it!"

"Believe it. Anyway, go back to eating and listening, would you?" Walther continued in his light, amused way.

"The Baron sent me to Germany to find my cousin Conrad Zeller, who he knew was a Protestant pastor. Your church lost their pastor about ten years ago, right?"

"Right, around the time of my father's death."

"It was Renni Kiik, that old Latvian Baptist, right? He got your father buried in a Protestant cemetery in Latvia but had a heart attack after the funeral and didn't return."

"I'd forgotten that."

"The Zellers were in Dusseldorf, at a small church there, ready and willing to leave Nazi Germany. Conrad was never very good at dissembling, you know."

Petras stared at him. "No, I didn't know. I thought he did a rather good job of it once he got here. I certainly believed him."

"Now you mustn't judge Conrad by Hans's behavior; Hans was a born Nazi. He's been a terrorist from the time he could walk."

Petras grunted, recalling the times Conrad Zeller had tried to indoctrinate him into middle-class German moralism, rather than Christian righteousness, in Petras's opinion.

"I think I'm losing your attention. The most important part of the story is, of course, Luisa. She's Conrad's cousin, on his father's side, not his mother's, who is my aunt, you know. I thought this would help him lose interest in Rima, Petras."

Petras stared at Walther, gratitude rising like a heat wave in his chest. How to thank him?

"Pavel decided any beautiful German woman would do for a breeding machine, so he 'bought' her."

"Bought her? Why was she willing to be sold?"

"She likes nice things, but she likes safety more. She thought here in this little backwater she'd be safe and snug in a lovely little castle, little thinking it was right on the Soviets' route to Klaipėda. Silly woman."

"You don't like her?"

"She's all right. Not very deep, you know, not like Ona. She was a real human being. But Luisa's a better person than Pavel."

"Who isn't?"

At that point a servant entered the hall and told Walther there was a phone call for him. Walther suggested that Petras eat his fill while saving some for Vanya before he returned to work. "You don't want to work all night. I'll be back soon." To the servant he said, "Do what you can to help Petras. Vanya is too weak to work now."

The man, a Lithuanian Petras didn't know, nodded and set to helping where he could by standing halfway up the ladder and reaching for the pieces of glass to save Petras's having to climb all the way up and down each time. As a result, Petras could see he'd finish in only an hour or two more. He would be glad to be done; he was exhausted, but at least the beautiful glass was safe, or nearly so. They would still need to find a place to hide it.

Soon Walther returned, and Petras asked him where he planned to put the glass.

"In the cellar, of course, under all that loose stone. I think we can make it look undisturbed with a bit of effort."

Petras nodded. "Perhaps."

"I've got a few men coming in tonight to help. I can trust them to keep a secret. You can sleep a bit while we do that."

Petras shook his head, ran a hand over his face. "Sleep sounds good, but not before this glass is moved. I wouldn't feel right about not supervising it."

"Always the perfectionist. That's why the Baron wanted you alone to do the window." He paused. "Did you ever think, though, that perfectionism is the devil's best way to torment us?"

"What? No, of course not! We must always try to do a perfect job."

"Do our best, yes, but perfect? How human is that? The devil likes to taunt us with our failings, you know."

Petras glared at him. "Sophistry, that's all. God wants perfection from us."

"No, I don't think He does, but we won't argue that right now." He paused. "A word of warning: your drive for perfection makes you a perfect tool for someone as power-mad as the Baron. Be careful."

Petras snorted. "Nonsense. Where did you get such stuff?"

Walther smiled. "Think about it."

Several village men arrived at that point and interrupted their talk.

"How many people are in on this secret, Walther?" Petras asked with heavy sarcasm.

"Don't worry about it. I can trust these men."

Petras looked at them all, examining their faces closely. All Lithuanians, at least, rough, simple peasants, all of them. No one in the city or Church power structure. Except for one, at the back of the group: Vidas Tomas, the policeman who had tried so hard to solve Ona's murder. He raised one eyebrow at Petras, but said nothing.

At Walther's directions, they began lifting well-wrapped canvas parcels and carrying them to the back stairs, down to the cellars. No one spoke, no one offered any suggestions on how to do it better. Within an hour, they were done. Walther slipped them each an envelope, of money,

Petras figured.

Through it all, Vanya slept away. Petras envied him. He was near dropping where he stood.

Walther asked Petras to follow him upstairs.

"What for?"

"To give you a bed."

"Not upstairs. Don't you have a servant's room down here or something?"

"All full. Just come this way."

"I don't want to."

Walther ignored him. "I'll put you in the blue room. No one is due to arrive, and you may as well have the best guest room."

Petras was too tired to argue. And perhaps none of his democratic ideals mattered anyway.

Once he stepped into the opulent room, however, he realized they did matter. The blue and white velvets and laces, the ornate furniture and the heavy oil paintings sickened him. He undressed quickly, the sooner to turn out the light. He lay in the bed, which was too soft, and fumed for perhaps five minutes, but his fatigue got the better of him and he fell asleep.

CHAPTER 26

Petras slept hard. He awoke late the next morning, panicked, thinking that he had failed to get to work on time. He threw on his clothes, washed his face and rinsed his mouth, then dashed down the stairs. Walther was waiting for him at the bottom of the stairs. Smiling at him, he said, "I hope you slept well. Vanya is up and feeling much better; he's waiting in the dining room for you. I've ordered breakfast."

"I can't wait for breakfast! I'm late to work!"

In his usual cool and calm way, Walther gestured before him to the dining room. "I've already taken the liberty of calling Antanas and telling him you worked most of the night on saving the Baron's window. He thought it was splendid of you."

Petras darted a glance at the man. Splendid? Just how

serious was he? "But I can't take time to eat."

"You must. I would feel we've failed in our hospitality to you if you didn't. Besides, Vanya wants to talk to you."

"Okay, okay." Irritated but resigned to wasting time, Petras entered the dining room. A large, long room with high ceilings, decorated in white and gilt, he could imagine it filled with rich, powerful people, not peasants like him. He sighed. How much longer until he could leave here and return to his world?

Vanya, who had been sitting with his chin in one hand and staring into his full plate, looked up and beamed at Petras when he walked in. Vanya looked only marginally cleaner than he had the day before. His hair spiked up around his head as if he'd run his fingers through it all night and never combed it. "Petras! Come in! I want to talk to you for a bit. Isn't this room something? It's mine for a short time, you know, and I plan to enjoy it."

"Enjoy it? How? It feels so evil!"

"But not at its heart, I don't think. I spent so many months in the cellars and learned much about it."

Petras shook his head. "How can that be?"

"Believe me. It was built in love, although also with some greed. Catherine was greedy for attention and love, but our baron, the one she built the Castle for, she really did love, I think." He pointed to the food on the sideboard. "Help yourself."

Petras looked at all the food arrayed there and realized how hungry he was. He mumbled thanks to Vanya and served himself large servings of meat, hot *kugelis*, and coffee. Before he began to eat, however, he prayed silently. *Dear God, this is how people are sucked in by the Powers, isn't it?* The Powers – money, sex, and earthly power – not bad in and of themselves, but capable of taking over a person's life if he wasn't careful. Like alcohol or greed.

Vanya talked and talked while Petras ate. He didn't say much, however, merely indulged in idle chitchat. He didn't even talk about his time underground. Once Vanya paused for a breath, Petras said, a lump in his throat, "Tell me about Ona's death. Were you there? Did you see anything?"

Vanya stared at him, his mouth working. He sat back. "No, I didn't see anything. I heard a very bad fight, though. Then she disappeared."

"When was this fight?"

"Some days before the night she disappeared – I can't recall the date. It was very cold the night she died."

"So what did you hear, of the fight, I mean?"

Vanya squirmed in his seat, and a look of pain crossed his face. He wouldn't look Petras in the eye, but at last he said, "It went on for days. He was so cruel to her." His tone had reverted to a childishness that hadn't been there just moments before.

Keeping his voice low, to avoid frightening Vanya, Petras persisted. "What happened?"

Vanya swung his head back and forth. "I don't know, really. I just know he was mean. But I tried to help, I did."

Petras watched fear and anxiety play across Vanya's face, and he figured he'd get no more from Vanya at this point; his own anxiety to get out of the Castle and out in the town to see what was going on was rising unbearably. He threw his napkin on the table, rose, and crossed to Vanya. Putting a hand on the man-child's shoulder, he said, "I'm so glad you're out of the dungeon, Vanya. Thanks for all your help." He paused. "If you need me, I'm in Biržai now. Don't hesitate to come to me. I'll help you all I can. And you can meet our son, Gintaras. He reminds me of you."

Vanya raised his eyes, full of tears, to Petras's face.

"Thanks. I'll come, sometime. And I'm sorry, Petras."

"What for?"

"I didn't help her. I'm so sorry."

Petras nodded, unable to speak, and turned and left the ornate, self-indulgent room.

Walther Funk was nowhere to be seen, for which Petras was thankful. He grabbed his coat from a hallstand by the door and went out the front door, to see Pavel's long, low car sitting there. A storm was building on the horizon, and a stiff wind from the east spit in his face.

The Baron's driver, whom Petras didn't recognize, exited the car and gestured to Petras. He was short and heavy and dark, ham-fisted with a bottle of vodka in one thick hand. He lifted his cap with the other and bowed slightly. "I'm to take you home, or wherever. And the sooner the better; the roads are getting clogged."

"Okay, thanks." Petras hesitated; he didn't want to enter the back door the driver held for him. "Can't I sit in front with you? I'm not used to the VIP treatment."

The man's broad, ugly face split in a wide grin. "Sure you can. I'll welcome the company." He stuck out his hand. "Shake. My name's Rimgaudas; good to meet you, Petras. I've heard a lot about you, you know, driving this car and listening to the Baron carry on."

"Oh? What did he say?"

"He was a bad-tempered sort, so I took what he said with a grain of salt. He didn't like you, but he respected how good you are with glass. It always sounded to me like you were busy sticking up for the underdog; since he was the one making underdogs, he didn't think much of that. But we did, those of us who worked for him."

"So who will you work for now, with him gone?"

Rimgaudas shrugged. "Who knows. So much change

in the air, who can predict? I'm thinking I'll join the navy. Want a slug?" he asked, offering him his bottle.

Petras tried not to cringe. "No. No, thanks." At least the man didn't seem drunk.

"Where to?" Rimgaudas asked.

The roads were jammed. "What's the story on the bus to Biržai?"

"Not running. The trains are running, but only to move Soviet troops in. I'm sure the buses will be commandeered soon by the Soviets. But I've got my orders from Walther to take you anywhere you want to go."

"What sort of person is this Walther that he tells you to do what I want? This doesn't make sense to me."

"What can I say? He's a good guy."

"But why isn't he like most people and covering his back at this time? He's going to be in a deep mire once the Soviets get here."

Rimgaudas shrugged. "He doesn't seem to think so. He's the type who always lands on his feet."

"Ah. Interesting." He crossed his arms and leaned back in the comfortable leather seat. He would never own such a vehicle himself, so it made sense to experience its opulence for a brief moment.

He watched passersby scurrying under cover as a cold sleet began to fall. Some women tried to flag down a passing bus, but the bus didn't stop, and they looked shocked. They all looked so tired and washed out, ready to be home at their own fires. Didn't they know yet that the buses were being commandeered for military movement?

"Poor souls. Miserable weather," Rimgaudas said. "It's good to be undercover in this weather. I have to be thankful I've had this cushy job for as long as I have."

Petras nodded. "Yes, I guess so."

"It couldn't last forever, though, that I knew. I'll find something else, soon enough. The Soviets have to be better than the Nazis, don't you think?"

Petras felt his heart stop. At last he spoke. "I couldn't say. There's no way to know." A heavy gloom settled over him, for he knew the truth. How could things be any better if Lithuania wasn't free to determine its own course? How could they live under the Soviet heel?

They would all soon find out, and he feared they wouldn't like the results.

The car was so quiet Petras felt he was watching a silent movie unfold around him outside. Rimgaudas caught up with the bus two blocks down, where it stopped for a light. A woman with three small children, one a babe in arms, tried to board, but the door didn't open. The children were crying and the woman looked haggard, laden as she was with several shopping bags and the baby. She pounded on the door and still it didn't open. Smiling Russian soldiers inside the bus watched the woman. Some shook their heads, as if to say, *Doesn't she know we have important business here? She's just a peasant, but we're important.*

At last the bus started to pull away, and the woman tried to run to it. The cobbles were slick from the sleet, and the woman faltered. Petras watched in horror as she slipped and fell, her bags of groceries spilling out of her arms as she kept a tight hold on the baby, who was crying. Before his eyes and the eyes of her other children, almost in slow motion, the woman fell under the bus, the back wheels passing over her and the screaming baby.

"Stop the car!" Petras said as he threw open the car door and dashed out to save her. Almost a bigger shock because he'd been so protected, as if in a cocoon in the car, the icy sleet chilled him as it slithered down his neck.

But it was too late for the woman, as he knew it would be. She and the baby were dead.

"Oh, dear God, dear God!" Petras moaned. "Why?"

But he heard no answer.

CHAPTER 27

Petras and Rimgaudas waited for the police to come. The bus didn't wait; it moved on, oblivious to the wreckage of the woman's crushed body. The sleet kept falling, hissing against the pavement.

He realized someone needed to see to the children, a boy and girl about four and five years of age. The girl was sobbing softly, the boy looked pale and in shock. Petras walked over to them and put an arm around each of them, moving them over to a bench along the sidewalk. The girl stopped crying and sat on Petras's lap like a stone, but the boy began to shiver uncontrollably. He began an inhuman wail that tore at Petras's heart. He felt helpless, even as he held them. What could he do or say that would help them?

It was Vidas Tomas who came. With his usual quiet but intense efficiency, he asked questions of those who witnessed the woman's fall under the bus. Her name was Rožalija Gimbutienė, and she was known by many as a hardworking, conscientious wife and mother. She had two older children at home, in school. Her husband, a depressive, had left them just three months before, to go to Poland to find himself.

How would the children live now? Did they have family who could take them in? Would they be sent to an orphanage? Petras didn't even want to think about it. He thought they might be hungry, so he asked Rimgaudas to sit with them while he went to a shop, but the little girl would not let him leave her. So, carrying them in his arms, he walked three shops down to buy them some chocolate. Neither one wanted to eat; Petras fed the girl a bite at a time, but the boy wouldn't open his mouth. Petras cajoled him a bit. "Oh, please will you eat this wonderful chocolate? If you don't, it will go to waste. Won't you take a bite?"

At last the boy opened his mouth and let Petras feed him, but Petras doubted the boy knew there was food in his mouth. Shock, he knew. He opened his coat and wrapped them both inside, next to his body.

At last someone came to take the children, a family member. Unfortunately it was Caterina, the children's paternal aunt, the sluttish housekeeper who worked for Juodas. Petras felt torn; did he dare let the children go with her? Was she trustworthy enough? But she had a family claim, and he knew they belonged with their family. Neither one seemed to recognize her, but they didn't seem afraid of her either, so at last he unwrapped them and let her take them. The little girl clung to him one last moment before letting go.

He wanted to cry for them, but he didn't dare. Swallowing his grief, he returned to the car and asked

Rimgaudas to drive him to Biržai. He wanted to see his family, see for himself that they were safe. He sat hunched over in the seat, hands on his knees, kneading and flexing in his compulsive need to do something that mattered.

The roads were crowded with buses and trucks all leaving Šiauliai. The trip dragged on and on, what with more and more vehicles attempting to get on the main road and out of the region. With the road blocked with traffic and the huge snow-covered pines hulking at its edges, Petras began to feel claustrophobic. He figured it would almost be faster to get out and walk home.

"I bet many of the private cars are leaving for Latvia or maybe crossing the Baltic to Sweden," Rimgaudas said.

"Will it be better there?"

"In Sweden, at least. Latvia I'm not so sure about. I have family there, and they say conditions are the same there as here."

Petras grunted. "Poor devils."

At last they pulled up in front of Petras's house. He tried to see it from Rimgaudas's eyes. Set back from the road, birch and linden trees dripping from the rain around it, the house looked quiet and safe.

"Will you come in for coffee?" Petras asked.

"Thanks. I'd appreciate it. I need to think about where to go next. I don't think I can return to town."

The house was empty when they entered, and Petras felt alarmed. But it wasn't long before he heard Rima's voice, speaking lightly to Gintaras. "We had a good walk, didn't we? It rained and rained, but Baby didn't get wet." She noticed Petras and Rimgaudas. "Oh! I'm so glad you're home." She smiled and nodded to the visitor. "Hello."

"This is Rimgaudas, the Baron's driver," Petras said, feeling lame but not able to explain the situation well in a few words.

"I thought that car out in front was the Baron's. And you rode in it? How wonderful!" she said brightly.

"Yes. Is there coffee on? Rimgaudas has a long trip ahead of him, and I offered him some."

"Certainly. I'll serve you in a few moments." She unbundled Gintaras and kissed his cheek. The baby reached for her hair and pulled it with a chuckle. To Petras she said, "Could you hold him for me for a bit? It's so good to have you home early."

Petras took Gintaras. "Oh, my, you're getting heavy, big boy. How does your little mamytė carry you all day?" The image of the dead woman and her baby under the bus flashed unwelcome across his mind, and he wanted to cry once again. Instead he held the baby close to him fiercely, until Gintaras struggled to get away. Petras spread a blanket on the floor in a thin shaft of light from the window, placed Gintaras on it, and gave him a silver rattle to play with.

Rimgaudas examined the child. "So this is the child in question, huh? The Baron said the boy was his, but he couldn't claim him because he's dark. What a crazy man. Anyone with any sense would see what a fine specimen he is."

Petras bridled. "This is my child, no matter what the Baron 'says.'"

Rimgaudas held up a hand. "Don't bite my head off. I'm only repeating what I heard. He was like a boar, hot to mate with any female. He was filthy, you know. You hear a lot, driving for a man like Pavel Gerulaitis. And I was always able to detect which was real and which wasn't. Don't think the man fooled me."

Petras looked intently at him. "Tell me, did you know my sister, Ona?"

"But of course! Quite a classy lady. Too good for him, and he knew it."

Petras swallowed, trying to gain the courage to ask the man his question. "Do you think – well, do you know whether he killed her?"

Rimgaudas returned his look. "I know what people said. Maybe he did. But you'll never prove it. He's gone now anyway."

"But I want peace about it, you know."

"He was taken with her, her looks and poise. Yet she defied him at every turn."

At that Petras felt a surge of pride. Tough, strong Ona.

"He was determined to have blond children. Stupid, I know, but that's what drove him." He paused. "I'll tell you what I think happened."

Petras nodded, trying to spur him on.

"I think he raped her and used her until she got to a point where she wouldn't take it anymore. She tried to escape – that's the word about the Castle – and he found out and killed her and put her in the lake. But Petras, you'll never prove it. He didn't ask for help that time, like he did to get rid of his wife, Ana, and her baby."

Petras felt overcome with horror, and the warmth of the room, the cooing of the baby, the fragrance of fresh coffee and hot bread all accentuated his horror and made him dizzy. How did something so bestial co-exist with such a peaceful place as his home? He couldn't reconcile it in his mind with the warring images – Ona dead, Joelis and his people trampled by Hans and his men, poor dead Ana and the baby, Rožalija Gimbutienė and her children – contrasted with the sweet, healthy baby on the blanket at his feet, kicking his fat legs in a shaft of northern light.

He had to keep his horror hidden, however, for he heard

Rima coming in with a tray to serve the men coffee and bread and cheese. "Eat up. I need to get Gintaras ready for his nap. We had a good walk this morning, and I'm sure he's tired. Did you know the Palauskas children are coming down sick? I went to see them because they make Gintaras laugh so, and the oldest one was spotty and feverish and the younger two were cross as bears."

Petras stared at her, horrified. "Did you take him in that house?"

"We were in the parlor briefly. The children were out in the hall, wanting to come see him – I'm sure they were feeling cranky with being confined."

"You took him in the house?" Petras repeated.

Rima's face fell. "Oh, Petras, just for a few moments."

"You know what Gerardas said. He said to keep him away from illness."

"But this was nothing, just childhood stuff. And Leda was bored too, so she wanted a bit of company, as did I. It gets too quiet around here at times. You didn't even come home last night –"

"I called Gerardas!"

"– and we waited and waited for you. Do you expect us to sit here with nothing to do while you live your exciting life in town?" She stopped, shocked at her own words. "I'm sorry, I didn't mean that. But it does get a bit boring."

"Oh, dear God in Heaven," he groaned and sat heavily in a chair. He put his head in his hands and moaned. "What if…?"

Rima frowned and shook her head. "Petras, you're overreacting. He's a healthy child, and he'll be fine." She picked Gintaras up and whisked him out of the room.

She didn't return for the next thirty minutes, and the men sat silent, Rimgaudas eating as if he were starving and

Petras staring at his cup of steaming coffee, until it cooled and steamed no more.

Rimgaudas said he needed to get on his way. "I think I'll go to Klaipėda and sign up on a freighter. Anything to get out of Lithuania." He gestured toward the back of the house. "You didn't tell her about the troop movements."

Petras shook his head. "I will have to, later." He shook hands with Rimgaudas. "Thanks for the ride. Take care."

"I will. I'm like Walther – we both land on our feet."

"I hope so. That's a good prospect."

"You'll be fine, and your boy. He'll catch a light case of measles and be fine, grow a bit more and get into mischief, and all will be back to normal."

"I hope so," he said again.

CHAPTER 28

Gerardas came to dinner that night, and Petras told everyone about troop movements in Šiauliai. By then, everyone knew the Germans were leaving Lithuania, the Soviets moving in, breathing down the Nazis' necks as they goose-stepped out of the country. "Good riddance," Gerardas said. "Now we have to pray the Soviets will leave soon too."

"Don't hold your breath," Petras said.

"You know something that we don't?" Mamytė asked.

"No, I guess not. I just believe we're in for a long siege."

Petras brought up the Palauskas children's illness. "Do you know what they have?"

"I'm sure it's measles." Gerardas turned to Rima. "You keep that baby away from there for the next month. Who knows how long it will take to finish its course with them?"

Neither Rima nor Petras spoke.

Mamytė's eyes flew open. "What? What is this? The baby's been exposed to those children?"

Rima pulled her napkin out of her lap and threw it on the table. She then pushed her chair back and left the room.

Alarm on her face, Mamytė watched Rima go. "Should I go to her?" she asked.

"No, leave her be."

Gerardas paled. "What, Petras? Tell me."

"She took him to visit there this morning. She said she was in the parlor, the children in the hall, away from Gintaras. She says it was nothing."

"She says, she says." Gerardas rose. "I'll go home and round up some B vitamins to give him a shot. Perhaps we can ward this off. It could be serious for him, young as he is."

Petras nodded dumbly. He felt it was too late to stop whatever had been put in train. "If you think it will help."

"I don't know, but it could." The little doctor bustled out of the house, promising to return quickly.

Petras played with the baby while Mamytė cleared the table. "I'll serve dessert and coffee when he returns," she said.

"Okay. Thanks." He sat for a bit in the warm room. The heat made him drowsy, so he decided he needed some fresh air. He wrapped Gintaras warmly and got the buggy from the front hall to take him for a walk. The rain had cleared up, and the sky was crystal clear.

"I don't know, Gintaras. What do we do if you get sick? Oh, a little cold is okay, but what if it's something worse? You're big and healthy, but is that a guarantee against something bad?" He remembered stories his parents had told about all the illnesses that were rampant during the

Great War, diseases like Spanish flu that took off hundreds of thousands of people, most in their prime. It could happen again.

He shook his head. "We won't think about that right now. Your grandmother is praying for you, for your health and safety. If anyone's prayers work, hers do."

The baby cooed in his buggy, kicked his blanket off, and Petras stopped to rewrap him. "You don't want to catch a chill, little one."

Gintaras laughed at him, and Petras smiled back. The smile hurt, though; it reminded him too much of other children who weren't warm and happy and safe right now. "I'll do my best for you, little one, as will your mamytė and granny and Doctor Gerardas. You are a precious gift."

A couple was walking toward him, and Petras flushed. He fervently hoped they hadn't heard him talking nonsense to a baby. But he thought not; they were young lovers with eyes and ears only for each other. Had he and Rima ever been like that?

After about twenty minutes he turned around and headed back home. Gerardas would be there soon, and he didn't want to make the doctor wait. He glanced around to be sure no one would hear, then spoke again to Gintaras. "Some day, you'll have to meet your Uncle Vanya. I think you'll like him. He's a gentle soul, not bright, but good. That's not a bad way to be." He knew this child was bright; please God that he would be good also.

The light inside the house seemed too harsh when he walked in. He nearly turned around and left again, but he rejected the idea. Time to face the others.

Rima was beside herself. She grabbed the baby out of his arms and held him close. "Where did you take him? Why did you just leave without telling me?"

"Sorry. You were upset, Mamytė was busy, and I wanted some fresh air. He's fine – I took good care of him."

At that Rima's face crumpled and she started to cry. "And I didn't! You think I exposed him on purpose!"

Seeing his mother was upset, Gintaras began to cry.

"Oh, Rima, please! Don't cry, don't make him cry. You're probably right, he'll be fine."

"You think I'm a bad mother!"

"Rima! Look at the child! His face is round and fat, and his thighs are like oak trees. How could I believe such a thing? I just wish you'd taken Gerardas's warning to heart. You dismissed his words, yet he spoke them with the greatest sincerity and deepest concern for the baby's health."

"I'm his mother! I know what's best for him!" By now Gintaras was howling and sucking his fist.

Petras sighed. "But of course. Feed him, won't you? He thinks he's starving."

Gerardas arrived soon after and took a few moments to prepare the shot. Donata asked if she could help, but he told her to sit and rest her bones.

Gintaras was sleeping peacefully, sated now, in his mother's arms.

"What are you doing?" Rima asked.

"Giving him a shot."

"But you'll make him cry."

Petras snorted. "It'll be the first time he's cried?"

"Don't get sarcastic with me, Petras," she snapped. To Gerardas she said, "Are you sure this will protect him?"

"Of course I'm not sure! But it's the best thing I can do at the moment. Besides asking Donata to pray."

"I'm already praying," Mamytė said.

Gerardas gave Gintaras a shot in the hip, and he screamed loud enough to make Petras's ears ring. He laughed involuntarily. "If his constitution is as strong as his lungs, he'll be fine."

Rima took him from the doctor and carried him off to bed. They could hear Gintaras still crying for several minutes, not easily comforted.

Gerardas grinned. "That's a fact." He turned to Donata. "Do you have any hot coffee for me? I missed out on a cup earlier."

Mamytė stood and bustled out of the room. "Right away, right away!"

Gerardas laughed. "What a treasure she is! You know, Petras, I may be needing to come to you soon to ask for her."

"Be sure you come on your knees. It will take a lot to win her away from us, you know."

Gerardas laughed and thumped his chest. "I'll win her, never fear."

Once Donata had served the coffee and some cherry cake, Petras turned on the radio. "I want to get the news about Šiauliai."

It wasn't good, and what there was, was sketchy. Petras felt frustrated that he couldn't see what was happening. At least the Nazis were on the run. Once the news report was over, a short program of classical music came on, and they all – Mamytė, Gerardas, and Petras – sat in silence to listen. It was Russian music, large and melodramatic and heavy, and it fit the day. Petras thought again of the poor woman and her baby, run over by the busload of heedless Soviet soldiers. Perhaps he could cry for her, later, in the night where no one would see.

He wished he could confide in Rima, but he knew better.

CHAPTER 29

For the next ten days, because of troop movements, Petras was unable to get to work, which he found difficult to tolerate, so he made work for himself, either at home or for neighbors. He repaired a rickety old woodshed for the aged Kaminskases down the street and ran errands for them and some other housebound older people in the town.

On the first day of his enforced idleness, he biked to Gerardas's house to use the phone. "You'll have to put one in, Petras," Gerardas said.

"Yeah, yeah, I will. Later."

Once Petras reached him, Antanas told him not to worry, that there was no work anyway. "Actually," he corrected himself, "there's plenty of work, but no way to get it done." There was no public transportation, and private car owners couldn't buy petrol. "This time of transition will end soon."

"For good or for evil?"

"Who knows? We're alive, what more can we ask for?"

Of course, Gintaras got sick. Petras was eating his breakfast before going out to chop wood, but Rima and the baby had slept in a bit. It was a cold, gray day, conducive to sleep. Petras was so tired of not being able to get to his job, however, that he ached to get outside and put in some physical labor.

Gintaras awoke feverish and cross, and Rima looked at Petras over the baby's head, her eyes wide with fear. "What can I do, Petras?"

"Perhaps he's just teething."

She shook her head, tears forming in her eyes.

"Okay." Pulling on his coat, Petras gulped down the last of his coffee. "Feed him, bathe him, get the fever down. I'll go get Gerardas."

Rima began to cry. "Oh, what can I do?"

Mamytė came and took the baby from her. "Let me bathe him. You sit and eat some breakfast." She kissed the baby's forehead and winced. "Oh, my, too hot, little one."

Rima ignored the advice to eat and trailed off after Mamytė, too anxious to settle anywhere.

Petras dashed out the door, thankful to have a job to do. What if...? But no, he wouldn't think that way. He grabbed his old bike and pedaled furiously down the road to find Gerardas. The road was fortunately dry, but the air was heavy, damp, and cold.

Before he reached the doctor's house, however, he heard the rumble and roar of huge trucks out on the main road, and it struck terror into his heart. He rode to the main crossing, where he stopped and watched the Soviet trucks lumber by, twenty, thirty of them, loaded with tanks and heavy artillery.

The relentless nature of the onward-moving juggernaut told him there would be more mothers and children to fall beneath the vehicles carrying Russian soldiers to their assigned destinations, and no one would care much. The dead, defeated bodies were mere rubbish in the way of important things, like the military desires of a huge state.

At that point tears came, and he sobbed as he faced his helplessness and his rage and his fear. There was nothing he could do but to continue in his own predestined path, to continue to do his duty as he saw it. He cried his pain out, then wiped his eyes on his coat sleeve. The trucks passed out of his sight, and he squared his shoulders, remounted the bike, and headed on to Gerardas's.

Gerardas was eating his breakfast. "It's amazing you caught me home. I was up most of the night with the Adamkuses; their children are sick too, one, I fear, with diphtheria." He ran a hand over his face, which was drawn and gray with fatigue. "Not good."

Petras told him about the trucks out on the main road.

"Yes, I saw a convoy when I returned home a bit ago. They're wasting no time getting into place here."

"No. Yet there've been no shots fired, right?"

"Not that I know of." He rinsed off his breakfast dishes, took a last sip of coffee, and found his coat and medical bag. "You want to ride with me? We can load your bike in the car."

"No, I need the activity. I'm about to jump out of my skin."

"Okay. I'll follow in the car." He put a hand on Petras's shoulder. "Don't worry too much. Gintaras's illness may be minor. We'll treat him the best we can. Do you think Rima will need a sedative?"

Petras shook his head. "I don't know. I doubt she'd take it. She'll feel she has to be on duty every minute he's sick."

"I'll take something anyway."

Petras nodded.

"Run along then. I'll be there before you."

Petras rode hard to get back home. The temperature had dropped perceptibly, and a light snow had begun to fall, and he took care not to slip on the slick streets. Gerardas drove sedately past him in his old car, and Petras was glad to have him on the case.

Once he reached the house, he saw a brown Russian car parked in front. In it were the two Communists who always seemed to be around at the Šiauliai pub that he sometimes visited. They were dressed in brown, of course. The Communists always wore brown, dull brown. Why did that offend Petras? It had to be preferable to the opulence of the Baron's Castle.

"Petras," one called, the one Petras remembered was named Sergei. His breath puffed out white in the frigid air, and he tugged at the fur hat on his head.

"What do you want?" he asked, ungracious.

The man placed himself in front of Petras's path into the house. The man was right in his face, and Petras stepped back. "We want to make you an offer." He smiled, reminding Petras of a snake.

"Me? Why is that?"

"We have an administrative aide position; we need a Lithuanian in place. Your name kept coming up."

Petras gazed at him. "I have a job."

He waved his hand in dismissal. "A craft. This would put you on an inside track with the Party."

"I'd need to think about it."

Sergei stared at him. "Don't take too long. This is a real

opportunity for you, and you shouldn't miss it."

Petras wanted to tell him no, shout no at him. Instead, he controlled himself, controlled the automatic shake of his head. "I'll consider it. Now, if you'll excuse me, my child is quite ill."

Again Sergei made that dismissing wave. "A child's disease. It'll soon be over. But the Soviet Union will be here forever."

"Whatever you say. Excuse me."

Rage building in his head, he turned his back on the men and felt their eyes boring into the back of his head. Picked into pieces by the mighty German and Russian hawks, that was how he felt. How he wished he could smash in their faces.

Gintaras was quite ill by the time Petras got back. Mamytė sat holding him in a rocker, with Rima hovering over them, wringing her hands. The child's fever was dangerously high, and his eyes looked vacant. "What is it?" Petras asked Gerardas, alarmed.

"I don't know yet, but I'd guess we'll soon see a rash. I imagine it's measles."

"Oh, dear God!"

"Now, Petras," Mamytė said as she rocked the baby by the fire, "you had measles and you're fine. Don't borrow trouble."

He flushed. "Of course, you're right."

"But this is different!" Rima said.

"Yes," Mamytė said, "because he's yours. But you must accept the fact that everyone you know, or nearly so, has had measles. Pray, don't fret."

Tears rose in Rima's eyes, and she dashed from the room. To pray, Petras hoped. It would keep her mind occupied.

Gerardas examined the baby and decided that so far, at

least, he was not seriously ill. "Now you know I have a special interest in this little one, so I'll do my best for him. Can't be here every moment because I have other patients, but I'll do my best." To Mamytė he said, "Donata, don't keep him too wrapped up or let him get too warm by that fire."

"I should take him outside and cool him off?" she asked facetiously.

"No, of course not, but don't burn him up either."

"Yes, sir." She looked down at the sleepy child and smiled. "Isn't he lovely?"

"Yes, he is," Gerardas said. He gathered up his things. "I'll be running along, but will be back later."

Once Gintaras was sound asleep, Mamytė laid him gently in his cradle. "He won't fit in this much longer, you know," she said to Petras. "He's growing so much."

"Do we have a larger bed for him?"

"I don't think so. You may need to make one."

"Good idea. I'll get right on it." He paused a moment, though, to watch Gintaras sleep. The baby's cheeks were flushed with fever.

"I'll watch him," Mamytė said softly.

Petras nodded. "Right."

He spent the next few hours in the small barn in back, working on building a larger, sleigh-shaped bed for Gintaras. At least he had something to do; anything, almost, was better than sitting and doing nothing. The fragrance of the new wood comforted him.

He thought about the Communists' offer of an administrative job with the Party. He shook his head. Mamytė would not approve; the atheism and materialism of the Party was anathema to her. It came to him, however, that he might not be able to refuse them.

CHAPTER 30

Rima came out to call Petras for lunch.

"How's Gintaras?" he asked.

She shrugged. "He's sleeping."

He looked closely at her. He could see the old, wild despairing look in her eyes, the tangles of her worry. "Rima, we'll get him through this."

"You can't know that."

"No, but I believe it."

They all sat silent through the meal. Petras was sure it was delicious and he told his mother so, but it struck him as so much sawdust. Yet he told himself he was being foolish to fret this way about measles. It could be miserable but brief, and the child would be back to himself in a week or two.

He felt rather than heard the rumble of a vehicle pulling

up in front and the slam of a door. Looking at his mother and Rima and scowling, he got up and said, "Who can that be? Gerardas back already?"

When he opened the door, he saw Pavel coming up to the house, and he stiffened. What could the man want?

He glared at Pavel as he walked toward the house.

Pavel smiled coldly. "Oh, such a welcoming face." He pushed past Petras to enter the house.

"What are you doing here? I thought you'd made tracks for Germany!"

"I did, but I remembered you have something of mine."

"The window? It's safe, buried in the cellar of the Castle."

"That's good." He looked around the room. The scuffle of a chair being pushed back in the next room drew his attention, and he strode out of the room, with Petras trailing behind, mystified. "Where is he?"

"He?" Petras repeated, fear clutching at his heart.

"There he is," Pavel said and crossed to the cradle by the fireplace. He leaned over and scooped the sleeping child up. "Gather his things," he said sharply to Rima. "Now."

"What are you doing?" she whispered, horrified. "You can't take him. He's sick." Gintaras woke up and looked frightened. He began to cry.

Pavel looked at the child. "He doesn't look sick. His lungs sound plenty strong. Hurry, and get his things together."

"No, I won't!"

Gintaras now was screaming and reaching for his mother. She tried to take him from Pavel, but he jerked the baby out of her reach.

"Fine. I guess I can buy plenty of clothes for him."

"You can't take him! I'm nursing him. He's never had

cow's milk!"

The Baron shrugged. "Many babies thrive just fine on it." With those words he turned and strode out of the room.

Petras struggled to regain his voice. "What are you doing?" he asked.

"Taking what's mine."

"Why? He doesn't look Aryan. You have a beautiful, blond Aryan wife."

"She lost the child she was carrying. He's of my blood at least. Look at him, nearly a spitting image."

"Actually, he reminds me more of Vanya. What will you do with another Vanya, bury him in a dungeon?"

With one hand Pavel reached out and struck Petras across the face. Petras felt blood spurt from his nose and trickle down his face.

"Imbecile. You let him out, didn't you? Now you have another mental defective roaming Lithuania. Keep him here, that's all I can say."

He rushed out of the house and to the waiting car. Petras ran after him. Was Walther driving him? No, there was no chauffeur. Pavel opened the door, thrust the baby into the front seat, and climbed in, starting the car and roaring off before Petras could stop him.

Petras stood in the road and watched the car disappear toward Šiauliai. He raised his hands and let them fall helplessly. He didn't have a car; how would he catch up with the man?

Gerardas! He'd have to use Gerardas's car.

The next few hours passed excruciatingly slowly. Petras borrowed Gerardas's car and asked for a brief driving lesson. It wasn't hard to drive; he'd certainly felt how gears move and how brakes work while riding in other vehicles. Gerardas's car was old but solid, and trustworthy.

Petras felt a pang of remorse. "How will you get to your patients?"

"I can borrow from the Kaminskases. Run along, now!"

Rima insisted on coming too.

"You can't!" Petras nearly shouted at her. "You'll slow me down!"

Her face set like marble, she said through clenched teeth, "I'm coming. And that's it, Petras." She got her coat and two changes of clothing for the baby but didn't change out of her thin leather shoes.

"Don't you think you need boots?" he asked.

"No, we'll be in the car."

"Cars have breakdowns."

She opened the door. "We don't have time to waste. I'll be fine."

A fresh snow began to fall, but it wasn't heavy yet. The snow worried him, though, considering he was a novice driver, but he felt he had no choice but to drive through it, and quickly.

He drove like a wild man. Fortunately, the roads were clear and nearly free of traffic. He didn't know why that was the case, but he was thankful for it. He figured it could have something to do with his mother's prayers.

Rima said nothing. She had brought a rosary that Petras had never seen her use before, and she clicked through the beads as he drove. A second set of a mother's prayers; perhaps not a bad idea.

When they reached Šiauliai, he drove straight to the Castle. It was the only place he knew where he might find the man, but he realized it wasn't likely Pavel had gone there. It was too obvious – but then, the Baron knew Petras didn't have a car, probably figured he was helpless, stranded in the country, so why not go to the Castle?

Once they pulled up to the Castle, there seemed to be no signs of life around the building, but he saw Pavel's car at the side door, so he stopped down the road a bit to think about what to do next. By this point the snow was heavy, and Petras felt as if he were trying to peer through thick lace curtains.

"What are you doing?" Rima asked in alarm.

"Thinking. I don't know the best way to approach this."

"I do. I'll go to the Castle, you go get the police."

"Why warn him off too early? We've got to think this out."

"My father and brothers! Let's get them first."

Petras considered that. "Okay, and I'll get Vidas. But we have to hurry."

She gave him a strange look. "I'd say so."

"Why do you look at me like that?"

"You were sitting here wasting time, and you tell me we have to hurry?"

"Oh, Rima, save it."

He turned the car around and headed for the Baltrunas house. He hated to face her father, as angry as the man had been about their wedding. Would he care enough about the child to help rescue him? "You leave me here and run on to get Vidas," Rima said.

"How will you get back to the Castle? It's too cold to walk and you aren't wearing boots! I wish you'd dress warmer!"

"Oh, Petras, stop it. I'll remember next time. Anyway, Alfonsas bought a truck, I heard. He can drive us. See, there it is." She pointed to an ancient black truck behind the house, then threw the door open and jumped out of the car while it was still moving. "I'll see you at the Castle."

This new assertive Rima – well, did he like that? He thought so. Would she prevail over the whimpering one? He hoped so.

Once she was gone, he remembered that Eugenijus was supposed to be gone. Hadn't Walther told him that? But they'd seen smoke from the chimney: someone was there.

The snow fell relentlessly, and he had to hunch over as close to the wheel as possible to see through the windscreen. He arrived at the police station, relieved, and entered to find Vidas sitting at a desk, talking on the phone. He looked up and smiled at Petras and then went back to listening. His jaw tightened, and Petras figured it wasn't good news. He looked around the utilitarian office and wondered what it was like to be a policeman. He doubted he'd like the job.

At last Vidas hung up. He stood and offered Petras his hand. "How are you? To what do we owe the honor of your visit? I hope it's good news for once."

"No, not at all. Pavel – " Here his voice broke, and he was fearful that he'd start crying. "He's taken the child, and Gintaras is ill. Rima has been worried sick as it is, and now this." He was horrified to feel hot tears falling.

Vidas led him to a bench and eased him down.

"I'm sorry," Petras said as the sobs racked his body. "I'm such a child still, trying to be a man."

Vidas put his arm around him. "It's all right," he said softly. "Go ahead and cry. It'll do you good." Vidas waited patiently for Petras to cry out his despair and to get control of himself.

"I'm wasting precious time. We have to go to the Castle and get the child back. Pavel's car is there, so we're hoping that's where the baby is. We need you to go with us. Rima has gone to her father's house to get him and her brothers, but who knows how they'll greet her? I think I should have gone there myself."

"Old Eugenijus is dry at the moment, and he has told me he regretted his last episode with Rima. Let's go. I think you can hope for the best."

He stood and grabbed his coat. "How did you get here?"

"A friend's car."

"Can I ride with you? Our one official car is gone for the day." Vidas rubbed his face with one hand; he looked very tired. "I may as well give you the news: that phone call was from regional office. The Soviets are due here any time, to stay. They plan to use the Castle for their administrative headquarters, so we need to get the child out of there. Let's go."

Petras felt sick. There was no time to lose. He had to get Gintaras and Rima out of the city before the Soviets came. "How long do we have?"

Vidas grabbed his coat. "I don't know. An hour or two, or a week or two," he said, grim-faced.

CHAPTER 31

Petras, Vidas beside him in the car, sped to the Castle. Snow was still falling, and night was drawing in.

When they arrived, Rima, her father, and her brother Alfonsas were already there. Eugenijus looked cross until he saw Vidas, at which point his face nearly split open in a wide grin. "Oh, thank God, reinforcements that will matter. The rest of us are worthless. Petras stood there and let the Baron take the child right in front of his face."

Petras bridled but decided against arguing with the man.

"That's not exactly how it happened, Father," Rima said. "I don't think you'd have been able to stop him either. He took us by complete surprise."

Petras smiled shyly at her in gratitude.

"I'm sorry, Rima," Vidas said. "We'll get him back."

She burst into tears. "He's sick! Please help me get him

back as soon as possible." Petras put an arm around her.

"Yes," Vidas said. He tugged at his coat and squared his shoulders. "Let's go."

He led the way up the front steps, Petras and Rima on his heels. Stopping, he turned to them to say, "I think you should stand behind us all. Eugenijus and Alfonsas should flank me, and you two shield yourselves behind them. I think, I hope, we'll face less resistance from him than you two would." To Petras he asked, "How much of his household staff is still here?"

"I don't know. Most of them left the day he did, with his wife and Conrad Zeller. Walther was still here, but I had the feeling he wouldn't stay."

Vidas stroked his chin. "You know, now that I think of it, you two" – he pointed to Petras and Rima – "need to get out of sight. Hide around the corner. I really fear he'll turn nasty if he sees you."

Petras nodded, Rima shook her head. He put his hand on her arm and turned her back. "Listen to him. He's right." He led her down the stairs and off to the left, but he stayed as close to the building as he could, to hear any conversation if it was possible. He was shaking with anxiety.

Rima was shivering.

"You cold?" he asked, wrapping his arms around her.

She shook her head. "No, just so frightened."

He pulled her close. "I know." They stood there in each other's arms for a few moments. "The cellar!"

"What?"

"Walther showed me a way into the cellar. We'll get in that way. But perhaps you should wait here."

"No, I'm coming with you," she said firmly.

He held her hand and dashed around to the back of the Castle. He searched for the coal chute. Had the false nail heads been replaced since he and Walther had freed Vanya? How long ago that seemed now. But even this morning seemed long ago.

No, the nail heads had not been replaced. He removed the doors and helped Rima down into the cellar. He noticed her hands and feet looked blue. "You're cold."

"I'm okay! Or I will be once we get him back."

As quietly as he could, Petras followed her into the cellar. It was dank and cold, and it seemed unused. The pile of rubble from Vanya's prison still lay on the floor – the rubble used to cover the stained glass, too.

"What's that?" Rima asked.

"Pavel had his brother walled up in there for months."

"Oh, dear God! His own brother! But why?"

"To teach him some lesson, who knows what. Walther Funk did his best to keep Vanya fed and somewhat sane. Once Pavel left two weeks back, Walther and I got him out. It was amazing what good shape he was in, weak, of course, but Walther had made sure he could get out in the sun at times when Pavel was gone."

"Incredible."

Petras took her hand and led her through the labyrinth of columns and sunken baths. The cellar was made up of many small rooms, some hidden off the main walkway, with no seeming logic to their use. The low ceilings and rubble under their feet kept them moving slowly and cautiously.

"What are these?" she asked, pointing to the oblong stone receptacles.

"Used to be hot springs baths, I guess."

"I smell the sulfur. Like hell."

He nodded. "I think the way goes through there," he said, pointing ahead to a stone staircase. Light filtered weakly through the opening above the steps.

It soon became clear, however, that the stairs led only to some old, unused kitchens that were walled off from the rest of the house. "We'll have to go back down and try again. There's got to be a way upstairs through here."

They kept going through the cellars, one feeding into another, with steps up and down to reach the different levels. The stone floor felt frigid to their feet. The farther they went, the darker it got. "I wish I'd brought a torch," Petras said.

After some minutes he stopped. "I don't know. I can't really see now."

A soft rustling off to the left made Rima squeal and cower in Petras's arms. She was shivering so hard, he could hear her teeth.

"Hush!" he said, straining to see through the murky cellar.

"That you, Petras?" called a voice.

A shock ran through him. "Who is it?"

"Me, Vanya."

"Vanya! What are you doing here?"

"Hiding. Pavel came back." He paused. "But what are you doing here? And who's with you?"

"It's me, Rima," she said.

"Oh, Rima! Are you all okay?" Vanya asked.

"No!" she said, beginning to cry again. "He's got my baby!"

"Pavel? Why?"

"He took Gintaras, who knows why," Petras said, "but we don't have much time. Can you get us upstairs?"

"Of course. I know every corner of this castle, you know."

"I'm not surprised. I remember how you darted in and

out of the ballroom while I was working on the window."

They heard scraping and the ring of a boot against stone. "I'll get you out in a minute." He appeared next to them and laboriously searched through his pockets. "I'm sure I have matches here somewhere."

"Hurry, hurry!" Rima said through gritted teeth.

"I'm hurrying." Silence. "No, I can't find them. I can find my way through without a light, though." He grabbed her hand and said, "Come."

Petras thought of the Bible verse about the blind leading the blind, and he thought it fit their situation. But he also believed that, better than anyone else, Vanya knew his way around in the Castle, blindfolded or even truly blind.

Rima sobbed. "For the love of God, hurry!" she cried. "I can't stand this."

"Oh, don't cry, Rima," Vanya begged, tears in his voice. "I'll get you out."

Petras felt as if he wanted to jump out of his skin. This whole mess felt crazy. Surely the baby was fine, though. Surely!

At last Vanya led them to a staircase deep in the bowels of the Castle. "This is the third subbasement," he told them. "We're almost to the secret passage for the ballroom."

"Hurry, hurry," Rima whispered.

They made their way upward, a much steeper incline than any they'd taken before, up or down. "This is it," Vanya said, "right through here." He pulled Rima through a narrow hall that was completely dark, except for a thin strip of light about twelve feet ahead of them. Petras held on to Rima's other hand as tight as he could; his hand was sweaty from nerves, and he feared he'd lose hold of her.

"Be quiet now," Vanya whispered as he pushed open a thick door, well hidden behind some heavy drapes.

And there was the ballroom, odd-looking now with the stained glass window gone and the opening boarded up.

"At last!" Petras whispered. "Where do you think Pavel has the child?"

"Walther said he was furnishing a nursery on the third floor. Let's try there. I'm sure it's the same room that was our nursery when we were children."

Vanya gestured to them to wait while he carefully opened the door onto the main hall on the second floor. He nodded his head, and they all left the ballroom. From below, they heard voices coming from the front foyer. Vidas was speaking calmly; Pavel was arguing. Rima's father and brother were silent.

"Does he have Gintaras with him?" Rima asked, her voice muffled with tears.

"I don't know," Vanya said. "I'll look."

"It's not likely he has him down there," Petras said. "Just be quick and let's head up to the nursery."

Vanya tiptoed to the banister, looked down to the foyer, and returned, shaking his head. "Upstairs, likely."

They removed their shoes and dashed up the stairs on the balls of their feet, careful, quiet. Once they reached the head of the stairs, they could hear, behind a closed door, the sound of the child crying.

"Oh, dear God in Heaven, thank you, thank you!" Rima cried out, softly. "He's there!"

"You're sure it's him?" Vanya asked.

"I know his voice," she said.

She raced past Vanya and got to the door first and turned the knob. "No! It's locked!" She turned a twisted face to them. "Get me in there!" she ordered.

"Sure. Just be patient, Rima," Vanya said. "You need

to believe I can get you into any room in the house."

"Well, then, do it, now!"

"Rima! Give him a chance."

She clenched her jaw – he could see the muscles turn white under the skin – but she kept silence.

Vanya looked down the hall, toward a small marble stand with a large Chinese vase on it. "In that vase. We always kept an extra key in there."

Rima started after it, but Petras grabbed her arm. "Hold on."

Vanya found the key and put it in the lock; it turned easily. Rima pushed past him and toward a crib across the large room, painted white, an icy cold room. There was no fire, no nanny anywhere, just the baby lying sobbing in a white metal crib. She grabbed him up and hugged him so hard he squealed; then, realizing who it was, he began to cry even harder than he had been. He grasped her hair in his fists and pulled. "He's mad at me," she said, nearly laughing through her tears. "I can't blame him." She kissed his face all over. "Oh, his fever is so high! What has the monster done to my child?"

Petras removed Gintaras's blanket from the crib and wrapped it around him. "Let's get him home," he said.

"Sit down in that rocker and feed him," Vanya said. "He's surely hungry."

"Yes," Petras said, "but we need to get out of here first. Take us back to the cellars."

"But why? It's so cold and dark and dirty for a baby!" Vanya said.

"To make sure Pavel doesn't find us up here. Let's go." He pushed Vanya ahead of him, gently, and took Rima's elbow to lead her out of the room.

"I can get out an easier way. That okay?" Vanya asked.

"Of course! Let's go," Rima said.

By this time, Gintaras had stuck a fist in his mouth and put his head on her shoulder.

"He looks heavy," Petras said. "Want me to carry him?"

"No!" She buried her nose in his hair.

"He's falling asleep," Petras said.

"Let's hurry!" Vanya said. "At least he won't cry now."

"True. But who knows for how long? Lead on, and let's try to avoid the cellars if we can."

"Follow me," Vanya said.

He led them down two flights of service stairs. "I'll check the new kitchens. I'm sure they're empty."

They waited in the hall and listened for voices from the front of the building. Petras thought he heard muffled sounds, but he wasn't sure.

Vanya darted into the kitchen and back out to gesture to them. "It's clear!"

At that point, the voices from the foyer increased in volume, Pavel shouting and obviously coming toward the back hall.

CHAPTER 32

"Hurry!" Rima said. "We've got to get out of here!"

"Yes, yes, of course," Petras said. He felt torn, drawn to see what was going on in front and to help combat it, yet pulled to get his wife and child out of this monstrous building. A heavy thud shuddered through the door closing off the back servants' hall from the main front hall. "You both go!" he yelled. "I'll follow!"

They dashed toward the kitchens in back, but before they entered, Petras turned back to see Pavel enter the hall, followed by Vidas, Eugenijus, and Alfonsas.

"You get out of here!" Pavel shouted to the men behind him. "I've got important work to do, to save my home from those barbarians!"

"It's too late," Vidas said quietly. "Come with us and save your life."

Pavel realized Petras was also in the hall. "You! What are you doing here?"

"I...I'm just checking on how they closed off the opening for your window that I removed. As cold as it is, I didn't want it gaping open. It seems fine."

"Why didn't you come to the front?" Pavel asked.

"I thought you'd prefer I come to the back. It was open. I knocked and no one answered..."

"Shut up with that blithering. No one's interested. I'd wager you're here to get that brat back. He cries all the time – how did you spoil him so fast?" He was shouting now, and his face was purple, swollen with rage.

The Baron was losing control, and Petras smiled. "It was easy. He's very lovable, you know."

"Why do you look like the cat who's swallowed the canary? He's gone already?" Pavel lunged, but Petras dodged him, and he ran into a wall.

Petras could smell alcohol on him. Surely he was drunk.

Vidas grabbed Pavel as he reeled away from the wall. "Hear, now, let's not do this. Run along, Petras, we'll take care of him."

"No!" Pavel shouted. "I'll kill him! He's entered my home illegally – who knows what he's stolen! Arrest him, or I'll kill him now."

Pavel left them, dashing through the hall door back into the foyer. All four men followed, Petras in front.

Vidas yelled at Petras. "Get out of here, you fool! He's insane!"

Petras glared at Vidas. "This is the end. I can't endure the pain and humiliation my family has suffered from him any longer. I'll kill him if he doesn't kill me first!"

Once they reached the foyer, they saw Pavel remove a rifle from a display cabinet standing between marble pillars in the front hall. He opened the gun to see if it was loaded, but before he could cock it and fire, Petras took a running leap and tackled him, forcing the gun out of his hands to clatter across the marble floor. He grabbed the man by the throat, knocked him to the floor, and began choking him.

"Stop it, Petras, let go!" Vidas yelled. "You can't kill him!"

"I will," he grunted through clenched teeth, "with pleasure. Tell me, or you'll die. Why did you kill Ona?"

Pavel pushed Petras off. "You idiot. You never understood anything, did you? I didn't kill her."

"Then who did? No one but you could have done it!"

"You didn't stop to think, did you? Who could have done it? That cur Hans Zeller, that's who. He killed her and bragged about it. I got him removed from Šiauliai for it. And you never even suspected. What an idiot you are."

Shocked, Petras sat back on his heels, mouth agape. Hans? How could that be? Hans Zeller? "Did you put him up to it? Was he one of your henchmen?"

Pavel snorted. "That fool? He was dangerous and stupid. And in love with your sister for years. But you all merely despised him. Actually, I did too. I couldn't use him even as a subordinate."

"I'll kill him!" Petras whispered through clenched teeth. "But you first!" He grabbed Pavel by the throat and choked him, pounding his head on the marble floor.

At that point the front door opened, banging against the wall. Sergei and three other Communists barged in. They looked at the two men grappling on the black and white marble floor, the others just standing and watching.

Sergei looked shocked. "What's going on?" he asked.

While Petras struggled to hold Pavel down on the floor in his frenzy to kill the Baron, Pavel scooted himself toward the rifle, which he finally reached. He stretched long fingers toward it and grasped the butt. He inched it towards himself, straining against Petras's hands.

"Watch it!" Eugenijus yelled.

Sergei pulled a gun from inside his heavy brown topcoat and cocked it, leaned close to Pavel, gun against his head, and said calmly, "Let it go, Gerulaitis."

Pavel grunted and dropped the rifle.

"Get up, Petras," Sergei said, still in his cool, calm voice.

Petras scrambled backward as fast as he could. He feared Sergei would as likely shoot him as Pavel.

Pavel lay still, then kicked his foot to hook around behind Sergei's, but he wasn't fast enough. Sergei pulled the trigger, the muzzle butted up to Pavel's head, and the Baron recoiled backwards, brains, blood, and bone spilling out on the black and white floor. At last he lay immobile.

Petras put his hands over his ears to shut out the horrible reverberations in the marble foyer.

He had hated the man for so long, his mortal enemy, and now Pavel was dead, past hurting him or his family anymore. But a Russian had killed him. Did that put Petras in Sergei's debt now?

He stared at Vidas and the Baltrunases, who all looked gray with shock.

The door opened slowly behind the four Communists, and Sergei swung around, aiming his pistol at whoever it was entering the foyer.

Vanya peeked around the door, wide-eyed. "What – ? He's dead." He looked at the Russian. "You killed him?"

Sergei thrust the gun into Vanya's chest. "Who are you and what do you want?"

"I'm his brother."

"Grab him!" Sergei said to his comrades.

"No, wait!" Vidas and Petras said together.

Vidas stepped in front of Vanya. "He's not like Pavel. He's gentle. Let him go. I'll vouch for him."

"He's been a tremendous help to me," Petras added.

Sergei lowered the gun toward the floor.

"Where's Rima?" Petras asked Vanya.

"I'm here," she said, sidling in around the door, carrying the sleeping baby in her arms. She stared at the body on the floor, the gun in Sergei's hand. "Pavel's dead." She began to cry. "I wish I could feel sorry for him, but I can't." She looked down at the child. "May I go into the study and feed him?"

Sergei turned chivalrous and said, "Of course, come in." He turned to Vidas. "I'm not sure I can let you have this man. I'll have to interrogate him."

"No!" Rima cried. "Please don't! Vanya won't hurt anyone, but you will hurt him, badly. Let him go," she pleaded.

Sergei rubbed his chin. "We'll see. You know, I'm here to take over this building now. Since Gerulaitis was a Nazi sympathizer, he has no claim to it. Nor do you," he said to Vanya.

Vanya shrugged. "I don't want it. My brain isn't too good, you know, and I can't run a place like this."

Sergei examined his face suspiciously. "Is he for real?" he asked Petras.

"Very much so," Petras said and put an arm around Vanya's shoulders. "Very real."

While Rima fed and changed Gintaras, Sergei searched all three floors in the house as well as the cellars for any hidden Nazis but found no one. He repeated to Petras his offer of a position with the Communist Party.

Petras flushed. He felt he owed Sergei something, but

he hoped not this. "I need some time to think, Sergei. I'm in a bit of shock at the moment."

Sergei smiled charmingly. "I understand. Take your time."

"Thanks," he mumbled.

Rima's father and brother clapped him on the back and congratulated him on rescuing the child. "That was almost as exciting as an American western, I'd say," Eugenijus said, his face genial after three glasses of Pavel's French brandy. "Come visit us from time to time when things settle down."

"I will, that is, we will. Your grandson is quite a boy. He's not himself today, but you'll get to know him better once he's well."

"Sure thing." Then the Baltrunases left.

Vidas stayed, asked if there was anything he could do to help. "I know you're feeling relief and grief too. This was a terrible thing."

Petras nodded. "Yes. I can't tell what I'm feeling. Mostly sick, I guess. What makes a person like Pavel? He was once a dear, small child like Gintaras, I'd guess. What went wrong?"

Vidas shook his head. "I don't know."

"And Hans, a killer too. I can't take it in. But I should have guessed. He's gone now, who knows where? Will he ever pay for killing Ona?"

Vidas heaved a great sigh. "Well. I can't say."

"Do you think we should take Vanya home with us?"

Vidas lifted his shoulders. "I'd suggest asking him. He's not a child, and you can't force him one way or the other. I can find a place for him for a short while."

Vanya didn't want to leave Šiauliai. He took Vidas up on his offer of a place to stay until he could find work.

Oddly, Petras felt rejected. Vanya was Gintaras's uncle, and it seemed as if they belonged together.

"Biržai's too small for me, you know. I do better in a city. But I can come visit."

"Okay." Petras felt he could live with that.

He helped Rima gather up Gintaras's few things. "How is he now?" he asked her.

"Fever, rash on his stomach," she said, sounding exhausted. "But he's quiet. He's not suffering, or in distress."

He nodded. "Good. Let's go home."

"Yes."

Chapter 33

The next few weeks were very strange. Petras felt in shock still, from the horrible fear of losing Gintaras and sneaking around the Castle to reach him and to get him out and to safety, then watching Pavel shot to death. And learning that Hans had killed Ona. That fact hurt Mamytė deeply, her beloved pastor's son the killer. She'd always tried to make allowances for the boy, cruel as he had been.

Petras knew it made no difference, that Hans and not Pavel was the killer. Pavel was dead, but Hans was still alive, and he knew he would never have closure.

Soon after he learned that Juodas had been arrested as a Nazi collaborator. Some said Caterina had informed on him. Petras felt as if he were floating off in space without a tether. He'd never liked Juodas, but his heavy, dark, looming presence had been like a fence, a boundary around his world, .

and now the edges weren't there to keep him on the earth.

Then, the growing reality. Something was very wrong with the child. He had suffered through a severe case of measles. They had sat up with him at night, bathing his body, rocking him and singing to him to get him through the night hours. The fever had affected his mind, it seemed, and of course Rima blamed herself for his decline. She got up at night and sat crying in a chair by the front window.

They took him to the health retreat at Likėnai, in hopes that the waters would benefit him. Nothing.

Mamytė and Rima prayed and prayed, Rima with her rosary. At times Petras thought the clicking of the rosary would drive him wild, that Mamytė would think the beads were heathen, but one evening she said something that calmed his fears.

"Our Lord hears her prayers, and if the beads help her pray, we're thankful for that."

"Okay, Mamytė. I'm sure you're right."

Gintaras survived, but vastly changed. He was too quiet, too passive. He ate halfheartedly, he grew thin and gray, he moaned a lot but didn't really cry out. It turned Petras's stomach to watch him seem to fade away before his eyes.

Gerardas seemed helpless. "I don't know, the high fever, I'd guess. Or maybe the fear and shock of being taken from his mother, I don't know. Just keep feeding him and holding him."

It was the longest, coldest winter of Petras's memory. He couldn't make it into the city to work, so he made work at home, but it was all so pointless. The Soviets had taken over the country, but he was too preoccupied with worries about Gintaras and his family to care.

When April came, there was a freak snowstorm. Petras noticed that daffodils, usually so heart-lifting, were blooming in the snow. Petras stared at them, feeling they were out of place, and couldn't make sense of them.

At home there was no change. Gintaras was weak but alive. He barely seemed to notice who was around him.

Mamytė cried at night, where no one could see her, but Petras knew, for her eyes were red and swollen every morning. But all day she put a good face on her grief.

And Rima became as passive as Gintaras. All the glimmer and light were gone from her face.

Gerardas told them about a doctor, Stasys Bučas, he'd heard of in Šiauliai who thought he could help Gintaras. "Maybe you should move back. Why don't you give it a chance, at least? And you could go back to work, Petras. I think this enforced idleness is very bad for you."

Rima's eyes lit up. "What can this doctor do for him?"

"I've heard Bučas has had good success with vitamin therapy. I don't know – you can try it."

"Let's go, Petras," Rima said. "I want to try."

They made plans to pack up and move back. Mamytė's house in Šiauliai was empty; the tenants had moved out with the Germans.

Using Gerardas's phone, Petras called Antanas to ask him if he still had a job. Antanas offered to come get them in his truck. He asked Eugenijus and Alfonsas to come too, with their truck. And Gerardas followed along, with Donata, Rima, and the eerily silent baby in his car.

A sad procession. Would Šiauliai be a better place for them now? Who could tell? But at least they were doing something.

It was a beautiful spring. The white apple and pink cherry blossoms were breathtaking, and the fragrance of the earth raised Petras's hopes for a cure for the baby. Yet the heart had gone out of Rima, although she went through all the motions of taking care of the house and Gintaras. Petras would ask her to come for evening walks with them, but she always refused. Still, Petras took Gintaras out in his carriage almost every night, talking to him and pointing out special things. He introduced him to the people they encountered, lifted him up to show him the neighborhood dogs, helped him touch the apple and cherry trees.

Yet the child never smiled. Gerardas thought he seemed depressed.

"Babies don't get depressed," Petras growled.

Gerardas shook his head. "I'm not so sure." He took Gintaras from Rima and jiggled him up and down, gazing into the child's eyes. No reaction. "Perhaps with time," he'd say, "the cloud will lift. Keep feeding him well, holding him, letting him touch things."

Gerardas asked Donata to marry him whenever she felt the baby was strong again and Rima confident enough to take over his care on her own. He planned to move to Šiauliai to join the new doctor, Stasys Bučas, at the clinic he was opening. "I think the man can help children like Gintaras. I'd like to be part of that."

Petras went back to work with Antanas, but it was clear the presence of the Communists was affecting orders for art glass. "Everything is so dull and utilitarian!" Antanas shouted one day. "It's boring!"

In late May Antanas had a heart attack. Petras was there. Antanas asked him to send for Eugenijus Baltrunas. When Petras's father-in-law arrived looking near death himself, Petras made to leave the sick room, but Antanas called him back. "Eugenijus, before I die…"

"No!" Petras said.

"Before I die," he went on, "I'd like to know you've forgiven Petras and asked him to forgive you."

Eugenijus turned bright red, then turned to glare at Petras. He didn't speak for a long time. "Why?"

"You're both good men, you both love Rima. It's not right to hold grudges."

Eugenijus still kept silence, as did Petras. "Okay," Eugenijus said at last. "I apologize, Petras. I think you're a good man, and you're a good husband to Rima. I wish you hadn't…"

"No," Antanas said, "stop with just the apology. Old news is old now."

"I forgive you, Eugenijus, and I hope you can forgive me," Petras said humbly.

Antanas smiled and turned his face to the wall. He died three days later. It was left to Petras to decide whether he should take over Antanas's business. There was a good income but not steady. How would he support his family? Stasys didn't charge much at the clinic, but it was a lot for them. He didn't think the business could provide enough work for him.

Sad and dejected though he was about it, he went to work for the Communists at the administrative headquarters for the collective farms in Ginkūnai. And he was back in the despised castle again. His office was a partitioned-off part of the ballroom, under the large window that once held Pavel's stained glass. Petras tried not to think of the glass hidden in the basement; he feared Sergei and the other Communists would read his mind and find it there.

One good thing about the placement of his office: he was flooded with a clear north light as he worked. It was good light for an artist. At times, when his work was caught up, he would sit and draw scenes from his childhood, his memories of his father, Ona, and other family members and friends. The light reminded him of brighter days in his childhood, when he'd sit alone and draw as he listened to Mamytė and Tėvelis chatting in the parlor and to Ona practicing her violin.

Much of the Castle's opulence had been toned down, for which he was thankful, but the dull brown of the walls, ceiling, and floors bored him. Nothing about the place could please him. From time to time, Vanya popped in through one of his secret passages to chat with Petras. He could make Petras laugh when nothing seemed laughable.

One day Petras said, "I wish you'd come visit us. I'd like for you to get to know Gintaras and for him to know you. He's so silent and withdrawn. Perhaps you can draw him out. He is your blood kin, you know."

Pleasure lit up his eyes. "I'd like that.

That evening Vanya joined Petras on his walk home. Once they reached the house, Petras could see it had been a bad day for Rima, by the wild look in her eyes and her matted hair. His heart sank, but he knew he could do nothing.

He picked Gintaras up from his crib and introduced him to Uncle Vanya. Vanya smiled a lopsided grin at him and tickled his tummy. And Gintaras reached for his finger and smiled back.

So galvanized by the signs of interest and life in Gintaras, Petras nearly dropped the child. "He smiled!"

Vanya shrugged. "He's a child. All children smile."

"He hasn't smiled for weeks, not since he got sick. Come look, Rima, he's smiling."

Rima lifted her head slowly and walked across the room to them as if in a dream. She took him from Petras and looked at his face, and the baby's smile faded. Gintaras twisted away from her and reached for Vanya. Her face collapsed, and she burst into tears.

Petras took Gintaras from her and told her to go wash her face and do her hair. "You're frightening him with such a sad face."

She scurried off to do his wishes, and Petras said, "Let's go for a short walk. You're not starving, are you?"

"Hungry, but I can wait. I learned how while I was in the cellar."

Gintaras reached for Vanya again, and Petras handed him over.

"I don't really know how to hold a baby," Vanya said.

"You can hold him a bit while I get his carriage out. If you get tired, you can put him into the carriage."

"Well, I don't want to make him cry."

They walked out under the setting sun for nearly an hour. Petras talked to Gintaras about the trees and introduced him again to the neighbors as they passed, and encouraged him to pat the dogs. For once, the child showed some interest.

"Vanya, I can't begin to thank you for coming. You've awakened him."

"His mama's face is scary. She needs to smile and talk to him."

"Yes. Will you tell her so?"

He nodded. "I'll try. You know, I tried to make friends with her when she lived at the Castle for a while, but she was so afraid. Tell her she doesn't have to be afraid of me."

Petras clapped him on the back. "I will. You're a good man."

"My brain doesn't work too good, but I do my best."

"I think it works just fine, Vanya."

CHAPTER 34

Life continued on in a rather desultory manner for Petras. Until the day the Germans came back, drove the Russians out, and took over Lithuania again. And the news began to arrive of massacres of Lithuania's Jews. And some Liths helped the Nazis; not many, but any at all were too many.

Petras's anger rose again, the way it used to when he had faced Pavel and his cruelties. It was the helplessness that fed the fury in his heart and brain.

With the Soviets gone, he was out of a job again, and in danger of execution at the hands of the Germans. He did his best to stay invisible but still live a somewhat normal life by keeping busy with repairs for folks in the neighborhood. For the first time in his life, he wanted to be a totally nondescript person. But without his art, he felt dead inside.

In late summer he decided to go to Joniškis to check on Joelis, whose family had disappeared from Šiauliai. Petras had not a clue where they'd gone.

By now Petras had a car, an old one but serviceable, so he left early one day to drive to Joniškis. It was cold and rainy, which Petras took as a good sign: easier to hide in a gray light than in a bright one. There were a lot of German troops being moved along the road, and he felt sweat trickling down his sides and back. He didn't want to draw their attention. He kept an eye out for Hans Zeller – what would he do if he saw the man? Would he run him down with the car and kill him? No, not wise. He'd never escape from the Nazi troopers all around him.

He pulled into town to find the streets deserted of all but a few Nazi soldiers. At that point he thought maybe the gray weather was not good because anyone outside in the pouring rain was obvious and therefore suspect.

He left the car behind the church and raced through the back streets of the artificially quiet town. He knew where the Jewish ghetto was, but didn't know precisely where to find Joelis and his uncle's family.

He took a back alley behind a row of very old pink-stone, single-story buildings. About halfway down the alley, he noticed the twitch of a curtain to his right. There was a door ajar next to the window, and he went to the door and called softly inside. "Joelis? Are you there? Does anyone know my friend Joelis, from Šiauliai?"

He heard a hiss and a scrabbling noise, then a thud that shook the ground, barely perceptible beneath his feet. He waited a minute before pushing the door open. The small entry hall was empty, with doors to adjoining rooms closed. In the weak shaft of light from the door behind him, he saw dust motes rising from a crack in the floor. A dead giveaway to a trapdoor, he thought.

He checked behind all the doors but found nothing. He returned to the crack in the floor and stood staring at it, hands on hips. What to do?

Quickly he went outside, searched for some dirt between the cobbles in the alley. He returned to the house, knelt and sifted the dirt he'd found in the alley across the crack. Next he paced around the room, leaving his footprints evenly across the floor.

Petras put his face down close to the trapdoor and whispered, "God keep you safe, whoever's in there." Slowly he stood and brushed the dirt off his hands and sighed deeply. He would never know who was in there, would he?

As he prepared to leave, he heard a rustle behind a door he'd checked when he first arrived. He turned slowly and peered through the narrow crack in the door. He couldn't see anything.

As he stood there, the door began to move toward Petras, creaking slightly in the reigning silence. He shivered with fear and squinted his eyes to be able to see who it was. *Please, not a German*, he begged.

His eyes met the eyes of a skeleton, dark, burning black eyes in chalk-white skin under spiky black hair. The skeleton was wearing the dusty black coat of a Jew, with a Star of David on his sleeve.

"Joelis?" he whispered. "Is it you?"

The stranger didn't speak, just stared at him. Petras reached a hand out for him, but the man didn't respond, except with a slight movement away from him.

Something in the expression of the man's mouth told him it was Joelis. "Okay, I won't touch you." He stood there staring back at Joelis. "How can I help?"

"I told you," Joelis whispered, his voice raspy. "I told

you to pray for us. Did you?" He made a motion of dismissal. "Never mind. It's too late. They're moving into Joniškis right now, you know, to kill us all."

Petras nodded. "I know. I'm here to help."

Joelis laughed. There was no humor in the laugh. "How would you help?"

Petras jerked back as if burned. Tears started in his eyes. "I don't know. Isn't there anything?" He pointed to the trapdoor. "Who's down there? Can we get them out? How many are there? I have a car."

"There are forty people down there," Joelis said, his voice flat.

"Forty! How can that be? There's not enough room!"

"There's a tunnel under all the ghetto, and small rooms dug off the tunnel. We dug them with spoons."

"I can't believe it!"

Joelis ignored him. "We found many dead bodies, bones of people, buried under there. We didn't know who they were, but we tried not to disturb them too much." He rubbed his face, which was lined with his fatigue. "So. You're going to get all of them in your car? Cars have changed a lot since I've been here, huh?"

"Sorry. No, I can't take all forty. But maybe a few at a time. Can't we try? You and four others, perhaps? Your mother and sisters – where are they?"

"Here. You saved them too, you know."

He felt faint. "How?"

"Your visit alerted my mother to the arrival of the soldiers. She took the girls out back and across the wall into a shop there. The shop owner fortunately said nothing. Three hundred children killed that day, did you know that?"

Petras shook his head. "How could they – so inhuman! I can't understand it." He shook his head. "So now – how

hem out of here?" As he asked it, fear raced up
low would he hide five Jews in his car? One
never. "How about food? Can we go get food
re they all as starved as you?"

do we get them out of here?" As he asked it, fear raced up his back. How would he hide five Jews in his car? One maybe, five never. "How about food? Can we go get food for them? Are they all as starved as you?"

Joelis laughed again that humorless laugh. "Some as starved as me, some more so. Some dead."

"Oh, dear God, I'm so sorry."

"Don't be. You saved my life once. You saved my mother. Sometimes I hate you for it."

Petras raised his hand, then let it fall, helpless. "Sorry."

Joelis thought for a long time. He jerked his head toward the door. "Let's go. We'll get food, try to bring it back in. I can't see anything else to do." He patted his coat pocket, as if checking for keys or his identity card. "Oh. Another thing. Stop saying you're sorry. It drives me crazy."

"Sorry." Petras gulped once the word slipped out of his mouth.

Joelis's eyes flashed. "Enough already!"

"Okay! But why?"

"It does no good to be sorry. You've helped me twice now. That does some good." He ran long, skinny fingers through his hair, making it stand up more. "I think. I'm still thinking about that. Perhaps you'd have done me more good to let them kill me that November."

Petras felt heartsick. "You really mean that?"

"Nah. But quit jawing. We need to move fast."

"Which way?"

"Don't you know the way? How did you get in?"

Petras sighed. Joelis was never easy to talk to, always taking conversations in a different direction from where Petras thought they were heading, but now he was really difficult. His mother had said he'd changed since that day at the Gymnasium. At least he was speaking. "This way."

Petras stuck his head out the door to check the alley. Nobody. "Let's go." With Joelis on his heels, he headed back up the alley. He could hear thudding noises off toward the town centre, but he didn't know what they were. Something warlike and Germanic, he was sure. He spat on the ground. Even thinking about Hitler's war effort gave him a sour taste in his mouth.

Joelis stayed so far back that, at times, Petras was sure he'd lost him. At last he said, "You're more familiar with this town than I am. Why don't you lead?"

"I'm keeping my eye out for Nazis. I have built-in detectors for them." He grinned, reminding Petras of the old Joelis. "Besides, I don't know where your wondrous steed is stabled."

Petras jerked his head off toward the side street where he'd parked. They ran through back alleys and archways under shops and apartments, and as they ran, they heard the sound of boots on cobbles and bricks. Petras broke into a sweat.

Always the sound of the boots was a street or two over from them. Petras kept to the back ways as much as he could, making the journey to his car even longer and more nerve-wracking. But he didn't know how else to safeguard Joelis.

At last he saw his car. Relief washed over him. "There it is," he whispered, but as usual, Joelis was too far behind him to hear. "Catch up, will you?" he panted, once Joelis was close enough to hear him. "Why are you lagging so far behind?"

"Testing for Nazis, what else?"

"Well, do it inside the car, will you?" Petras opened the back door for him. "Get on the floor, and I'll throw a blanket over you." He got an old gray blanket from the boot and spread it carefully over Joelis.

"Wake me when we get there." He frowned. "Where is there, by the way? Where are we going?"

"Anywhere we can, out of here."

Petras slammed the door and went around to the front. He started the car and pulled cautiously out into the street. He saw two or three other civilian cars ahead of him, which gave him hope he could pull this ploy off. It suddenly seemed to be a singularly stupid plan. Going back to Šiauliai seemed to be the only recourse, but could he evade the Nazis on the road?

As he proceeded carefully down the side streets and approached the edge of town, he saw a solitary Nazi soldier watching him from an empty street corner. The soldier looked familiar.

"Hans!" he said.

"What?" Joelis asked, his head up and right behind Petras's right ear. "Hans Zeller? Where?"

"Get down, you idiot! He'll see you!"

"I want him to," Joelis said in a snarl. "He's precisely what I've been looking for."

"What do you mean?"

"Hush. Don't talk."

Petras looked over his shoulder to see Joelis pull a gun from the pocket of his coat. "Joelis! No! Where did you get a gun?"

"From a Soviet friend, who else? And I've saved it just for Hans, you know. Open your window."

"Why?"

"Oh, just shut up, Petras, and open the window." He stuck the muzzle of the gun out the edge of the car window, just an inch or so. "You'll need to duck when I yell, so I don't ruin your hearing with the blast."

"Too late. One ear is already ruined, from the time Hans killed Saulis that November."

"Stop talking and get ready to duck. Pull alongside him."

His stomach churned. He hated Hans, wouldn't mind seeing him dead, but this seemed so devious. Did that matter if a person was going to kill another? Was it somehow more honorable to be open about it than deceitful?

When he pulled alongside Hans, the noise of the car drew the Nazi's attention. Hans looked at him and smiled. "Well, Petras! Long time no see."

Petras flushed, jammed on the brakes, turned off the motor, and threw open the front door. The streets were blessedly empty. "Oh, good God, how can you speak so coolly, as if we were friends, as if you were innocent? You who killed my sister?" He hurled himself at the stunned Hans, who didn't have time even to put his hands out to ward Petras off.

Petras knocked Hans to the ground and started pummeling him. "You killed her!"

"Wait! Let me tell you – I was trying to help her!"

"Oh, sure you were." Petras didn't believe him but stopped to listen anyway.

"She'd climbed down a rope or something, some sheets, maybe, from her bedroom window! She fell the last few feet. I helped her up, and she thanked me. Then – I don't know what came over me. She was already used, already used by the Baron, so why shouldn't I use her too? I tried to kiss her and she slapped me."

Petras put his hands around Hans's neck. "And then what?" he asked through gritted teeth.

"Just what you just did – I lost my temper and choked her. You could have done the same!" By now Hans was whining, and Petras prepared to slap him.

Joelis scrambled out of the car behind him. "Stop, Petras! You're going to get us caught! Get off him, or I can't get a clear shot!"

Petras punched Hans once more and then drew back. Hans peered at Joelis, and his eyes, swollen already, narrowed to slits. "You Jewish filth! Who are you to speak in my presence?"

Joelis laughed and stuck his gun under Hans's nose. "Even now, huh, you are so cocky? Move, Petras!"

Petras's head swam. He didn't know what to do. The image of Ona's face in death, however, came to the forefront of his thoughts, and with it the certainty that Hans would never come to justice under the law.

Hans began speaking through gritted teeth. "Today, Joelis, you will die. The SS is here to kill off you and all your kin, all of them, forever. I'd heard you were here in Joniškis, so I came here to seek you out myself. Here you are, and I will laugh to see you beg for mercy!"

Joelis laughed, and Petras suspected at that point that he wasn't sane. "I don't think so." He slowly moved the gun muzzle all over Hans's face and watched him squirm and sweat begin to bead on his forehead. "You don't know precisely when I'll pull the trigger, do you?"

"You'll never pull the trigger. Petras will be my witness to what you've done!"

With that Petras saw red. He pushed Joelis aside and grabbed Hans by his collar and jammed his head against the pavement. "I am your witness, that you killed my sister. And I will be glad to see you die!" With that he kicked at Hans. "Toad!"

"Get back, Petras," Joelis said. "For the last time, get out of the way. You're wasting time." He held the gun up
.

to Hans's temple and fired. Hans twitched and then lay
still. "Get in the car! Let's go!"

Petras began to shake. Confused, he stared at the boy
he'd grown up with who now lay dead. He felt an absurd
elation. He'd actually attended in the execution of Ona's
killer. That was good. Wasn't it?

He got in the car, waited only a moment for Joelis to
get himself under the blanket, and started off down the
road. "Wait!" he said, and pulled over to the side of the
road. "Pitch the gun out the window! If you're caught, it'll
be your death."

"You're right, it will. I plan to kill myself. I won't be
taken, Petras," he said in a low, quiet voice.

Petras gave up and pulled back onto the road and began
driving. Ahead of them about fifty yards he saw about fifty
Nazi soldiers marching a large group of Jews at gunpoint
down the road and into a field of blooming, bright yellow
rape. His head started to pound and he began to shake.
"Joelis!" he whispered. "Don't come up to look, but I think
it's the end."

"What do you mean, don't look?"

"The Nazis – and all the Jews lined up!" Petras pulled
over to the side of the road. He went around to the boot
and pulled out a change of clothes he'd brought with him
in the morning, not knowing how long he'd be gone. He
tossed the clothes into the backseat. "You need to change
clothes. I'll throw your regular clothes in the boot here.
You lie on the seat, covered up as if you're sick. It's the only
chance we have to get you through."

Joelis stared at him, black eyes burning in his white
face. "I don't want to get through. The Nazis are going to
kill them, and I want to go too."

"But Joelis! After all we've been through! I've got to get

you to safety!"

A tear trickled down Joelis's face. "Thank you. But I'll never be safe."

"No," Petras said, steel in his voice. "I'm not arguing with you. Change now, give me your clothes, and get on the back seat."

Joelis returned his glare and shrugged. "Okay. I'll give it a try. But you know this may get you killed. If you let me hide here, if they stop us, you can say I had you under gun point and made you drive me out."

Petras shook his head. "No. Get changed."

The Nazis had started herding the large group of Jews, about five hundred, Petras thought, off into a field to the right of the road. They marched them off to a line of oak trees along a creek bed. Petras could hear shouting, and his blood froze. The guns – they started firing the guns.

"Oh, God," he whispered, "oh, God, no." He stood frozen for fifteen minutes, unable to move, letting the tears stream down his face. At last the guns were silent. He could smell blood and excrement drifting over the breeze, heard the Germans yelling and some even laughing.

"It's over, isn't it?" Joelis asked, his face pinched. He started gasping, as if he couldn't breathe. "All of them?"

The fusillade of gunfire started up again and went on for nearly half an hour, and Petras went off to the side of the road to vomit. He sat in the dirt at the side of the road and held his head in his hands. He couldn't believe it, he couldn't believe it. How could he have stopped it, how could he have made a difference? He couldn't come up with a single thing he should have done differently, but he was sure there was something, something, anything.

The soldiers were so preoccupied with killing off Joniškis's Jews that they never noticed Petras and Joelis. At last, Petras pulled himself together and took Joelis's clothes from him, threw them in the boot.

"Stop. Throw them in the alley," Joelis said. "If we're stopped…"

"Okay," Petras said, seeing the sense in that. Once he disposed of the clothes, he checked on Joelis's pose as a sick person. It was a good disguise – he definitely looked sick, to death.

Petras didn't try to drive particularly carefully, just efficiently, to get them away from there. They didn't speak all the way back to Šiauliai. It was dark when they got to the house, and Petras nearly had to carry Joelis inside.

"What is it?" Mamytė asked, when she heard Petras come in. He told her all about the slaughter of the Jews in Joniškis, and she began to cry. He didn't tell her about the execution of Hans Zeller.

Looking half-asleep, Rima came into the parlor then. Petras told her about the occurrence in Joniškis. Mamytė left the room to get supper on for the two men, and Rima sat down hard in a chair and stared at Joelis and Petras. She didn't speak. Shock drained her face of color as it filled her eyes with horror.

Mamytė came back in carrying a tray with two large mugs of hot tea with milk and sugar. "We heard on the radio tonight about the massacres all over Lithuania. How could they, how could they kill God's chosen people?"

Joelis didn't seem to have the strength to pick up his mug, so Rima held it for him and helped him take small sips. When Mamytė returned with potato soup, cheese, and fresh bread, Rima fed him a bite at a time.

Petras wondered whether Joelis would be offended by food from a non-kosher kitchen, but decided it wasn't worth worrying about at this point.

"How's Gintaras?" Petras asked Mamytė when he got her off to the side.

"He had a good day. Vanya came and took him for a walk, and he laughed at Vanya's antics."

"And her?" he asked with a tilt of his head to Rima.

"Vanya told her to stop with the long faces and start laughing and talking with him, and she listened to him."

Petras nodded. "Good. It's about time for her to wake up. The baby's alive. He'll be fine, just different."

"Yes," she whispered. "He's just fine."

CHAPTER 35

Petras had nightmares for a week, of the people hidden under the floor in Joniškis and of the ones who were marched out of town and shot. He didn't dream about Hans's death at all.

He and his family kept Joelis hidden for the next months while he grieved. Petras watched him closely, to see if killing someone had fundamentally changed Joelis. His face was drawn and gaunt, but was that because of the gymnasium and all its horror?

Because of the presence of the Nazis, there was no opportunity to return to Joniškis to check on the forty Jews hidden under the ghetto, although Petras never gave up looking for a chance to go back. Months later he learned most had gotten out and fled to the Soviet Union.

The Nazis tried to form SS troops in Lithuania, but

the country refused to cooperate, the only German-occupied country that did. Several national leaders sent letters of condemnation to Germany to protest the massacres of 200,000 Jews, 90% of Lithuania's Jews. As a result, universities were closed and many intellectuals sent to concentration camps, Dachau, Stutthof, Birkenau.

The Nazis fought the Soviets over Lithuania and over the city of Šiauliai, and nearly all the public buildings were damaged in the fire fights. The Church of Peter and Paul miraculously escaped all but minor damage, in spite of its large, imposing steeple, and all the Catholics in town said it was because of God's favor.

Petras and his family stayed inside much of the time, and he did his best to stay busy. The air strikes ended, with the Soviets winning and the Nazis on the run.

Robert Branson came by nearly every day to keep Petras posted on what was going on. Petras didn't understand why Branson had taken an interest in them, but he was grateful for it. His visits felt like a lifeline to a saner world.

Life returned to a semblance of normality, although Petras knew it was only a matter of time before the Soviets moved back in.

One day Rima spoke to Petras. "Remember you wouldn't go to the Hill of Crosses after our wedding?"

"Yes. And?"

"Can we go now?"

He stared at her. "Why?"

"It's time. I want to give thanks for some things and ask forgiveness for some things. My saint's day is next week. I'd like to go then."

He shook his head. "It means so much to you?"

"Of course!"

"If you wish."

They drove Antanas's truck. Gintaras loved the ride and waved at bystanders from his mother's lap by the front window. It was a gray, blustery day, which matched Petras's mood.

When they arrived, about ten older women milled around, placing flowers at the foot of the crosses, weeding and cleaning up the grounds. The wooden and iron crosses, many with ancient symbols of the sun and moon on them, reflected Lithuania's paganism as well as its Christianity. Petras shivered, for the spirit of life and death filled the Castle mound studded with mementos of martyrs to Lithuania's struggle with Russia and Germany.

Rima placed a small, plain cross halfway up the hill. "To remember all we've lost and all we'll win, some day," she said.

Still the fighting went on, and Petras did his best to keep their home peaceful.

Rima stayed stable through it all, was playful and talkative with Gintaras, who mirrored her animated expressions, but she was solemn with Joelis. She became his handmaiden as much as she was able, what with the responsibilities she had with the baby.

"You're so good with Joelis," Petras said on one of their late-evening walks with Gintaras in his carriage.

"I know what it's like to grieve."

"Yes, I understand."

"Do you think we'll ever have a normal life here in Lithuania?"

"I don't know. I just don't know."

"We'll have to do the best we can, I guess."

He stopped under a July tree* in bloom and took her hand and kissed the palm. "I'm glad to have you back, Rima."

"Thank you for being patient with me."

"I'm not always patient," he said.

"Patient enough. I love you." She took her hand back and started pushing the carriage. Gintaras looked at his parents and smiled, then stuck his thumb in his mouth and gazed up at the night stars. "He'll be fine, won't he?"

"Yes," Petras said. "Perhaps a bit slow, but still a lovely child."

"And you don't mind raising him?"

"Of course not. You know he's always reminded me more of Vanya than of Pavel."

"I must tell you," she said as she stopped walking again. "I'm pregnant, but with your child. It will be different this time, won't it?"

Different, yes, he thought. He put his arm around her shoulder and drew her close to him and kissed her. A group of teenaged girls was passing by, and they giggled. Rima blushed, and Petras kissed her again.

"Joelis will be leaving soon," Rima said, once they began walking again. "Where will he go?"

"I'm not sure. I talked to Sergei in Moscow, and he thinks he can get him a pass. He'll be safer there."

"That's hard to believe."

He shrugged. "Sergei says they'll drive out the Germans completely soon and return, and we'll all be safe from the Nazis."

"Out of the frying pan into the fire."

July tree: *liepa* [LYEH-pa], the linden or lime tree

"Yes." He paused. "Rima, I will have to work for the Communists when they come back, you know."

Saddened, she shook her head. "It hurts you to do that."

He didn't look at her.

"You do it to support your family, and I'm sorry you have to swallow your pride this way."

He turned and put his hands on her shoulders. "I wouldn't give you up, though, to salvage my pride. So I must say it's worth it. You understand?"

"Yes," she whispered.

"It can't be forever."

"How long, do you think?"

A vision of a large black bird hovering over Lithuania flashed through his mind. Suddenly he couldn't breathe, suffocated as he felt under the bird's oppressive shadow of evil threatening his land. Would they survive it?

At last he answered her. "I can't guess. A year, five years, fifty years?" He groaned. "Fifty years? Surely not. But the last time the Russians ruled us, it was seventy-five years. 'Kas bus, tas bus, o Lietuva nepražus – What will be will be, but Lithuania will never perish.'"

"Please God that's true." They walked along in silence for a while. "Time to start teaching Gintaras Lithuanian in secret?"

"Time to smuggle books in from Latvia again?"

They returned to the house. They could see Mamytė and Gerardas by the front window drinking tea in the lamplight. "It looks cozy, doesn't it?" Petras asked.

"Safe, from Nazis and Communists."

He shivered. "We can only pray so."

"You believe in prayer now?" she asked.

He laughed. "I always did. I never gave up asking, only to be told no. But I've been told no so many times in the past few years, maybe once more won't hurt me."

"You're a good person," she said shyly. "I'm glad you picked me."

He kissed her again, and Gintaras laughed at them this time. Petras picked him up with one arm and wrapped the other arm around his wife, and they went in.

About the Author

Laurel Schunk has written six books – four adult mystery/ suspense novels as well as two easy readers for second graders. In *A Clear North Light,* she has begun a three-book saga about Petras Simonaitis and his family in pre-World War II Lithuania. Schunk visited Lithuania in 1996, when she interviewed fifteen people about how living under Nazi and then Soviet domination affected their faith lives. From Nazi massacres of Jews to the Stalin-ordered exiles into Siberia, she has turned their heart-wrenching stories into a three-generation epic of ordinary people living heroically under impossible circumstances. *A Clear North Light* covers events beginning in 1938 and ending in 1940.

A CLEAR NORTH LIGHT

Book One of the Lithuanian Trilogy

1939

Petras

THE EAST WIND SCATTERS

Book Two of the Lithuanian Trilogy

1965

Gintaras

THE JULY TREE

Book Three of the Lithuanian Trilogy

1990

Eligijus